DANGEROUS SEA

Also by David Roberts

Sweet Poison
Bones of the Buried
Hollow Crown

DANGEROUS SEA

DAVID ROBERTS

Constable • London

Constable & Robinson Ltd
3 The Lanchesters
162 Fulham Palace Road
London W6 9ER

First published in the UK by Constable,
an imprint of Constable & Robinson Ltd 2003

ISBN 1-84119-572-3

Printed and bound in the United States of America

For Elisabeth
and in memory of Eustace

I am grateful to Peter Lester for permission to consult
the Cunard Archive at Liverpool University

Cassio: Oh, let the heavens
Give him defence against the elements,
For I have lost him on a dangerous sea

. . . .

Brabantio: Thou art a villain.
Iago: You are a senator

Shakespeare, *Othello*

February and March 1937

1

'Damn and blast it! Oh sorry, Connie, but, hang it all, just look at it!'

It was late February and London was cold, wet and miserable. After the warmth and colour of the auditorium, Bow Street seemed distinctly uninviting. Peering out through the rain from the portico of the Opera House, Lord Edward Corinth wondered how he would ever locate the Rolls. He grasped his companion by the arm and said, 'I don't think Page will find us in this mêlée. Perhaps I ought to go and explore.'

As he finished speaking, however, the Duchess pointed. 'Look! Over there, Ned. There he is.'

Somehow, the chauffeur had found his way to the front of the queue of taxis and cars, and Edward, relieved and admiring, wondered if he had had to resort to bribery or if it was sheer force of personality. Page approached them holding a large umbrella open above him. Edward gratefully released his sister-in-law into his charge and prepared to follow but a tap on the shoulder arrested him.

'Lord Edward – it is you, isn't it?'

The man who addressed him was small, narrow in the shoulders and altogether unprepossessing. His fraility was emphasized by his bald head, wispy ginger moustache and weak blue eyes which nevertheless glowed brightly from behind wire-rimmed spectacles. He had raised his black silk hat to greet Edward and now replaced it.

'Lord Benyon, how are you?' Edward responded, with genuine warmth. Benyon might resemble an undernourished bank clerk from one of the novels of H.G. Wells but he was, in fact,

3

a distinguished economist and one of the Chancellor of the Exchequer's trusted advisers. It was not a total surprise to see him at Covent Garden because Edward knew he was a close friend of Sir Thomas Beecham, the director of the Opera House.

'That was my sister-in-law you saw being escorted to the car. May we give you a lift or have you a car of your own?'

'That's very good of you, Lord Edward,' said the little man. 'If it's not taking you too much out of your way, I confess we would be very glad of a lift. I don't fancy my chances of finding a taxi in this weather. I live in Gerald Road. Do you know it? Almost next to the police station.'

'Of course. Noel Coward lives in Gerald Road, doesn't he? I went to a party there once, with a friend of mine who was rather a good singer.'

'Yes, indeed. Not that, I'm afraid, we see anything of him. He moves in much more glamorous circles. Oh, forgive me, may I introduce my sister, Mrs Garton?'

Edward raised his hat to a lady so tightly wrapped in her cloak he could only see a pair of blue eyes above a rather pleasant smile, and then looked anxiously after Connie. 'Very good. Let us sally forth. I don't know how long Page can defend his position from the mob.'

A girl in a threadbare dress and a rain-sodden hat thrust a bunch of violets at him. Irritated by this new delay, he moved his arm to brush her aside and was immediately ashamed. How could his minor inconvenience compare with what this girl had to endure? He fished in his trouser pocket and came up with a half-crown which he pressed in the girl's hand. Her gratitude made him even more embarrassed and he saw Benyon smiling.

'As my friend, Verity Browne, would say, these girls don't need charity. They need education and a proper job,' he said sheepishly.

They elbowed their way through the crowd which continued to stream out of the Opera House. They ducked and dodged as umbrellas were opened all about them, spokes prodding spitefully. Water dribbled off black brollies on to shawls and capes, down necks, ruining top hats and making patent-leather shoes glisten. Women, clutching their evening bags in one hand and holding their long dresses clear of the wet pavement with the other, protested in shrill squeals. The scent of rotting vegetables from the market made Edward momentarily nauseous.

When they reached the sanctuary of the Rolls, Connie was already ensconced in the back but made no objection to taking Benyon and his sister home. Connie had not met him before but they had many friends in common and were soon at ease with one another. Edward relaxed and, as the car turned into the Strand, prepared to devote himself to Mrs Garton.

'What did you think of the opera?' he asked her. 'Wasn't Erna Berger a magnificent Queen of the Night?'

'It was heaven. *The Magic Flute* is a favourite of mine, Lord Edward, and Erna Berger . . . how could anyone sing with such purity of tone? I really can't find the right words without resorting to cliché. And Tiana Lemnitz . . . her Pamina! I believe we were privileged to hear it.'

Edward said, rather michievously, 'So what do you think it's all about? I mean, not that absurd Masonic abracadabra stuff. What's it *really* about?'

'Human cruelty,' she replied rather surprisingly. 'Beneath all that heavenly music, there is the story of harsh and unjustified punishment. It's hardly surprising Pamina tries to kill herself.'

Benyon, seeing Edward was rather taken aback by the seriousness of his sister's remarks, said, 'Well, we must enjoy it while we can. It may not be a privilege we will have again, to listen to such singing. Sir Thomas was saying to me the other day that he was literally bankrupting himself putting on what the press are calling a Coronation Season. Unless he can find money from somewhere, it will have to be his last.'

'Oh, but that's terrible!' Connie exclaimed. 'We can't let Covent Garden close. Can't the government do something? Surely, London must have an opera house. If the Italians can fund La Scala and that's not even in Rome . . .'

'Maybe, but the government puts guns before music.'

'Some would say about time too,' Edward put in drily.

'Well, I wouldn't,' Connie said stoutly. 'My son, Frank, told me Sir Thomas had been at Eton not long ago and it had been a revelation. Let me see, what was it they played? I remember, Mendelssohn's *Midsummer Night's Dream*. Frank said it was better than the record he has of Toscanini. Of course music is more important than guns, Ned.' She shivered. 'Though I'm not saying we don't need guns, more's the pity.'

There was a silence and then Edward said, with an effort, 'I was very sad to hear about Inna. I would so much have liked to come to the funeral but unfortunately we were out of the country . . . Verity and I. Your wife was a very remarkable woman, if you will allow me to say so. I don't know exactly what it was she said to Verity but it had a great effect on her. She had some sort of block writing her book on Spain but Inna showed her how to overcome it. I honestly believe she is the only woman Verity admired unreservedly.'

'That's very good of you,' Benyon said, visibly moved. 'It was a great blow to me, though of course we knew the cancer wouldn't . . . give her very long. Perhaps you think it wrong of me to be at the opera within two months of her death but . . .' Mrs Garton leant over and took his hand, 'when she was dying, she begged me to go on doing what she knew I had to do to keep sane – music, going to all my ridiculous meetings and committees. She knew that if I stopped and . . . gave way, I would never be able to survive. Inna was my life, Lord Edward, but I feel her with me now, by my side . . .' He made an effort to pull himself together. 'Forgive me for talking this way. It must be Mozart. He sometimes has that effect on me. Now, tell me, you were in Spain over Christmas, were you not? I read something about it in the paper.'

'Yes,' the Duchess interjected. 'Frank gave us all a fright by running away from school to join the International Brigade.'

'And Verity and I went to Spain to fetch him back,' Edward said grimly. 'We caught up with him on Christmas Day just outside Madrid. He was manning a machine-gun, would you believe?' He could hardly keep the admiration out of his voice. 'Anyway, we dragged him back by the scruff of his neck and he hasn't stopped complaining since. He's resolutely refused to go back to school so, at the moment, he's sitting at home in a deep sulk while we try to think what we are going to do with him.'

'I see,' Benyon said meditatively. 'Look, what are you doing at lunch tomorrow? I have a ghost of an idea but I need to mull it over and talk to someone first to see if it's practical.'

6

'That's very good of you,' Connie said. 'Of course you're free tomorrow, aren't you, Ned?'

A little nettled at being taken for granted, Edward had to agree. The car drew up in Gerald Road, a narrow street of substantial houses with a small police station at one end endearingly decorated with window boxes. When Page opened the car door for them, Benyon said, 'Please don't get out, Lord Edward. The Athenaeum at one o'clock? Excellent!' Turning to Connie, he added, 'Thank you so much for the lift, Duchess. I must tell you, my wife thought very well of Lord Edward and my dear Inna was a shrewd judge of character.'

The Athenaeum, in Pall Mall, was just a five-minute walk from Brooks's, Edward's club in St James's Street, but in atmosphere it was a world away. Brooks's had its share of members who slept the days away in the deep, leather armchairs but these were by no means the majority. Members of Brooks's were, for the most part, aristocrats, diplomats and politicians – Tories to a man, despite the club's Whig origins. At the Athenaeum, Edward anticipated bumping into bishops, judges and senior civil servants. The thought did not excite him. As he entered the atrium with its sweeping staircase leading to the great rooms on the first and second floors, he was as usual put in mind of a cathedral and he could not prevent himself grinning when the first person he saw, after he had given his name to the porter, was the Bishop of Worthing, Cecil Haycraft, whom he had met at Mersham Castle.

'Lord Edward! I didn't know you were a member, but how nice to see you. How is your brother, the Duke? I heard that he made a very good speech in the Lords on the Education Bill.'

'Thank you. He is well but, as to my being a member here, I have to disappoint you. I am just a guest.' He decided to tease the Bishop who rather prided himself on being modern and unstuffy. 'I am surprised that *you* are a member. Isn't it a little . . . old-fashioned for a man of your advanced views?'

The Bishop blushed and Edward repented his impertinence. 'I'm just joking – forgive me.'

The Bishop's face cleared. 'Of course, and you, Lord Edward, how are you and how is that delightful friend of yours, Miss Browne?'

There was the very slightest sting in the inquiry. Verity Browne was everything the Athenaeum feared and despised. She was a woman and, if that was not bad enough, she was a Communist and, worst of all, a journalist. And yet, for some reason which he could not quite define, Edward found more satisfaction in her company than in that of any of the women in his social circle. The society women he met at dinners and at balls – though, as a matter of fact, he no longer went to balls – bored him.

Verity did not bore him. She was elusive. She was infuriating. She liked to make fun of his preconceptions and prejudices. She accused him of belonging to a class which history had decided to consign to the dustbin and she was consistently disparaging of his efforts to be a *chevalier sans peur et sans reproche*. Despite all of this – and to his friends' amusement and puzzlement – he found himself completely in her thrall. Perhaps it was that she did not toady to him, the son of a duke, as so many of the women in his set appeared to do. Perhaps it was because she forced him see the world from a different perspective, or perhaps it was just something 'chemical', as the modish phrase had it. On several occasions he had been on the point of proposing marriage to her but for one reason or another he had never got the words out. He knew she was more than likely to say no, so there was some relief in not having forced the issue.

Verity was aware of Edward's feelings for her – how could she not be? – and sometimes thought she reciprocated them. She certainly liked and admired him. His courage, his intelligence, his enterprise and – there was no getting away from it – his social position made him attractive and she had come to depend on him in moments of crisis. If only he would be satisfied to be her lover. It wasn't just that, as a committed Communist, it was against all her principles to marry into the aristocracy. If she decided she wanted to do something perverse, she would not be put off by the derision of her comrades in the Party. No, she genuinely felt she was unsuited to marriage. Her strongest emotions were political rather than personal, or that was what she told herself. She was a foreign correspondent – a demanding and occasionally dangerous job which she had been told often enough was man's work. And there was war everywhere, in Spain and soon throughout Europe. A great battle with Fascism was looming and she was determined to be part of it. For the forseeable future, there was going to be no chance that she could be fulfilled by building a cosy nest for her man and bringing his babies into the world. She did not like babies or anything which restricted her movements. She was ready to accept she was selfish but at least she wasn't cruel enough to marry a man and lead him a dog's life. If there was one thing upon which she prided herself it was being honest.

'Verity is well. She has just completed a book on the war in Spain, for the Left Book Club. I am sure you are a subscriber.'

The Bishop was not sure if he were again being teased and finally decided he was. 'I am indeed a subscriber. You have me in your power, Lord Edward. If it came to the notice of the club secretary, I would probably be drummed out.'

He smiled and Edward liked him for it. Further discussion was cut short by the appearance of Lord Benyon on the staircase above them.

'I thought it might be easier to talk confidentially in one of the card rooms and then have lunch, if that's all right with you.'

Benyon ushered him into a small room redolent of cigars. Two card tables, covered in green felt, stood abandoned in one corner and on a horsehair sofa opposite sat Major Ferguson.

'I gather you two know each other,' Benyon said.

Edward nodded and took Ferguson's outstretched hand. He had met the Major a few weeks previously and knew him to be one of those shadowy policemen whose authority was not to be questioned and whose sphere of operations was wide but amorphous. Special Branch had been set up during the Fenian troubles of the 1880s but was now responsible for state security which, according to Verity, in practice meant harassing the Communist Party while tacitly approving Sir Oswald Mosley's activities. Edward had no idea if this was true or merely left-wing paranoia.

Major Ferguson was not physically impressive. He was

shorter than Benyon who was himself not much above five feet. He wore a bristly military moustache, not unlike the Führer's. He was almost bald. His brown eyes were masked by spectacles thick enough to suggest his sight was very poor. He was saved from the instant anonymity he no doubt fostered by a scar above his right eye.

'Lord Edward!' Ferguson exclaimed, pretending for no reason Edward could imagine that bumping into him like this was just some happy accident. 'Much has happened since we last met.'

He was referring to the Abdication of the King and the murder of two people connected with him. 'Your investigation was commendably thorough and you got to the bottom of it all with the minimum of fuss. Congratulations.' He shook Edward's hand with unexpected vigour.

'Very kind of you but . . .'

'But what am I doing here? Shall I tell him, Lord Benyon, or will you?'

'You go ahead.'

'Right you are.' Ferguson was playing the hearty 'good fellow' you might meet on a racecourse but Edward was not deceived. This man, despite his insignificance, was dangerous. 'Cigarette?'

Edward was about to take one and then remembered Ferguson favoured a particularly noxious Egyptian brand. Ferguson laughed to see him hesitate. 'I had a small bet with myself that you'd remember.' He replaced his cigarette case in his breast pocket and they all sat down.

'Major Ferguson hasn't got long. He won't lunch with us so I knew you wouldn't mind if we disposed of our bit of business before eating,' Benyon said apologetically.

Edward nodded, rather bemused. 'Business? What business?'

'Not business exactly,' Ferguson said airily. 'A week from now Lord Benyon is going to the United States ostensibly to accept an honorary degree from New York's Columbia University. He is also giving two lectures – one to the New York Press Club and another to a group of influential businessmen. He then goes on to Washington and will have a meeting with Mr Lauchlin Currie, the President's chief financial adviser, and will give two more lectures there before returning home.'

'I see. And how does that . . .?'

'Affect you?' Ferguson had a habit of completing people's sentences. 'I'll tell you, but I need hardly say that this is all in the strictest confidence.'

'Except certain people already seem to know!' Benyon broke in.

'Yes. There's a leak somewhere right enough, at the very top of government, but we haven't yet put our finger on who the wagging tongue might be. Anyway, Lord Benyon has a much more important object in going to Washington than giving a few lectures, interesting though they will no doubt be,' he said, smiling insincerely at Benyon. 'The real purpose of the trip is a private meeting with President Roosevelt and two of his closest advisers. The Prime Minister has, as you know, begun to strengthen our armed forces in the light of the international situation . . .'

'Too little and too late!'

'Probably, Lord Edward,' Benyon agreed, 'but there's no point in crying over spilt milk. The fact is that millions of pounds are being spent on rearmament but Britain is no longer the financial power it used to be. Neville Chamberlain – and, whatever I think of him as a human being, he's a sound man to have as Chancellor of the Exchequer – has said that the fifteen hundred million pounds the government plans to spend on the Navy and the Army in the next five years is almost certainly inadequate. The Chancellor will have to raise taxes and borrow at least two hundred million. That's not going to be easy. Most people are quite unaware of it but, to be blunt, Britain is bankrupt, so far as a country can go bankrupt. Most of our foreign investments had been disposed of by 1918 and it's little more than sheer bluff that we can sit as equals at the same table with our North American friends.'

'And your object is to borrow money off the United States?'

'Beg, borrow or steal,' Benyon said emphatically. 'We cannot fight another war without American financial support. Roosevelt has made it plain that the United States will not come in on our side if there is a war. Fifty thousand "doughboys" were killed on the Western Front. It may not be many compared to our losses but American public opinion is absolutely firm in its opposition to any policy other than isolationism.

No more young Americans will die on the battlefields of Europe.'

'I understand and I wish you good fortune, Benyon. You have clearly got a Herculean task ahead of you but I don't see how I can be of any assistance.'

'We have it on good authority,' Benyon went on as if Edward had not spoken, 'that the German government knows the real purpose of my visit and Major Ferguson says they will do anything . . . *anything* to ensure its failure.'

'Meaning?'

'We have definite information that they would not stop at murder,' Ferguson elaborated.

'Oh really, Major! Are you asking me to believe that agents of the German Reich would resort to murder to stop Lord Benyon reaching Washington? With respect, surely that is pure John Buchan.'

'Not at all!' Ferguson said a little huffily. 'Our agent in the German Chancellery is adamant that this threat is to be taken seriously and his information, gained at great personal risk, is not to be dismissed lightly.'

Edward felt himself reproved. 'Well, I am sorry, but you must admit it seems preposterous. The new Germany is not to my taste and I have been convinced for some time that war is inevitable but surely no European government will resort to murder. They are not a bunch of thugs.'

'But that is just what they are, Lord Edward,' Ferguson said fiercely. 'Hitler has never had any compunction in murdering even his closest associates when they have outlived their usefulness. Think of the Night of the Long Knives in June 1934. Röhm and all his Brownshirts were murdered at a word from their Führer. You have heard of these prison camps they have set up? There's one near Munich about which we are beginning to hear frightful stories. Without trial, without possibility of appeal, the Nazis imprison their enemies in these places and most are never heard of again.'

'Jews . . .' Edward began.

'Not only Jews. Communists – anyone who causes them any trouble.'

'And the German public knows about this?'

'They know something of it but it is dangerously "unpatriotic" to object . . . to speak out in defence of the country's "enemies".'

'I am not naive about the Nazis, Major Ferguson. I do understand what you are saying but to put it another way – and I am not meaning to belittle Lord Benyon's mission – would they *bother* to attempt to kill him? Are there not many more obvious . . . targets?'

'I don't think you fully understand, Edward.' Benyon unconsciously dropped into an intimacy which his listener considered a compliment. 'My mission is of the utmost importance. If war was declared tomorrow, we might stave off defeat for a week, a month or – at the most optimistic estimate – three months. We cannot win – we cannot survive – without American aid.'

Benyon was deadly serious and a cold shiver ran down Edward's spine. 'The French?' he offered up.

Benyon was contemptuous. 'A "busted flush", as our American friends would say. I believe they could not withstand a German invasion even as long as we could. They have no English Channel to "serve it in the office of a wall".'

'But I still don't see how I come into this. I am flattered you have taken me into your confidence but surely, Ferguson, you have Lord Benyon protected?'

'On British soil Lord Benyon has protection day and night but out of England . . .'

'How are you travelling to the States, Benyon?' Edward asked.

'On the *Queen Mary*.'

'That is almost the same as being on British soil.'

'Not so, Lord Edward,' Ferguson said. 'We have a passenger list but who is to say if it is accurate or complete? The *Queen Mary* carries some seven hundred First Class passengers and an equal number in the other two classes. Lord Benyon will keep himself to himself as far as is possible without arousing comment but there is always a chance . . .'

'. . . someone might take a pot shot at me.'

'*Dulce et decorum est pro patria mori*,' Edward quoted. 'I have always considered that to be a particularly insidious lie.'

'Sweet and honourable to die for one's country?' Benyon

said thoughtfully. 'But don't forget that Horace's next line, if I remember it aright, is *mors et fugacem persequitur virum* – Death hunts down the man in flight.'

'Our agent believes that it is on the ship they are most likely to attempt to . . . do their dirty business.'

'But, Ferguson, you can surround him with your people on board.'

'It is not that easy, Edward,' Benyon said earnestly. 'The difficulty is that I do not wish to draw attention to my mission. If it is to succeed, secrecy is of the essence. If the press were to get hold of the real reason for my trip, it would be a disaster. Our enemies would make hay with our obvious weakness and the American public would imagine they were about to be duped by "perfidious Albion".'

'One of my men will pose as Lord Benyon's manservant,' Ferguson said, 'but what we really need is someone who can mingle easily with the other First Class passengers and keep an eye out for any potential threat.'

'And you want me to be your *homme de confiance*?'

'Don't be offended,' Benyon said hurriedly. 'It would be a great pleasure for me to have you on the *Queen Mary* as my guest – or rather the government's guest. I will have a great deal to worry about and to feel that you were there to . . . well, to keep an eye on me, would be a great relief.'

'Are you taking anyone else with you?'

'My secretary, Marcus Fern. I call him my secretary but really he is my assistant – a brilliant young man. I don't know if you have met him?' Edward shook his head. 'He's a very able young banker and one day he'll be Governor of the Bank of England, I'm convinced of it. It's very pleasing he has consented to accompany me on this trip. He's at Samuel Montagu – David Keswick spotted him. Fern is one of the new breed of City men – self-made – his father was a schoolteacher. We need more of his kind, in my view, if London is to retain its position at the centre of the financial world.'

'My dear Benyon, as I have said, I am very flattered to be asked and I don't underestimate the importance of your mission but, to be honest with you, I am determined to find myself a real job – a permanent position where I can put my shoulder to the wheel. There's a war coming and I want to be in a position to make a contribution . . .'

'I appreciate your patriotism. I must tell you I am fully informed of what you have achieved in the past two years. I know it is a fault of yours to undervalue yourself. You are building something of a career as a "trouble-shooter", as the expression is. You may think you are unknown in government circles but I assure you that this is not the case. I happen to know that only the other day Vansittart was speaking of you to the Foreign Secretary in the most complimentary terms.'

'May I think over what you have told me?' Edward said at last. He had a feeling he was being ungracious. Benyon was not a man to overstate the importance of his mission. 'When exactly are you sailing?'

'In five days.'

'Good Lord! On Saturday? Oughtn't you to have dealt with all this weeks ago?'

'Although my lectures were planned some time ago, the extra element was only added a few days ago.'

'And the warning from our agent,' Ferguson added, 'came through the day before yesterday.'

'I see,' Edward said doubtfully.

'Twenty-four hours. We need an answer not later than Wednesday to permit us to make other arrangements if you decline to accompany Lord Benyon.' Ferguson spoke stiffly as if he had expected Edward to have agreed immediately.

'There's one other thing, Edward,' Benyon said, looking at him anxiously. 'I thought it might be useful to take a young man with me to run errands and carry my briefcases, make sure I catch trains and so on, and I wondered if your nephew Frank would take the post. You said he was rather at a loose end. Of course, I would have to meet him and see if we would get on but he obviously has pluck and determination. I like the sound of him.'

Edward smiled. How clever! Benyon had offered to solve a problem which only minutes ago had seemed intractable. He was being offered the gentlest of bribes but could hardly take offence. He said, 'You know Frank considers himself a Communist? In fact I believe he's a member of the Party.'

Major Ferguson grinned. 'We know but we believe, under his uncle's watchful eye, he will do nothing to embarrass Lord Benyon. However, I must emphasize that neither he nor anyone else can be told the real purpose of the mission. Only Mr Fern and yourself know that. Even my man, Barrett, who will act as Lord Benyon's valet, does not need to be told. You understand?'

Major Ferguson was suddenly grim-faced.

'I understand,' Edward said.

2

Verity Browne looked up into the smiling face of the young American and smiled back. His name was Sam Forrest and he was the emissary of John L. Lewis, the United Mineworkers chief.

Lewis was the most powerful labour representative in the United States. When asked by a reporter what he believed, he said without hesitation, 'The right to organize, shorter hours, the prohibition of child labour, equal pay for men and women and a guarantee that all who are able to work shall have the opportunity for employment.' When the reporter added, 'And a living wage?' Lewis roared, 'We demand more than that: a wage that will enable the worker to maintain himself and his family in health and modest comfort, purchase his home and educate his children.'

Lewis was not a Communist, nor was Sam Forrest, but they did believe in the reform of capitalism and Forrest had been sent to England to meet workers' leaders and see what the two labour movements could do to help one another. Forrest's three-week visit was almost over. It had been a considerable success and he was returning home on the *Queen Mary* in five days' time thoroughly pleased with himself.

'Why don't you come with me, Miss Browne? You could report on our struggle and meet some of our leaders. Maybe go to Chicago. There's a major move going on there in the meat-packing industry. Maybe you could sell your book to a New York publisher and give some lectures on the war in Spain. Anyways, I'd sure be glad of your company.'

Verity was taken aback. She liked this young man a lot – his

17

open smile and lazy drawl had got under her skin – but she had never contemplated prolonging the acquaintanceship. She had followed Forrest from meeting to meeting, reporting for the *Daily Worker*, the official organ of the Communist Party, and had even managed to get a small paragraph into the *New Gazette* about a meeting in Coventry which had been broken up by the police.

'Oh, I couldn't do that.'

'Why not?'

'I'm supposed to be giving a lecture in Scarborough next week.'

'Where the heck's Scarborough?'

'My employer, Lord Weaver – he'd sack me.'

'Well, who cares? Get a job on the *New York Times*. Don't be so defeatist.'

'I'm not being defeatist,' Verity said indignantly. 'I'd have to get permission from the Party.'

Forrest could sense she was weakening. 'No problem there. I was talking to one of your people and he was saying they ought to have better liaison with their friends in the United States. Got any more reasons not to come with me? I could introduce you to some useful people.'

'I need to be back in Spain. Madrid can't hold out much longer.'

'Look, Miss Browne . . . Verity,' the big man said, taking her by the arms, 'I guess Madrid can fall without your help. You'd only be gone three weeks, a month at the most. It would be good for your career. This is our century. Europe's finished. Come with me. You won't regret it.'

Lord Weaver, Verity's employer and the proprietor of the *New Gazette*, was enthusiastic. 'I like it. We should have more people in the States. Hopkins is a good man but he can only cover so much. He reports from Washington and Washington isn't America. Write some pieces about how ordinary people live, about the way machines are transforming the lives of housewives.' He held up his hand as he saw Verity open her mouth to object. 'I don't mean report on women's topics. It's simply that what happens in America happens over here five years later. You know, "I saw the future and it works."'

'That was said about Russia. But you really mean it, Joe. You want me to go?'

'I think it's a great opportunity. Godber will have a fit,' he laughed. Godber was the paper's editor. 'He really can't stand you. I can't think why.'

Verity grinned. 'I suppose it won't cost too much. I can go steerage.'

'Certainly not! The *New Gazette*'s prestige is at stake. I don't suppose Sam Forrest is going steerage.'

'No,' Verity agreed. 'First Class.' It had surprised her that this representative of the people was travelling in such style. When she had asked him if there wasn't a contradiction there, he smiled and said. 'My union's one of the most powerful in the country. I wouldn't be taken seriously by the employers or anyone else if they think I can't afford to travel with the high-hats.'

The Party, too, as Forrest had forecast, was enthusiastic. Verity was summoned to meet Ronald Kidd, her area organizer, a man of about fifty with a flowing mane of white hair and black eyes which burned with ardour for the cause. Verity liked him but was rather more afraid of him than she was of her other employer, Lord Weaver. Kidd was emphatic. Of course she must accept Forrest's invitation.

'Get to know as many of the union leaders as you can and write about the class struggle for the *Daily Worker*. We've neglected to build up strong ties with our friends in the United States. That was why we were so ready to welcome Mr Forrest. It's important we don't let this opportunity pass just because we have so much on our plate here in England. I'll give you the addresses of friends of ours in the Youth Congress, young people with the right ideas – not all Communists. And here are some back issues of *New Masses* – that's the official journal of the Communist Party in the States.'

'I didn't know they allowed Communists in the United States.' Verity remarked.

'I have a pamphlet here somewhere on the history of the Party in the States,' Kidd said, opening a desk drawer stuffed with leaflets. 'It's very different from ours. The Party spent many years trying to establish separate unions and organizations but, in the last year or two under the leadership of Earl Browder, a magnificent man – from Kansas I believe – the CPUSA has changed tack. The new directives from Moscow mean we co-operate with any group opposed to Fascism. In the States, Party workers have joined the CIO, the Committee for Industrial Organization, whose president is John Lewis, young Sam's boss. Ah, this is what I was looking for.' Kidd produced a small stapled pamphlet from a cardboard file. 'This will tell you all about it. But don't spend too much time trying to meet Party members. As I say, your task is to develop relationships with the union bosses. For the most part, they are as capitalist as their employers but, in their struggle for workers' rights, they are our allies. Our enemy's enemy is our friend. You understand?'

'Yes, I suppose so.'

Kidd opened the pamphlet and began to read. ' "The IWW" – that's the Industrial Workers of the World,' he explained, 'the Communist Party in industry, you might say – "was founded with a statement that the working class and the employing class have nothing in common. Instead of the old slogan: a fair day's wage for a fair day's toil, the IWW says abolish the wage system. An injury to the members of one industry is an injury to the whole working class and has to be met with strikes and sabotage."' He pushed his glasses up his nose and looked sternly at Verity. 'That is what we believe even if for the moment we have to compromise. Never forget it.'

Verity left Kidd's office – a modest affair over a garage next to a church in Bermondsey – confused but excited. Her restless spirit was stimulated by the promise of a new world to explore. She decided she would drop in on her friend Edward Corinth and show off a little. It did not strike her as odd that she chose to talk over her orders with a member of the despised 'upper class' rather than another Party member.

'Miss Browne, my lord.'

'I do wish you would sound a little less funereal, Fenton. Miss Browne would be very hurt if she could hear you.'

'I did hear him,' Verity said, sweeping into the bedroom uninvited and kissing Edward on the cheek. She turned to Edward's valet. 'I sometimes think you don't trust me, Fenton.'

'Madam!' The rebuke, if on the chilly side, was not totally humourless. He didn't trust her as far as he could throw her which, since she was small and very thin, was a considerable distance.

'I know, Fenton,' Verity sighed theatrically. 'You are being protective, but surely you can't blame me just because, whenever Lord Edward comes to any event in which I have a starring role, he always gets himself a bloody nose?'

She was referring to the Cable Street riots and a lecture she had given in the East End the previous autumn which had ended in fisticuffs. 'Anyway,' she went on, 'I bring you tidings of great joy. I am leaving the country. I shall trouble you no more. I am off to the United States of America – on the *Queen Mary*, no less.' With a sweep of her hand, very much in the Isadora Duncan mode of expression, she swung her arm sideways, knocking a china ornament off the mantelpiece. 'Oops, sorry,' she said, bending to pick the pieces up off the floor.

'Please, miss, let me do that,' Fenton said, with an implied sigh of forbearance. 'I shall return shortly with a dustpan and brush.'

Verity looked around her and noted the suitcases open on the bed and on the floor beside it.

'But you, too, look as though you are about to take a trip. Are you off to Mersham?'

'A little further actually. Please put down my hairbrush. It's a particular phobia of mine not to allow anyone to touch my hairbrush. And that goes for my shaving tackle too,' Edward added, deftly removing the razor from Verity's outstretched hand.

'Oh, that's what it is, is it? I thought it had to be the exhibit marked C – the murder weapon.'

'Please, Verity, I've got a lot to do before I leave. I really don't have time for idle chatter. I have to be at Southampton not later than one pip emma tomorrow and I've only just started to get everything together.'

'Well! That's a coincidence. I too have to be in Southampton

21

tomorrow. I suppose there's no possibility we are going to be shipmates?'

'God forbid!' Edward said, putting his hand to his forehead in imitation of Sir Donald Wolfit playing Macbeth. 'But here's a coincidence,' he continued with heavy irony. 'As you have guessed, I also have a passage booked aboard the *Queen Mary*. We are, in short, to be tossing in the same barque for four, or possibly five, days. Let Joy be unconfined. I had counted on a few days' repose to get me in a fit state to cope with the mind-numbing energy of New York but, what matter . . .? To be with you . . . Just joking,' he added, fending off a cushion. 'Come over here and let me kiss you properly. Quick, before Fenton gets back.'

She offered him her cheek. 'I'm certainly not kissing you if you're going to be patronizing.'

'Sorry, V. But why are you going? I must say, it's quite funny! We both suddenly decide to go to America and end up on the *Queen Mary* together. We'll probably be in next-door cabins. No, wait! I will be in First Class and you will be with the Ellis Island immigrants, I assume.'

'You assume wrong. We newspaper men – and women – travel in style.'

'So, on the spur of the moment, you decide to go to America? Why, for goodness sake? Oughtn't you to be in Spain? I thought there must be one continent at least which is free of the mayhem you seem to bring to the places you visit.'

'I'm not a tourist. I'm a newspaper correspondent,' Verity said grandly. 'So I go where the news is and, if mayhem is your word for news, then you are quite correct. But seriously, are you emigrating, or what? No, I've got it! You're after that girl again, aren't you? What a lark!'

'If you mean Miss Pageant . . .?'

'Yes, Amy.'

Amy Pageant was Lord Weaver's daughter and was now a star on Broadway. Edward and she had had a brief affair and Verity had always been jealous of her, even though she had no right to be.

'As a matter of fact, I am accompanying Lord Benyon who is travelling to the United States to receive an honorary degree

22

from Columbia University and give several important lectures,' Edward said pompously.

'I see. And what precisely is your function? To carry the bags? I never heard you were an economist.'

'I am going as his personal assistant to smooth his way so he can concentrate on the important things.'

'I shall enjoy meeting him again. A very nice man, I thought. I was so sorry about Inna. Is he very unhappy?'

'He's one of those people who bury their unhappiness in work. But you still haven't told me *your* reason for being on the *Queen Mary*.'

'I am going to report on the workers' struggle. Our comrades in arms – how the ordinary American combats the tyranny of capitalism. Hard-hitting stuff.'

'That's for the *Daily Worker*, I imagine. What does Joe Weaver want you to do? If I remember correctly, the *Gazette* already has a correspondent in America.'

'The paper does have a Washington correspondent and, of course, takes stories from Reuters and other news agencies but Joe thought a series of articles on how the ordinary American lives and works would be interesting. The idea being that what the Americans do today, we do next year.'

'I see. Well, there we are then. We travel together. I look forward to it. Now, leave me to get on with my packing.'

'I don't know about travelling together, exactly,' Verity said casually. 'I am travelling with a chap called Sam Forrest. He's John L. Lewis's assistant. Have you heard of him?'

Edward was immediately on his guard.

'He's an American politician, isn't he?'

'He's head of the mineworkers' union.'

'He's not a "Comrade"?'

'No, he believes that reform within the constitution is the only way to avoid revolution. Roosevelt likes him – well, respects him anyway.'

'I look forward to meeting Mr Forrest,' Edward said courteously.

Verity was suspicious. 'I don't trust you when you're being reasonable. I hope you won't try and patronize him like you do me.'

'Tu ne quaesieris, scire nefas, quem mihi, quem tibi finem di dederint, Leuconoë, nec Babylonios temptaris numeros. I don't know why but old Horace has been rather in my mind.'

'There you are! That's just what I mean. You know I have no Latin. It wasn't thought suitable for gels to be taught Latin in the schools I attended. Anyway, wasn't Horace the one who liked little boys?'

'It's not my fault you weren't educated. The poet says, "You don't inquire – it's forbidden to know – what our end will be – whether this winter will be our last." Something like that . . . Oh, and "Don't play about with foreign affairs."'

'I can't think why they teach that stuff at Eton. It should be abolished. I don't trust your translation, anyway. I'm sure there was something about Babylonians in there.'

There was a silence as Fenton returned to the room and began sweeping up the remains of the china ornament.

'I'm sorry, V, I'm forgetting my manners. Have some coffee or something. I can't give you lunch, I'm afraid, I've got to go to the bank and so on and arrange some things for Frank.'

'For Frank?'

'Yes, he's coming too – to carry the bags as you put it. But don't tell him I said that,' he added hastily.

'Oh, that's good.'

There was another, somewhat awkward, silence. Edward's nephew Frank, the future Duke of Mersham, had not endeared himself to his parents by running away from school to join the International Brigade. The Duke had blamed Verity for turning him into a Communist and precipitating his flight to Spain. This was not entirely fair. It was true that Frank had been very taken with Verity and impressed by her commitment to the Party, and she had thoroughly enjoyed seeing a sprig of the aristocracy abandon his class prejudices and side with 'the people'. It helped that he was good-looking and half in love with her. However, she claimed she had never encouraged him, except by example, to go to Spain. If there was anyone to blame it was a young Eton master by the name of John Devon in whose company Frank had gone to war.

Verity had told the Duchess she would bring Frank home and, with Edward, she had done what she had promised. The two of them had travelled to Spain and tracked him down to a particularly nasty spot on the front line in the ever-moving battle for Madrid. The task of getting him back to England was made easier when his commanding officer had been informed that he was only seventeen. Frank had claimed to be twenty. He was immediately ordered out and had no option but to obey. He had spent the journey home in a deep sulk and had remained mutinous back in the bosom of his family. He understood why his uncle should wish to drag him home and listened guiltily as he lectured him on the distress he was causing his parents. However, he found it difficult to forgive Verity for what he saw as her betrayal. How could she of all people not approve of his leaving school to fight for the Republic?

The long and short of it was that Frank had arrived at Mersham Castle a week after Christmas and proceeded to make everyone's life a misery. If there was anywhere more pleasant to be imprisoned than Mersham, Edward could not imagine it, so he was not too sorry for his nephew. Bored and sulky, Frank had cheeked his father and reduced his mother to tears on more than one occasion. He had taken to hunting three days a week, choosing to jump the highest fences and run the greatest risks. His recklessness paid off. He was thrown quite badly, concussing himself briefly, and felt in some obscure way that he had made a point.

He still absolutely refused to go back to Eton and, though the Duke could get him into his old college at Cambridge easily enough, it was evident the boy needed to do something first to clear his head of what his father called 'this Communist nonsense'. There had been some talk of his going to the Cape or Kenya but Edward was against it. He had a feeling that, in his present mood, Frank could easily fall into bad company and turn into one of the lost souls who made their own and other people's lives a misery in the ill-named Happy Valley. Benyon's offer to take him to America came at just the right moment. He would have some sort of a job to keep him busy and he had more than once said how much he wanted to go to the United States, 'where people are valued for what they are, not for where they were born', he would add with bitterness.

The problem, as Edward saw it, was how to get Frank to go willingly. It was important for his self-respect not to be shipped off to the States like the naughty schoolboy he was. Edward suspected that, if his father or mother informed him of what had been arranged, he would rebel. It was better they said nothing other than that Lord Benyon had expressed a desire to meet him and he was to present himself at the Athenaeum the next day for an interview about a possible job.

Frank took the bait, intrigued that anyone should want to offer him employment but determined not to allow himself to be treated like a child. As Edward had anticipated, the two of them liked each other at first sight. It did not matter that Benyon was a middle-aged academic economist and Frank a schoolboy on the cusp of manhood who had been to the wars and returned with his tail between his legs. What mattered was they were both natural rebels. The Duke's son wanted an end to the class system and to help usher in a Communist utopia. The economist liked nothing so much as to ruffle the feathers of politicians, diplomats and businessmen. Benyon displayed like campaign medals the press reports of his spats with Montagu Norman, the Governor of the Bank of England and the most powerful man in the financial world, not excepting the Chancellor of the Exchequer with whom he had also had very public differences of opinion. It was good, too, that there was so little time to think about it. The *Queen Mary* sailed on the Saturday. Benyon made his offer on the Thursday and Frank accepted on the spot.

'That reminds me. How's the book going?' Edward inquired.

Victor Gollancz had just published Verity's account of her time as a foreign correspondent in Spain and in particular the siege of Toledo. Government forces had been routed by Franco's Moorish troops and a savage massacre followed. The book was called *Searchlight on Spain* and had borne the imprint of the Left Book Club.

'Too early to say,' Verity said, affecting nonchalance. She was actually consumed with excitement and it required a great effort of will not to telephone the publisher on a daily basis to find out how many copies had been sold.

'You got my letter? I thought it was very good. Very vivid and, as far as I could judge, accurate.'

Edward's praise meant more to Verity than she would ever have admitted and she had bought an album in which to keep his letter and others of a similar nature – though as yet she had not received any. Edward had been in Spain at the outbreak of the civil war and his was an opinion she valued.

'You really think so?' she was unable to prevent herself asking.

'I really think so. Now please, V, leave me. We'll meet at Philippi.'

'Where?'

'Philippi – *Julius Caesar* ... God help us, woman! Shakespeare.'

Verity had, she supposed, studied Shakespeare at some of the many schools she had briefly attended, but had no memory of this play.

'I can't think how you missed it. It's the classic account of how a Fascist tyrant is killed by a group of conspirators who themselves become tyrants.'

'Of course I've read it,' she lied, 'I just didn't recognize the quote, that's all. Stop being superior. I hate people who are always quoting things.'

'We shall meet on Southampton Dock,' Edward elaborated. 'Now please leave me.'

'Well, we will, dash it!' she riposted. She had meant to say something witty or even biting, but it would have to do. Damn him!

While Frank had been meeting Lord Benyon, Edward had been closeted with Major Ferguson in his dreary little cupboard of an office above a public house off Trafalgar Square. He was going through the reports British agents had sent detailing possible threats to Benyon.

When he had finished, Edward stood up and stretched himself. 'It doesn't amount to much, does it? It's all very vague. An overheard conversation, a copy of a letter recovered from a waste-paper basket, a hint from an official in the Reichsbank ...'

'No, it doesn't,' Ferguson agreed. 'It's one of the reasons Lord Benyon refused to have full police security. He thinks we are exaggerating the threat, and perhaps we are, but it is my duty to take no risks. I don't want it said that I didn't do all I

27

could to protect him. As you know, the man is important enough but his mission makes him *very* important.'

'And the moment Benyon is on American soil I can regard my duty as completed?'

'Yes. You will be met by FBI agent Henry Fawcett who will accompany Lord Benyon throughout his stay. Then, if it is convenient, you will return with Lord Benyon on the *Queen Mary* on March the eighteenth. By that time, he will have succeeded or failed in his mission so he will be in less danger but we musn't take anything for granted. Do you think you can keep him safe for four or, at the worst, five days?'

'God knows.'

'By the way, our chap in New York is Bill Stephenson – a Canadian. Officially, he's Head of British Passport Control in the United States. He has an office in Rockefeller Center. Here's his number, but only telephone him in an emergency. He likes to keep a low profile, you understand. He's one of the best.'

'I see. Your man, Tom Barrett, is staying with Lord Benyon the whole time . . . as his valet?' Edward had been introduced to Barrett the previous day and had liked the look of him. He was a twenty-seven-year-old Welshman possessed of attractive hazel eyes and a wide smile which revealed good teeth. He had played rugby for Wales and looked as though he would be a useful man to have by you in a scrap.

'Yes, he is one of our small band of trained marksmen.'

'Well, that sounds all right. Now, you said you had a list of the First Class passengers?'

'Yes. It may not be quite complete. There are changes right up to the moment the ship sails but here it is.'

Edward was handed a file containing some twenty-five sheets of names. 'It's all right,' Ferguson said smiling. 'You don't have to read this now. It's for you to keep and refer to as and when. I might say, the Atlantic crossing ought to be entertaining. Cunard like to have film stars and the like on board. It brings useful publicity. There are some famous names on the list like the stage magician, Jasper Maskelyne. Have you ever seen him? I saw him at the Palladium once. Quite extraordinary – he cut this girl in half in front of our very eyes . . .'

He noticed Edward looking at him in amusement, stopped and then went on more calmly, 'Apparently entertainers like Mas-

28

kelyne get a free trip across to the States in return for doing a show. There's also the black American singer and actor, Warren Fairley, and his new wife, Jane Barclay.'

'Of course! Fairley's been playing Othello at the Haymarket,' Edward said, as excited at the opportunity of meeting him as Ferguson had been about Maskelyne. 'I gather it was quite a sensation. The reviews were ecstatic. I meant to see it but because of . . . you know, having to dash off to Spain, I never did. Jane Barclay's some sort of starlet, isn't she?'

'Fairley met her on the last film he made. They were married immediately after it was finished – that was about eighteen months ago.'

'I see you have been doing your homework! Isn't Fairley a Communist?'

'He is and, as you can imagine, a black man who is also a Red married to a white girl has a rough ride in the States. Too colourful, if you will pardon the pun. It's one of the reasons he wanted to come and live in England. He gets too much harassment in the States from people who should know better. He only goes back to make films. There's one character who isn't going to like sharing First Class with him – George Earle Day. Ever heard of him?'

Edward looked blank.

'He's Senator Day from South Carolina and he doesn't like the English, Jews or anybody with a black skin. He hates Fairley worse than most. Their paths have crossed on several occasions. The last time, Fairley was making a speech against segregation in the city of Anderson and Day had him locked in the cells for a night. It caused an outcry in the press.'

'Hmm, he sounds just the fellow to make for an interesting trip. By the way, if he doesn't like the English, what's he been doing in London?'

'He's been . . . how shall I put it? . . . oiling a few wheels. He's hoping to be made ambassador to the Court of St James. Ambassador Bingham – a good man and a friend to Britain – has Hodgkin's disease and I am sorry to say is unlikely to recover.'

'Senator Day's a friend of Roosevelt?'

'Hard to say. More likely FDR wants him out of Washington.'

29

'But surely London is an important posting?'

'Yes, and at such a crucial time for us it could be awkward having an ambassador of Day's persuasion. He's an isolationist who believes England's ripe for Herr Hitler's picking. And he may be right at that,' Ferguson added grimly.

'Anyone else?'

'You'll find in that file potted biographies of anyone who is anyone. Oh, one more person to look out for is Bernard Hunt, the art historian and dealer. We have our suspicions of him.'

'What sort of suspicions?'

'We think he's probably a crook so don't buy any pictures off him.'

'I'll try not to,' Edward grinned.

3

As they drew up on the dockside and recognized the three black-and-red-ringed funnels of the Cunard Line, the sheer size of the *Queen Mary* silenced even Verity who had been talking all the way from London. Edward had crossed the Atlantic on the *Normandie* the previous year and now made every effort to act as if he was used to great liners but it was no good and he was soon swapping statistics with Sam Forrest, like boys admiring a new motor car.

'I read somewhere that if she was stood on her bows she would be taller than the Eiffel Tower,' Edward said.

'I guess she'll take the Blue Riband off the *Normandie*.'

'I'm sure she will. She can make thirty knots, or so they say. They deliberately made her bigger and faster than the *Normandie*, just for the hell of it.'

Verity piped up, 'I heard a funny story. Apparently, they were going to call her the *Queen Victoria* but the King – I mean George V, of course – misunderstood when Cunard's chairman asked permission to name it after a great queen and said Queen Mary would be delighted!'

They looked around for Lord Benyon's party which included Frank, who had already taken on his role as chief bag carrier and dogsbody, but there was no sign of them. The dockside was seething with people but it was ordered chaos. Each of the two thousand passengers seemed to have brought along their friends and relations to see them off. The smartly uniformed officials, clipboards at the ready, marshalled each passenger according to class and directed them to their designated gangway. Fenton summoned porters, who disappeared with the luggage, and then took their tickets for stamping, leaving Edward, Sam Forrest and Verity to go on board. Edward had been in two minds whether or not to take Fenton. He elicited from Ferguson that the government was not prepared to pay for *his* ticket. He decided finally it was worth fifty pounds to have Fenton by his side. In the unlikely event of there being any trouble, he was a good man to have around and anyway, damn it, if he was to travel in style he needed his valet.

As they crossed the covered gangplank into the belly of the ship, Edward, giving way to fancy, thought of it as an umbilical cord. But, oddly, they were returning into a kind of luxurious womb, not leaving it. They would have no responsibilities on board except to enjoy themselves – or rather that was true of most of the passengers. He had the responsibility of keeping Lord Benyon alive for the duration of the voyage. Surely, that ought to be possible, he told himself.

Verity was unable to restrain her excitement as she went on board. Edward noticed Forrest watching her with an affection-ate smile and, when he put his arm round her, he felt the familiar stab of jealousy. On their way down to Southampton in the Lagonda, Edward had resolved to seize the opportunity provided by being closeted with Verity for almost a week to ask her to marry him. Wasn't it said that shipboard romance was almost compulsory? Verity's excitement and evident good humour made him feel optimistic but he wished Sam Forrest had been a little less good-looking, that his chin was a little less rugged and his smile a little less engaging. He was young too – about Verity's age he guessed, maybe a year or two younger, say twenty-five or six – and he made Edward feel old.

Cunard had decided for some reason to call First Class Cabin Class but, whatever its name, it was the height of luxury. When Verity was shown into her stateroom by an obsequious stew-ard, the first thing she noticed was the white telephone beside her berth and she let out a squeak of excitement. 'Can we really telephone from our cabins or is it just so we can telephone other cabins?'

'No, madam. You can use it to ring another cabin, of course, but you can telephone almost anywhere in the world. There is a seven-hundred-line switchboard and five radio operators are on duty twenty-four hours a day. Shall I ask your stewardess to unpack for you?'

Verity gulped. It was true she had rushed round to Hartnell's for a new white linen suit and an evening dress – apparently blues, greens and yellows were the fashion – but she wasn't sure she wanted a strange woman inspecting her lingerie and finding it wanting. She glanced at the steward, who smiled as if he read her thoughts, and that decided her. She wasn't going to be ashamed of anything. With a tilt of her chin, familiar to all her friends, she said coolly, 'That would be kind.'

Sam Forrest, who had the cabin next to her, put his head round the door. 'May I come in?' he inquired, coming in anyway. 'Isn't this the tops, Miss Browne?'

'Sam, if we're going to be on a boat for a week – even a boat as big as this – you've got to stop calling me "Miss Browne".'

'Really? I appreciate that, and you can go on calling me Sam.' He spread his hands out. 'It gives me a real drive playing at being a Vanderbilt. I came over on a crate which I guess don't amount to a "hill o'beans", as my pop would say, compared with this. I just hope none of my folks get to hear about all this and think I need taking down a peg or two. Come and see my cabin. I even got a "barth", as you English call it. Oh, and by the way, this isn't a boat, Verity, it's a ship.'

The telephone rang, making Verity jump. She lifted the receiver gingerly. 'Verity, is that you? It's me ... Edward. You're on B Deck, aren't you? You've got to come up to A Deck and see where I've ended up. You'll be green with envy.'

'I doubt that but we'll come anyway.'

Edward wondered sourly if it was always going to be 'we' and if he would ever be able to prise Verity from Sam Forrest's side.

Lord Benyon had been allotted three of the eight special staterooms on A Deck. In fact, these were suites, each comprising a bedroom, sitting-room and bathroom. In the second suite, which Edward shared with Barrett, the sitting-room had been turned into a bedroom so that Barrett could be on hand in any emergency. Normally, servants had cabins in Tourist Class, where Fenton was lodged. Benyon had a double bed and, besides the usual furniture, there was a writing table and two easy chairs so that he could work as comfortably as if he were in his study at home.

Fenton appeared. He had dealt with all the paperwork, seen the luggage stowed and garaged the Lagonda to await their return. At that moment Verity and Sam Forrest knocked on the door and Fenton let them in.

'Fenton's arranged everything, V. All the trunks . . . everything. He's quite indispensable.'

'You're a marvel. Thank you so much. Isn't he a marvel, Sam?'

'Very much so. Thank you, Mr Fenton.'

'It's a pleasure, sir . . . miss.'

Sam seemed a shade embarrassed. He had never had a valet and had no idea how he should treat the man. When Fenton turned his back, he asked Verity, in a dumb show, if he should tip him. Verity shook her head vigorously. She didn't approve of valets on principle and she knew Fenton didn't approve of her on some contradictory principle which she had never properly understood, but she knew enough to sense that he would be insulted by being offered a tip.

'Gosh, this is luxury!' Verity said, opening a cupboard. 'Why, there's even a bar. Do we have a bar, Sam?'

'No booze in my cabin. I guess we aren't important after all.'

'Nor is Edward. It's Lord Benyon who has to be coddled. Where is he, anyway? Oughtn't he to be here?'

'I don't suppose he'll be long,' Edward said, but a small, hard nut of unease made his stomach contract.

An hour passed exploring their new home and marvelling as each new wonder revealed itself. At last, hooters sounded and instructions were given over loud hailers for visitors to make their way to the exits. Final tearful embraces and hearty handshakes ensued.

'Let's go on deck,' Edward suggested. 'What time have you, V? I wish Benyon wasn't leaving it so late.'

He was getting seriously worried. Was he going to have the embarrassment of sailing across the Atlantic without the man he was supposed to be protecting? They all trooped on deck to join the throng of passengers waving to their friends on the dock and shouting inaudible farewells. Edward scanned the quayside, his hand to his forehead. He noticed that some of the gangways were already being removed. He was just wondering if he ought to try and see the Captain and demand the ship be held for the latecomers when there was a blaring of horns and a Rolls-Royce swung on to the dock. It came to an abrupt halt by one of the gangways. Frank tumbled out shouting for porters. The car was immediately surrounded by ship's officers and stewards who obscured Edward's view. When the crowd parted, he could see Benyon, aided by Barrett and followed by a tall, red-haired man he assumed must be Marcus Fern, being ushered up the gangway. Fretting that Frank was not with them, he made to go down to the lower deck to greet them. As he did so, Verity called to him and he went back to the rail. He saw his nephew still on the dockside with two officials. They were checking which suitcases were to go in the hold and which were to be sent to the cabin. Looking up at the ship, Frank caught sight of his uncle and gave him a cheery wave. Then he picked up two heavy-looking briefcases and loped up the gangway.

Edward breathed a sigh of relief. 'Damn the boy! He would be late for his own funeral,' he muttered to himself and then wished he hadn't.

Half an hour later, her sirens sounding urgently, the *Queen Mary* was nudged away from the quay by blunt-nosed tugs, and turned her sleek black bows toward Southampton Water.

Verity and Edward began to make their way to Benyon's suite. A slim, anxious-looking man pushed past them through heavy swing doors towards the dining-room.

'Did you see who that was, V?' Edward said, lighting a cigarette.

'No, who was it?'

'Henry Hall.' Verity still looked puzzled. 'You know, the dance-band leader. He's on the wireless . . . Don't worry about it. You've obviously been out of the country too long.'

When they reached Lord Benyon's stateroom, Frank was there piling up suitcases. He kissed Verity and shook his uncle's hand. 'How's he shaping up?' Edward inquired of Benyon, trying not to sound like a mother hen.

'He's been invaluable. We had a smashed windscreen which delayed us. I hope you weren't worried.'

'I was rather. Mr Fern . . .?'

'I'm so sorry. I was thinking you two knew each other. Marcus, may I introduce Lord Edward Corinth. Edward . . . Marcus Fern, one of the ablest men in the City and a valued friend.'

Fern held up his hand. 'Please, Benyon. If we're not going to quarrel, you're going to have to stop flattering me. There are many abler men in the City than I, Lord Edward. By the way, I've been hearing all about you. Your nephew seems to admire you. I can't think how you do it. My sister's son thinks I'm a terrible bore, and perhaps I am.'

Edward smiled. 'You have the suite next to this, isn't that right? Then there's Barrett and me on the other side.'

'Yes, Benyon won't escape,' Fern said with a grin.

Edward glanced behind him. Verity was talking to Benyon – they seemed to have a real rapport. He was praising her book and she was blushing prettily.

'Will you excuse me for a minute, Fern? I need to have a word with my nephew. Frank, come into my cabin for a moment, will you?'

Frank followed his uncle obediently into the next cabin and Edward asked him to close the door behind him.

'Yes, Uncle? Did you want to say something?'

'I'm glad to see you're getting on so well with Lord Benyon.'

'Yes. I like him enormously. I think I'm going to be an economist.'

Edward repressed a smile. 'What made you so late? I was getting worried.' He tapped his pocket and fetched out his silver cigarette case. 'I thought you were going to miss the boat, literally, or were you just trying to "make an entrance"?'

'Oh no, nothing like that. We were late starting – some last-minute meeting of Mr Fern's overran. Then, on the way down, someone tried to stop us.'

'Whatever do you mean?' Edward looked up, the lighter in his hand half-way to the cigarette in his mouth. He removed the cigarette so he could speak more clearly. 'Who tried to stop you?'

'Can I have a cigarette?'

'Certainly not!'

'I hope you're not going to treat me like a child.'

'No, but ... anyway, what happened? Who tried to stop you?'

'We were bowling along just outside Micheldever ... it's a good road and we were going quite fast when there was a bang. The windscreen shattered and I thought a stone had come up from the road. Fortunately, Bannister, Lord Benyon's chauffeur, is very good. He brought the car to a halt at the side of the road even though he couldn't see a thing. God knows what would have happened if we had careered across the road into the oncoming traffic.'

'Golly! Was it a stone?'

'No. It was a bullet. I've got it here. I thought you'd like to see it. It went between Barrett and the chauffeur.' He passed Edward a metal object, flattened and misshapen but definitely a bullet. 'A .303, I'd say. What do you think?'

'Good Lord. Frank, I'm horrified. What did you do – call the police?'

'I wanted to, of course, but Benyon said we shouldn't. He said we'd get delayed and that was exactly what they wanted. I asked who "they" were and he said to ask you.'

'I'm not sure I can tell you.'

'I say, if I'm going to have people shoot at me, I think it's only fair I know what it's all about. I'm not a rabbit, you know. It would have been safer if you'd jolly well left me in Spain.'

'Damn and blast! Your mother would kill me if she knew I had put you in danger,' Edward exclaimed, rather unfortunately in the circumstances. He considered for a moment. 'All I can say is that Lord Benyon is due to have a very important meeting with President Roosevelt in Washington. It's top secret but it looks as though not secret enough.'

'And who wants to stop this meeting taking place? The Nazis?'

'Yes, if you must know, Nazis.'

'Gosh! How absolutely ripping.'

'Don't be an ass, Frank. This is serious, not some schoolboy prank.'

'Sorry, Uncle.' Frank sounded crushed. 'So we need to keep our eyes open?'

'Indeed, but I can't really tell you what to look out for. The main thing is keep all this under your hat. Barrett knows as much as you do so you can trust him but nobody else.'

'Not even Verity?'

Edward shuddered. 'Especially not Verity.' Frank opened his mouth to object but Edward stopped him. 'Verity is first and foremost a journalist and a very good one. You would put her in an impossible situation if you started pressing alarm buttons. Don't even tell her why you were delayed. It's nothing to do with her.'

'If you say so, Uncle, but, as you say, she's a very good journalist. I expect she'll get it out of Mr Fern – probably has already.'

'Frank! This is serious,' Edward repeated. 'You have to be discreet and I'd better impress it on Fern, but then, he knows what's at stake. The trouble is, we've no idea if there is anyone aboard who might try and finish off what your friend outside Micheldever started.'

'So Barrett's a policeman, is he? I thought he looked a bit tough for a valet. Wow, I really think I'm going to enjoy this trip.'

Verity, too, was enjoying herself. It was something of a paradox that, sincere as she was in her belief that wealth ought to be more fairly distributed, she liked the way the rich lived. She liked fashionable clothes, she liked to eat in good restaurants and she liked luxurious hotels. The *Queen Mary* was everything she admired. She had already explored the public rooms, each more splendid than the one before, decorated with paintings and murals by the most distinguished living artists. Cunard had decided to eschew the 'Stately Home' look in favour of a light and airy modern design. The First Class saloon – which Cunard called prosaically the Main Lounge – was perhaps the most magnificent room. Verity had pushed her way through heavy swing doors to stand, mouth agape, in this great space which pierced three decks. A hundred feet long, it had walls of a rich golden colour, the dull bronze metalwork contrasting with the dark wood panelling. She counted no fewer than thirty-two tall windows which illuminated a huge gilt panel featuring unicorns and peacocks above a massive onyx mantel-piece. At first she thought the huge room was empty – everyone was on deck or in their cabins – but then a deep, dark brown voice boomed at her from an armchair to the right of the fireplace.

'Magnificent, isn't it? Do you see, they have a stage and a cinema here too. I always notice that because so often I am asked "as a great favour" – that's usually how they put it – to sing.'

Verity walked over and said, 'You're Warren Fairley, aren't you? I must tell you how much I admire your work for social equality. I'm proud to call myself a Communist and your example has been an inspiration to us all. I've read about your work for the ILD.' The ILD was the International Labor Defense League, the legal arm of the Communist Party in the United States which was active in the defence of strikers and racial minorities, particularly blacks. 'You live in England now, don't you?'

'Well, Miss . . .?'

'Miss Browne, Verity Browne. You'll have to forgive me but I have never seen you on stage so I can't say anything about acting.'

Fairley solemnly rose from his chair, the book in his lap falling on to the floor along with an issue of *New Masses*, and shook Verity's hand. 'I am delighted . . . but surprised to meet a fellow Party member in the First Class lounge on the *Queen Mary*. But then life is full of surprises. It is so refreshing to meet a white person who likes my politics rather than seeing me as just another singer of Negro spirituals.'

Verity stooped to pick up the book he had dropped. '*Mary Barton* by Mrs Gaskell – what is it? I've never heard of Mrs Gaskell.'

'She was a friend of Charlotte Brontë. Wrote her biography in fact, but her novels are the thing. They're about working-class life in Victorian England – the North mainly. "Trouble-at-t'mill" – that kind of thing, but very good. Her descriptions of the industrial poor are required reading for people of our persuasion.'

'Golly! Well, of course, I will read them.'

'Here, take this. I've read it before.'

'May I? Thank you so much. I suppose I couldn't ask you to write in it for me, could I?'

He took out his fountain pen and wrote on the title page. When he had finished, he said, 'I expect you think it's an odd book for an American – a black American – to be reading but I think John Steinbeck must have read her too. Have you read *In Dubious Battle*? It came out last year. It's the story of a strike of migratory fruit pickers.'

'You must think me very ignorant but I haven't heard of him either. I have read Albert Halper's *Scab!*, though.' She saw from the look in his eyes that he did not consider Halper to be in the same league as this man Steinbeck. 'Oh dear! I have so much to learn!'

Fairley chuckled. 'At least you want to learn. I find so many people like to stay with their own ignorance. It makes prejudice so much easier.'

'I only read books which tell the truth,' Verity said, as though the truth was something finite and definable. 'I don't really read novels. They're . . . made up.'

'*Le récit est menteur et le sens est véritable.* That's La Fontaine – the story is a lie but the meaning is true.'

'I see . . . I think.'

'For the Marxist, the fundamental forces of today are those which are working to destroy capitalism and establish socialism. We can all agree on what is important – the economic crisis, unemployment, the growth of Fascism, the approach of a new world war. A writer today who wishes to produce his best work must go over to the progressive side of the class conflict.'

Verity nodded her head gravely. She wanted to ask whether Jane Barclay was a Marxist but didn't quite dare.

The contrast between the two of them was comical: the small, birdlike girl, her white hand almost enveloped in the powerful black hand, looking up in awe at the famous – not to say 'notorious' – face of the other. Verity was struck not just by the physical presence of the man – six foot three and with the broad chest of an opera singer – but by the dignity of his demeanour. Although she could not remember ever having read *Othello*, she recalled a line which had been drummed into her at school: 'Keep up your bright swords for the dew will rust them.'

She only half understood what it meant but it seemed to express just the kind of noble contempt for the rabble this man exuded and yet, paradoxically, it was to 'the rabble' he had dedicated his life.

'I suppose we ought to be on deck or something,' she said.

'I don't want to sound arrogant, Miss Browne, but I have made this crossing many times – though not, of course, on this great ship – so I can take my leisure here without too great a feeling of guilt. In any case, I told my wife this was where I would meet her. I am afraid I had to leave her and her maid to unpack on their own. I thought I might otherwise drown in lingerie. But don't let me stop you . . .'

Verity giggled. 'I was just exploring but I can do that any time. I would much rather talk to you . . . I mean, if I'm not being a nuisance. I expect you must be tired with strangers buttonholing you.'

'Not when they are young and beautiful with principles I can share.' His eyes twinkled and suddenly Verity found her insides turning over. This was a very attractive man, she found herself thinking, and to her annoyance she blushed. It annoyed her that, as a hard-bitten war correspondent, she should blush like a young girl.

'But why are you living in London? Or are you going back to live in America?' she asked hurriedly to cover her confusion.

'I am going to the States to make a film and address two political meetings on the issue of race but then I will come back to London. The authorities in my own country make it almost impossible for me to live peaceably there. To quote a hero of mine, Frederick Douglass, a runaway slave who travelled Europe arousing anti-slavery sentiment, ' "I go back for the sake of my brethren. I go to suffer with them; to toil with them; to endure with them; to undergo outrage with them; to lift up my voice in their behalf." '

What might have sounded grandiose or melodramatic in another man, resonated in the rich, *basso profundo* voice of Warren Fairley as simple truth.

'You will think I am very stupid but is there still much . . .

41

you know, what's the word – discrimination? I suppose in the South . . .'

'Miss Browne, you must not encourage me to lecture you. Yes, there is still a frontier across which no Negro can cross. There may be no customs posts or walls but it is a real frontier for all that. If a black man wants to move into a white neighbourhood in any city – I don't mean just in Atlanta, Georgia, but even New York or Washington – he will not be allowed to.'

'But that's terrible. Who would stop him? The police?'

'Yes, the police in the last resort but it would never come to that. The black face would see all doors closed against him. He would find no one prepared to sell to him and, if he wants to travel to another country, he may not be permitted to go.'

'But surely they can't stop you going abroad?'

'When first I applied for a passport to come to Europe, it was denied me. They called me a troublemaker and a denigrator of my country. I told them I was a patriot but they laughed. It took me three years and the agitations of many powerful white men before I was given my passport and it may be revoked at any time.'

'So there is a risk in going back to America?'

'A grave risk, Miss Browne, but a risk I intend to run.'

'You have many enemies then?'

He leant over and put his hand over hers. 'In the scales, just one of my friends tips the balance against all my enemies. I am what I am and I would echo that racist bigot, Martin Luther, whose views I abhor, and say, "Here I stand."'

Their tête-à-tête was interrupted by a shrill squeal. 'Why there you are, Warren. I've been looking all over for you. I looked in here before but I didn't see you and you must have been so engaged with this little lady you didn't see me.'

'Jane, honey, look who I have found! Another Comrade. I wouldn't be surprised if there are more reds in First Class than in Tourist. May I introduce Miss Verity Browne? Verity, Miss Jane Barclay.'

The two women looked at each other with instant loathing. Verity was not a frequent 'picture-goer' but she would immediately have identified Jane Barclay as a 'film star'. She might never have seen her fleeting appearance in *Blue Orchid* or her moment of fame as a streetwalker in *Sinners* but the woman who now claimed Warren Fairley was everything she ought to be. She was excessively blonde – platinum blonde, she thought it was called – with an hourglass figure and a dress which revealed more of her breasts than Verity thought wise.

'Pleased, I'm sure,' she said, putting a limp hand in Verity's. 'Now, sweetheart,' she continued, turning to her husband, 'your little girl's just dying for a Manhattan. While I was looking for you I discovered a cute little cocktail lounge complete with a good-looking boy behind the bar only too eager to satisfy my desires. Are you coming with me or am I to go unprotected into temptation?'

Jane Barclay spoke in a southern drawl which Verity thought was adopted for her benefit. Anyway, it was clear she was de trop so she said a quick goodbye and was favoured by Warren Fairley with a suspicion of a wink. As she made her way up on deck, she thought how odd it was that highly intelligent men left their brains at home when they chose their women.

Edward had also been making friends. He had gone with Frank to see how Lord Benyon wished to spend his first evening on board and discovered him deep in conversation with the man Major Ferguson had labelled a crook.

'Ah, there you both are!' Benyon said amiably. 'I want you to meet a good friend of mine, Bernard Hunt, the distinguished art historian. We were discussing the art on board.' Introductions were made and hands shaken. Hunt was a lean, tall man with the loricate, leathery skin of the chain smoker. He was smoking now, and his long, sensitive, nicotine-yellow fingers against his equine face made Edward want to wipe his own hand on his coat. There was something dirty about him. 'He was telling me Cunard consulted him on who they should commission to decorate the ship. It was a brave move of Cunard's chairman, Sir Percy Bates, to make the *Queen Mary* a showpiece of modern British art. It must have been quite a responsibility, Hunt?'

'It was! A great responsibility and a great burden. I was bound to make myself unpopular and I did.'

'Well, indeed,' Benyon said, smiling mischievously. 'My

good friend, Mr Duncan Grant, was commissioned to paint some murals and then had his sketches turned down. He was very much upset, as you can imagine.'

'That was unfortunate but, really, they were quite unsuitable.' Hunt quickly changed tack. 'Lord Edward, I would be happy to take you and your nephew on a tour of the ship if you were interested. The paintings in the private dining-rooms by Dame Laura Knight and Vanessa Bell – another of Lord Benyon's friends – are very pleasing.'

'Oh yes. I've seen Vanessa's paintings,' Benson responded. 'Her work is absurdly undervalued in my opinion but, of course, you'll say I'm *parti pris*.'

'That's very kind of you, Mr Hunt,' Edward said. 'I would very much like to look at the pictures with you, and Frank should come too. He needs further education.'

Frank looked at him with distaste. 'Sorry, not me. I'm playing squash with a man. Gosh, is that the time? I must run – that is, if you don't need me, sir,' he added guiltily, turning to Benyon.

'No, that's all right, Frank. I'm going to do some work. The steward tells me the long-range weather forecast isn't good and we might have a rough crossing. I'm afraid I'm not much of a sailor so, if I'm going to get anything done, I ought to do it now before I'm prostrated."

'Surely a modern ship like this won't roll very much?' Frank said.

'I have to say that on the maiden voyage, on which I was privileged to be a guest of Cunard,' Hunt put in, his face going a shade paler, if that were possible, 'she did "roll", sometimes quite alarmingly, and the weather was said to be good.'

'Who did those amazing paintings on the walls of the Verandah Grill?' Edward broke in, seeing Benyon looking apprehensive. 'I think that's what it's called, isn't it?'

'Those rather risqué pictures of carnival crowds?'

'Yes, that's right.'

'I'm glad you like them. They're by Doris Zinkeisen who is on board with us. I'll introduce you. If you're ready, Lord Edward, we might leave Lord Benyon to his work and your nephew to his exercise and walk round the public rooms.'

44

'Well, if you are sure that wouldn't be a bore...' Edward said politely.

'That's it! I've had enough! I thought I was fit but I'm licked.' The young American looked at Frank with admiration. 'You've hardly worked up a sweat and here I am on the floor.'

'Isn't it amazing!' Frank said.

'What?'

'This place. Having a real squash court on a ship.'

'Sure is, and I want to use it now, while it's calm. Can you imagine trying to play squash in the Bay of Biscay!'

He laughed and his broad smile revealed the perfect teeth of the well-bred American. Frank had struck up an acquaintance with him in the cocktail bar and they had liked each other immediately. They were of an age – Perry Roosevelt being the elder by two years – and had both been brought up among the rich and privileged. Frank had rebelled against his background, hating to have it so easy. His running away to Spain had been designed to assert his position as an adult but, in an odd way, it had made him feel more of a child than ever. When he had been hauled back home, he had been secretly quite relieved. He would never admit it but Spain had been frightening in a way he had never imagined. His uncle had been tactful – he had not dressed him down or patronized him – and even the Duke, his father, had not berated him as he had anticipated. His mother had been so delighted to have him back in one piece that she said not a word to him of the anxiety she had felt. All this restraint had the desired effect: Frank felt guilty – ashamed – angry with himself and the world in general.

This trip with Lord Benyon was a godsend. He had longed to go to America. He instinctively loved all things American and, though he had felt a little bored at being made a baggage handler, he had had, in the event, an exciting time of it. Within two days of meeting his employer he had been shot at and, though he was able to pretend – after Spain – that he was 'used to it', it had given him quite a jolt. It was all very well dodging bullets in a country at war but in the Hampshire country-side...? That was unsettling. He had been impressed by Benyon's behaviour under fire. He might not look 'a man's man', as they said in the body-building advertisements in the newspapers, but he had been coolness itself.

Mr Fern, too, had seemed unmoved by the experience but, when Frank looked at the papers he had in his hand which he had been discussing with Benyon, he was surprised to see that Fern had, quite unconsciously, crumpled them into a ball. Barrett had taken charge and no one had questioned his authority. He had been sitting in front with the chauffeur and, even before the car had come to a halt, he had smashed a hole in the fractured windscreen with his gloved hand. Once he had ascertained nobody had been hurt, he had ordered the chauffeur to continue to Southampton.

'That was a bullet, Lord Benyon, not a stone. We're lucky to be alive and we should get away before whoever it is takes another shot at us. If we lose a tyre, we'll be sitting ducks.'

'Shouldn't we call the police?'

'There's nothing to be gained by waiting here for the local police,' Barrett said decisively. 'They won't know how to deal with the situation. For all we know, the gunman may be repositioning himself as we speak. From the position of the hole in the windscreen, I would say he's somewhere over there.' He pointed a hundred yards ahead of them where several trees lined the road.

Everyone had looked nervous and the chauffeur started the engine so clumsily that it stalled and they had to wait a few moments before he could try again. This time it started, to the relief of all concerned. The chauffeur swung the car into the road and they sped off.

'Did you see anyone?' Frank asked Barrett.

'No, nor did I expect to. We're not dealing with amateurs.'

Frank had wondered just who they were dealing with but decided not to ask. In their heavy ulsters, Barrett and the chauffeur were reasonably well protected against the wind but they must have been cold, Frank thought. The rest of them in the back were protected by the glass partition. When they stopped for petrol half an hour later, Frank saw Barrett probing a hole in the upholstery with a knife. 'Ah, got it! I thought so.' He had handed the spent bullet to Frank. 'Keep it as a souvenir, if you like. It's no use to me. Let's hope it's the last of its kind we see. It must have missed my head by an inch, damn it.'

After their game they showered and, at Perry's suggestion, repaired to the bar. Frank would have liked to talk about being shot at with his new American friend but he stopped himself. Perry seemed 'a good chap' and was travelling First Class but, even so, he really knew nothing about him.

'You're related to the President?' he asked.

The direct question seemed to fluster Perry a little. 'I'm only a cousin . . . a distant cousin. It's a huge clan. My sister and I hardly ever get to see the great man except at major family gatherings. You know Mrs Roosevelt is also a cousin? It must be odd to marry someone and not change your name.'

'Your sister? Is she on board?'

'Sure. Talk of the devil, here she is. She's my twin.'

The girl who came towards them with the unconscious grace of the young was wearing a simple white dress, white stockings and a straw hat with a ribbon round it. She looked part angelic child – the kind you don't trust – and part tennis player, Helen Wills without her racket. She was the most beautiful thing Frank had ever seen and he fell helplessly in love before she had even opened her mouth.

'Philly, I want you to meet my new friend, Frank . . . Lord Corinth? Is that how I should introduce you?'

Frank did not hear what was said to him. He just gazed at the girl, his mouth a little open, proving that love really can strike a person deaf and dumb.

'Hey there,' Perry said, waving a hand in front of Frank's eyes, 'don't fall in love with my sister like all the rest. You're my friend. I found you first. Philly, Frank here's a duke or he will be one day, I guess. He's a genuine English aristocrat and don't pretend you've met any others because you haven't.'

Philly swung her long legs over a stool and said, 'A Gibson, please, Roger.' The bar steward looked gratified that the pretty girl already knew his name.

'And for you, sir?'

'Oh, a gimlet,' Frank said, trying to sound sophisticated. 'What's a Gibson?' he inquired, unable to sustain the fiction that he was a habitué of nightclubs.

47

'Gin and vermouth,' Philly replied. 'Just a martini really. I was trying to impress you.'

'You succeeded.'

Perry gave every sign that he was bored – or was it jealousy? 'Have you seen the swimming-pool? It's a killer. What say you? Shall we go use it before the *hoi polloi* find it? I need to shower anyway and so do you, Frank. Doesn't he stink, Philly?'

'I don't smell anything. Come over here.'

Obediently, Frank got off his stool and went over to the girl. She raised her face to his and sniffed. 'Closer,' she commanded and Frank lowered his face to hers. A whiff of scent made his head swim. He thought he must kiss her or die but, before he could do so, she said, 'You're right, Perry. He does stink.'

Frank looked from one twin to the other, bewildered and not a little in love with both of them. 'I'll go and get my costume,' he said with an effort. Feeling very thirsty all of a sudden, he swallowed down his cocktail and almost choked. The twins laughed.

The pool was the most luxurious Frank had ever seen. He guessed it must be over thirty feet long and maybe twenty wide. It had two diving boards and was faced with glazed terracotta tiles. The walls shimmered green and red while the mother-of-pearl ceiling added to the impression of being in a jewel box. Perry and he showered and then, laughing loudly to fill the emptiness of the place and hear the echo, pulled on their trunks and made a dash for the water. Out of the corner of his eye, Frank saw the girl leaning against one of the faience columns which supported the arches over the pool. She too had changed but seemed in no hurry to get into the water. Making every effort to impress her, Frank dived off one of the boards and resurfaced to find Philly had not even been watching. She had been fitting her bathing cap in a mirror on one side of the pool.

Frank pulled himself up on to the side and watched the water stream off him. It was quite warm but, feeling suddenly naked, he pulled a towel round his shoulders. Perry came to sit beside him. 'Fancy swimming in February in the middle of the Atlantic!'

'I don't suppose you'd last many minutes if you were

swimming in the Atlantic.' Frank paused but Perry made no comment so he continued, 'With a name like Roosevelt, I suppose that means you are going into politics.'

'I don't think so. Not immediately, anyway. I want to make money.'

'But aren't you rich?' Frank asked naively. 'Oh, I'm sorry. That sounds rude.'

'No, I don't mind. I guess we are rich compared with other folk but we're not rich by the standards of the rich, if you know what I mean.'

'But there's always going to be someone richer than you,' Frank laughed.

'Maybe, but not much richer by the time I'm through. You can't go into politics without money, anyway. I expect it's the same in England.'

Frank considered. 'Money always helps, I suppose, but politicians aren't rich the way you mean it. Stanley Baldwin's father was an industrialist – steel or iron, I think – and the Chamberlains are not poor but we don't have Rockefellers and Mellons like you do in the States.'

'Not even dukes? Aren't they rich?'

Frank blushed but tried to answer coolly, as if talking about how rich you were was something he did all the time. 'My father is rich in land but he doesn't have millions in the bank.'

'Did you go to Eton?'

Frank found there was something distasteful about being questioned so blatantly but he had, after all, started it. He knew it was the American way not to beat about the bush and, in theory at least, he approved.

'I went to Eton but then I went off to Spain before I was finished to join the International Brigade,' he said casually.

Perry was impressed. 'Wow! You've been to war? And all I've done is prepped at Grotton and now I'm at Harvard – just to please my Pop.'

'Your parents are here, on the ship?'

'My mother is. Pop's in Washington. They're divorced.'

Frank could not prevent himself being shocked. Where he came from divorce did not happen – or, if it did, it meant social ruin. He had heard divorce did not carry the same stigma in the States, but still . . .

They turned to watch Philly on the end of the board, preparing to dive. She was clearly waiting until she had their full attention. 'She's very beautiful,' Frank said, without meaning to.

Perry looked at him oddly. 'Don't let her sucker you. She's like that girl in *Great Expectations* – they made us read it at college – she has no heart. Don't say I didn't warn you.'

Frank wasn't listening. With a graceful bounce, Philly had dived. Clean as a knife she cut the surface of the water and then swam to the side to join them. 'Look,' she whispered, 'we're not alone any more. I'm going. I hate being looked at.'

This was so obviously untrue, Frank opened his mouth to object. Then he saw the old man and his wife at the other end of the pool climbing gingerly down the steps into the shallow water. She meant she only liked being watched by people she wanted to impress. He saw that now and it cheered him up no end. He understood that, for some reason, this wonderful girl wanted to impress *him*. He gathered up Philly's wrap and helped her put it on. He was tender and she shot him a look of gratitude which made his pulse race. At that moment, he would have done anything she asked him. He looked apologetically at Perry who was smiling compassionately at him.

4

Not many hours had passed since those who had boarded the *Queen Mary* at Southampton had looked about them with, as the poet Keats puts it, 'a wild surmise'. They had struggled to find their way about, found their berths and lost them again, expressed wonder and awe at the grandeur and luxury of their new abode while worrying, at least in the case of the females, at the inadequacy of their wardrobes. These same passengers now watched with amused condescension the absurd floundering of the lost souls joining the ship at Cherbourg. The 'old hands' chatted amongst themselves, no longer strangers, but an aristocracy bemoaning the necessity of absorbing these interlopers, many of them, it was whispered, 'foreigners'.

A sea voyage, it has been said, suspends time so that, whether it last four or five days, as would this transatlantic crossing, depending on the weather, or weeks, had the destination been Australia or India, the time would pass both very slowly and so fast that, when dry land was achieved, the days at sea would be immediately forgotten. Intimacies, even love affairs, fanned by the sea breezes or the music of Henry Hall's dance band, would dissolve in the dirty air of reality when feet were once again on solid ground. 'It was a dream,' a passenger would say to herself or himself. 'I must have been bewitched. Did I really give those awful people our address and *beg* them to come and stay whenever they were next in London or Leeds, Boston or Philadelphia? Did I really think this man handsome enough to kiss by the lifeboats? Or, the girl with her appalling mother – did I really ask her to spend the rest of her life with me?'

Fortunately, it was generally agreed, promises made on a luxury liner were as gossamer. There was a code or formula, Edward had once been told, which excused actresses' indiscretions on the film set – DCOL. Amy Pageant had told him it stood for 'doesn't count on location' and, when it had been explained to him, he was shocked and Amy had laughed at him. However, he was soon to think there must be a similar exculpation covering shipboard flirtations. He had happened to see his nephew deep in conversation with a pretty American girl. Frank said something – Edward could not hear what – and the girl threw back her head and laughed, exposing her exquisite throat. Frank half raised his hand as if to shield himself but had then laughed too, with the delicious complicity of the acknowledged lover. Edward sighed as he watched the besotted boy and then chided himself. Were he Frank's age, would he not be in love with this elfin child? Hadn't he seen Verity looking at Sam Forrest with just such intense fascination? He wondered if, after all, this was going to be the right moment to ask Verity to be his wife.

An elderly couple called Dolmen, who came aboard at Cherbourg, were immediately and instinctively judged to be beneath the notice of many of the English. It was generally held to be unfortunate to be foreign, a deliberate affront not to speak English and thoroughly reprehensible to be German. Mrs Dolmen fell foul of all of these tenets. She spoke no English and only a little French. Mr Dolmen spoke English with a heavy accent but Frank, who was the first to meet him – he had the cabin on the other side of his – rather liked the look of him.

He had no such feeling about the couple occupying the cabin on the other side. 'Major Cranton,' the man had barked, thrusting his hand out to Frank when they had happened to leave their cabins at the same time. His little moustache, wrinkling as he spoke, and military bearing advertised the truth of his assertion. From what Frank overheard – quite involuntarily – the Major seemed to have little time for his wife whom he ordered about as if she were his batman. The walls of the cabins were not thin but nor were they completely soundproof and Frank, registering this, hoped he wasn't going to be disturbed by the Major's parade-ground expletives.

Once they had left Cherbourg, it was time to dress for

dinner. Marcus Fern, who had been to the States on several occasions, agreed with Edward that it was important to make 'a good impression' on the first night, particularly as they were invited to sit at the Captain's table – a compliment they owed to being stars in Lord Benyon's firmament. So it was that, come seven o'clock, Frank could be found struggling with his white tie, cursing his starched shirt front and hopping about on one leg looking for an errant sock. Ready at last, he leant over the basin to peer in the mirror and prepared to do battle with his hair. Springy at the best of times, it could not be made to lie flat. He risked a little brilliantine but in the end gave up. He cursed for the last time as one of his gold shirt studs popped off his chest and down the plughole. Awash with pleasurable self-pity, he comforted himself that, whatever he wore, he would still feel inadequate when he saw Philly Roosevelt again.

He went to Lord Benyon's suite on the deck above where Edward, Verity and Sam Forrest were already congregated, drinking cocktails. He noticed that Sam had chosen to wear a dinner jacket, or tuxedo, as he referred to it to Frank who had not heard the word before. Instead of a waistcoat, Sam wore a white cummerbund. He looked rather dashing and Frank felt overdressed and half-throttled by his collar.

'Where have you been?' Verity demanded. 'I told Mr Forrest he needn't put on the whole soup-and-fish but never mind,' she said, seeing Frank's face fall, 'you do look very handsome in it. I would kiss you but I don't want to smudge my lipstick.'

If she was looking for a compliment from her young admirer, Frank did not oblige. He still hadn't altogether forgiven her for the part she had played in his ignominious return from Spain. In any case, for the last three hours there had been only one girl in his life and it wasn't Verity.

'According to my uncle, First Class passengers never wear dinner jackets on the first night at sea,' Frank replied, then, seeing the American wince, realized he had been rude. He added hurriedly, 'But what does it matter. It's all bunk anyway!'

Verity appeared not to have noticed the slight to her friend because she carried on as if Frank had not spoken. 'Sam wants to tell you about the Youth Congress and the struggle for workers' rights,' she continued bossily. Frank was unable to feel any enthusiasm for a political lecture and his face must have shown it because Forrest winked at him and after a moment's hesitation the boy smiled back. He decided that Sam was 'a good chap' for all he was an American. In fact, come to think of it, he was starting to like Americans more than some of his own people.

Verity looked at Frank sharply. 'What *have* you been up to? You've been up to something.' Then, remembering she had no rights over this young man, she added hastily, 'Not that it has anything to do with me, of course.'

'I was swimming. You said you didn't need me, sir,' he said, turning to Benyon.

'No, that was all right by me, my boy, but I'm not in charge of your political education.'

Verity looked a little put out. She had a feeling she was being teased. Given that her political example had led Frank – or so his family thought – to run away from school and nearly get himself killed in someone else's war, her attempt at 'educating' him might be seen by two or three of those present as something of a disaster.

'I'm hungry,' Edward announced to his nephew's relief. 'Shall we go in to dinner? I confess to being curious as to what the food will be like. I hear they have employed a famous French chef.'

'I agree,' Benyon said. 'All my instincts – and I should add the steward's instincts – suggest that we're in for a bit of a blow, so who's to say we'll feel like dining tomorrow night.'

'Don't say that,' Verity wailed. 'I really mean to live like a capitalist exploiter for a few days. I'll be devastated if I spend the whole trip writhing on my bunk, or whatever you call it.'

As they entered the restaurant through the silver-metal screens, they were all struck by the magnificence of the scene that presented itself to their gaze. Surmounted by a vast dome, the great room, the whole width of the ship and over a hundred feet in length, glistened in subtle, indirect lighting. A huge painting of the English countryside embraced the bronze grille doors which dominated the room. The tables laid with silver were reflected in glass wall panels but the brilliance was

54

tempered by the wood and bronze. Most striking of all, a huge map of the Atlantic Ocean, decorated with aeroplanes and stars, covered almost the whole of one wall. Remarkable though this was, it was made even more marvellous by a model of the *Queen Mary* which passed over the painted ocean between representations of London and New York, enabling passengers to plot the progress of their ship.

The head waiter, who now approached them, might have been welcoming them to the Savoy Grill or the Berkeley. Without being required to identify themselves, they were ushered the whole length of the restaurant to the Captain's table which rested on a slight dais. The Captain was not yet present but Verity was delighted to see, half hidden behind a huge swan sculpted in ice and dripping from the beak on to a silver salver, Warren Fairley and Jane Barclay. Proudly, she introduced them to the party and was glad to see the respect and warmth with which Edward greeted Fairley. She admitted, grudgingly, that, whatever his faults, Edward's manners were perfect. Rather unexpectedly, Edward considered, the Dolmens were also brought to the Captain's table as was Bernard Hunt accompanied by a lady wearing the most extraordinary coiffure which looked as though an exotic bird had died in her hair. This was Miss Doris Zinkeisen.

Miss Zinkeisen was one of the best-known names in theatre and film on both sides of the Atlantic. She had designed the costumes for *Nymph Errant* and *Wild Violets* and numerous Cochran reviews. She was a friend of many Hollywood stars who depended on her, on and off the set, to look their best and she had been appointed 'Personality Creator' to one film studio. She was also a successful artist and had her first picture hung in the Royal Academy when she was seventeen.

Hunt introduced her to the company, mentioning that she had been appointed by Cunard to decorate the Verandah Grill, one of the alternatives to the restaurant, in which First Class passengers could eat à la carte.

'What an honour!' Edward said politely.

'Well, you know,' she said, sitting down next to Edward, 'the idea appealed to me but I said I must be allowed to decorate the whole room – curtains, chairs, carpets – not just do the murals. They wanted something light-hearted and gay.

What a shock they got when I chose black carpets and deep red velvet curtains! They had in mind one of those awful twirly carpets you get in bad hotels. I said to them, "You're mad. With a black carpet, when a bit gets worn you can cut it out and replace it with another square of black. You can't do that with a twirly bit." They were thrilled. They'd never thought of that.'

'I haven't had a chance of seeing the mural in the Verandah Grill yet.'

'As for the mural, my dear, everyone says it's divine, but I wouldn't know. I was quite exhausted when I'd finished it but I think it *is* a success.' She cocked her head on one side and looked more like a peacock than before. Edward tried to keep a straight face. 'Do you know, darling, it was so long it wouldn't fit in my studio. I had to borrow another one and then people would keep on dropping in to chat. When it was ready I took it to Glasgow and, my dear, I found total chaos. Can you imagine! There was I surrounded by hundreds of workmen, all very jolly, and passing remarks in their broad and oh-so-sweet Scottish accents and exhibiting their even broader humour. One of the dear fellows said to me, "Och aye, she must be a polisher," because, you see, I had my overalls on. There were wires all over the place and they discovered the clock in the smoking-room below could only be regulated from up there. So do you know what, my dear, they calmly cut a bit out of my mural so the damned clock could be controlled! I do believe you could go through my mural like Alice through the looking-glass.'

'I say, how fascinating! You mean there are passages between the decks?'

'I guess so – service tunnels or something like that. Anyway, as I was saying, when the King came round to look at every-thing he stood in front of my mural for a long time and then pointed to an elderly lady I had painted and said, "How like my dear mama!" And do you know, it was! Quite uncon-sciously, I had painted Queen Mary into the picture!'

Miss Zinkeisen's flow came temporarily to a halt through lack of breath and she sipped her champagne. 'Now,' she said, 'do tell me, who are you?'

On the other side of Edward was Jane Barclay. He thought

56

she might be one of those empty-headed bottle-blondes who he supposed were bred in Hollywood but he was soon made aware that she was no fool and had a keen eye for pretension and patronage.

'Isn't Doris exhausting?' she said in a West Coast accent. She only used a southern drawl when she was annoyed with her husband as she knew he hated it.

'Miss Zinkeisen? She is rather but I like her and I certainly admire her energy.'

'Have you looked at the so-called art on this ship?'

'I have. Some of it, at any rate.'

'What do you think of it?'

'I –'

'It's so bourgeois, as Warren would say. So mediocre. At least, that's what I think but what do I know? Are there any good artists in England? This is all so – oh, I don't know – polite.'

Edward, taken aback by this frank criticism of Bernard Hunt's taste but inclined to agree, said, 'I know what you mean but –'

'And this food's disgusting.' She held up her fork, on the end of which a small shrimp dangled.

'Oh, I don't know,' he said. It rather shocked him to find someone daring enough to criticize any aspect of the *Queen Mary* but he had to admit to sharing a certain sense of disappointment, at least as far as the food went. The smoked salmon he had ordered was excellent but why surround it with gherkins? Still, it seemed preferable to the grapefruit cocktail or the scotch broth.

'Perhaps it's a bit dull,' he ventured. 'I gather it's better in the Verandah Grill. We might try that tomorrow night.' She grunted but made no other comment so Edward changed the subject. 'Are you making a film, Miss Barclay?'

She looked at him darkly. 'Is that some sort of wisecrack?'

'I'm sorry?'

'Are you the only person on this boat who doesn't know I've been – what do you call it? – blackballed by the studios?'

'Why is that?'

She looked at him to see if he was trying to insult her but decided he was genuinely ignorant.

57

'Because I'm with Warren, of course.'

'Because he's a Communist?'

'Because he's a *black* Communist,' she said vehemently. 'They don't like it when a white girl gets hitched up to a black guy.'

'But surely, in 1937 –'

'You really don't see it, do you? In the movies, black actors only get small parts, as servants, or do "turns" tap-dancing or what have you, bits which can be cut when the film travels south. Most of America – and I don't mean just the southern half – is still living in the last century. You know *Gone with the Wind*?'

'Certainly, it won a Pulitzer Prize, didn't it? I haven't read it yet but it's set in the Civil War, isn't it?'

'That's the one. Well, I heard that Sam Goldwyn, when he bought the film rights, thought of making it in modern dress.'

'He didn't realize it is a historical novel?' Edward hazarded, not understanding.

'He didn't want to have to cast blacks in major parts. Goldwyn has never read a book but you could say that about most Americans. People say we're a new country but our prejudices are ancient and we treasure them. To be black or a Jew . . .'

'But Mr Fairley is a great singer and actor as well as a political leader – he's not . . .'

'He's not any old "Negro", you were going to say?' Her bitterness was poisoning her, Edward could see that. 'Do you know, the shipping line made a fuss about us sharing a cabin?'

'But you're married?'

'We're married, but they chose not to believe it. Warren had to show them his marriage licence. It was humiliating.'

'That's terrible,' he said inadequately, 'but we think he's a great man.'

'You do? And that girl you're with . . . Miss Browne? . . . she's a Communist too?'

'She is,' Edward said, glad for once that Verity's politics were going to prove a social asset.

'Well, tell her to keep her mitts off my man, will ya,' she said, and turned her back on him.

He looked across the table at Verity who was deep in

conversation with Sam Forrest. He liked Forrest – who could not? – his open face and hearty laugh were a tonic. He and Verity looked like young lovers so he couldn't think why Miss Barclay thought that she might be interested in her husband. He mused for a moment. He had been on the point of asking Verity to marry him when they had heard of Frank's flight to Spain. By the time they had fetched him back, the moment had passed. It wasn't that he cared for Verity any less but he was coming round to the view that perhaps she was right when she said she wasn't the marrying type. She liked the attention of men like Forrest and he knew, if he were married to her, he would always be fighting jealousy. But more to the point, Verity was not a stay-at-home. After this trip to the States, the odds were she would be going back to Spain to report on the war there. If not Spain, then some other unpleasant, dangerous corner of the world. She had fought her way up to being a respected war correspondent. It was a unique achievement for a woman and she was hardly going to throw it away for a husband and babies.

When he looked at her again he saw she was now talking to Warren Fairley, and Jane Barclay's remark suddenly seemed less absurd. There was an intimacy in the way they were talking – their faces barely a few inches apart – that made him stop and reconsider.

There were still three empty seats at the table. One was the Captain's and he wondered idly who else was missing. Having crossed the Atlantic before, he knew that to come to the table after the Captain was seated, without a very good reason, was considered a grave discourtesy.

At that moment Captain Peel arrived, apologizing for being so late.

'No trouble, I hope, Captain?' said Mr Dolmen in a worried voice.

'Nothing to worry about – nothing at all – except that I'm afraid we're in for a bit of a blow.'

'Oh dear,' Lord Benyon said, his face falling. 'I'm afraid I'm not a very good sailor. However,' he added more cheerfully, 'I am reliably informed the *Queen Mary* is the most stable ship afloat.'

'And so she is,' the Captain said firmly. 'There's nothing to worry about, I can assure you, sir. Our ship is the product of modern engineering at its best. We're a long way from Masefield's "dirty British coaster butting through the Channel in the mad March days"!'

Edward tried to suppress his instinct that the time to worry was when the experts took it upon themselves to reassure you that they had everything in hand.

'But you're not eating, Mrs Dolmen?' the Captain said, with a hint of disapproval.

'We're vegetarians, Captain,' Mr Dolmen said in a low voice, as though this was something to be ashamed of.

'And have you been properly looked after?' Captain Peel inquired sharply.

Dolmen nodded and opened his mouth to speak, but the Captain prevented him. 'Good! Mr Dolmen, if you – and your wife, of course,' he added with a little bow, 'would find it interesting, one of my officers will take you round the engine room after dinner. Lord Edward,' he said, obviously keen to involve the whole table in general conversation, 'perhaps you are not aware that Mr Dolmen – or should I say Professor Dolmen – is one of Germany's leading engineers. Aeronautical rather than naval, I believe?' he said, turning back to Dolmen for confirmation.

'That would be very good of you, Captain,' Dolmen said in his thick German accent. '*Danke, Herr Kapitän. Ich möchte* . . . I would like to see the engine room.' His wife leant over to him and said something in his ear. '*Natürlich, liebling!*' he replied and turned again to the Captain. '*Meine Frau* . . . my wife asks whether it would be possible for her to see the kitchens. It is so wonderful that you can feed all of us.' He spread his arms wide, almost knocking off his wife's spectacles to encompass not just the First Class dining-room, huge though it was, but the other dining-rooms and restaurants below them.

'Oh, yes, I would so like that too,' Miss Zinkeisen said. 'I have been so busy with making my Verandah Restaurant perfect I have never seen the kitchens. I mean, I went round them on the maiden voyage but I was so exhausted and excited I couldn't take it all in.'

'That's settled then,' said the Captain genially. 'Two tours after dinner, but I expect the young will want to go dancing. Lord Benyon, perhaps you have work to do?'

'I do but I could not possibly fail to take up your invitation to visit the engine room. And Frank, you'll come, won't you?'

'Oh yes, sir, I would love to. Thank you, Captain.' He had wanted to spend the rest of the evening with Philly, if he could find her, but felt it would be rude to have said so. He thought longingly of the nightclub and fancied he could feel Philly's slim white arms round his neck as they danced the night away. Ah well! He had his duty to do and that meant sticking to Benyon, unless relieved by another member of the party. Who could guess what dangers there might be in the ship's entrails?

'You will come with us to see the kitchens?' Miss Zinkeisen said pleadingly to Edward. 'Or is it not manly to prefer kitchens to engines?'

'Of course, I shall come with you,' he replied gallantly. 'I am sure there will be another time when I can see the engines. I agree with you, Professor Dolmen,' he said, smiling across the table, 'that it is a miracle, comparable with feeding the five thousand, to keep all the passengers well fed. After all, when one is suspended outside real time with no responsibilities, as we are at sea, we eat and drink more than we would on land and probably to excess.'

At this moment the head waiter appeared, escorting a large, coarse-featured man about fifty years of age and a woman, presumably his wife, covered in jewellery which only served to emphasize her strong resemblance to a sheep.

All the men rose and the Captain said, with a hint of a reprimand, 'Ah, Senator and Mrs Day, we thought you must have been taken ill.'

'No, sir, but we should certainly have been taken ill if we had not changed our cabin. My wife is not a good sleeper at the best of times but the noise from the engines on this boat is very bad. Now the *Normandie* . . .'

Edward wanted to hide under the table. It was true that he had been surprised by the noise, or rather the vibration, from the ship's great propellers but to say as much to the Captain in front of important guests was close to an insult. The Captain, recognizing no doubt that here was one of those difficult customers who had to be endured, said with a smile, 'And are you happier in your new cabin?'

'The Purser has given us one of your executive suites or whatever you call them. It's better but I –'

The Captain cut him short by turning to the steward and muttering something in his ear. At once two waiters appeared with champagne. 'I'm afraid, Senator, we started our meal without you but we waited on you for the champagne. It is customary for us to make a toast. I hope you will all join me in wishing our great ship well?'

'I never touch wine,' the Senator said virtuously, 'and champagne is particularly bad for my stomach. A little bourbon and a brandy after dinner is all I can manage. Isn't that right, Marlene?'

The sheep-faced woman looked at her husband in what Edward identified as naked terror and said nothing. The Senator stared round the table and his eye rested first on Sam Forrest and then on Warren Fairley. 'What's that coon doing at this table,' he whispered to his wife so loudly that the Captain heard, as no doubt Day intended.

Captain Peel's face turned red and then almost purple. 'Senator Day, I hope I am wrong and I did not hear you make a personal remark about one of my guests.'

No one spoke, all present frozen in embarrassment and horror. Even Warren Fairley was speechless. The silence was broken by the rasping voice of the Senator, whose southern drawl sounded to Edward marinated in hatred. 'I was merely expressing my surprise, Captain, that you should choose to sit down to dinner with bolsheviks and –'

'Mr Day . . . I cannot allow you to continue. I must ask that you apologize to the table or leave us.'

'I shall certainly not apologize for expressing an honest opinion.'

'In that case . . .' the Captain said, rising, 'I must ask you to leave my table. The steward will see that you have a table to yourself.'

'I see, sir, you take the side of the enemies of our two great democracies. That is your privilege, though I confess to being mighty surprised. I shall be writing to Sir Percy Bates, your chairman, whom I was talking to at our embassy the other night and you can bet your bottom dollar you haven't heard the end of this. My friend Congressman Dies is setting up a committee to investigate un-American activities and I note several Americans at your table, Captain Peel, who I expect to see appearing before it. And you, young lady, if you hope to work in Hollywood you will have to do something about the company you keep.' He looked directly at Jane Barclay and she returned his stare unblinkingly. 'Come, Marlene, this is not a place where I could feel like eating.'

When the Senator had departed, the Captain turned to Warren Fairley and said, 'On behalf of the Company, I apologize for what that man said in your hearing, sir.'

'It's nothing, Captain, but thank you all the same.' The Captain turned away, believing that his apology had been gracefully accepted and the ugly moment brushed over, but Fairley was not finished. He spoke calmly enough but, just beneath the calm, they could all hear his intense fury. 'I am sorry to say there are many like Senator Day in my country, Captain Peel, which is why I prefer to live in England. These politicians from the southern states are good haters, I'll give them that. I put it down to sexual frustration, if you will forgive me for saying so, ladies. They like to lynch a Negro before taking their wives to bed and, when they are prevented as Senator Day was this evening, they spew out their filth like the devil in the Bible.'

Even Edward was surprised by Fairley's bitter words but he had no idea of the nature of the struggle in which he had been engaged for so many years. In a typically English way, Edward had expected Fairley to dismiss the affair with a wave of his hand and change the subject, as he would have done, but Fairley would never let such a moment pass without forcing its significance down the throats of the witnesses. Until the day arrived when he had no need to fight the unthinking racism of fellow Americans, he would always make his protest and he knew he would never live to see the battle won.

A waiter discreetly removed the two place settings and the Captain's guests inched apart from each other, covering over the space like a growing hedge. Everyone at the table was unsettled, as though they had each been physically assaulted. Frank whispered to Verity, 'I wanted to punch his mouth, and I would have done if he hadn't gone.'

Verity, unwontedly sensitive to the will of the majority though profoundly stirred by Fairley's words to the Captain, shushed him and made him talk to Sam Forrest about the union movement in the United States and the iniquities of men like Henry Ford. Forrest was a good speaker and Frank was soon absorbed in an account of the riots in Toledo, Ohio three years earlier.

'Ford's an anti-Semite and an enemy of the people,' Sam opined. 'He praises Hitler for his "realism". Whenever I hear the words "realism" and "pragmatism", in my mind I substitute "expediency" and "cynicism".'

'I thought he had given the ordinary working man the chance of owning a car he could afford and thereby given him freedom?' Edward suggested mildly, knowing this would provoke heated discussion and take people's minds off Senator Day.

Forrest rose to the challenge and told the table what he thought of Ford so powerfully and lucidly that Edward imagined the industrialist's ears must be burning. Fully launched now, Forrest continued on the more general theme of the workers' struggle, Verity looking on adoringly.

'The American Workers' Party, to which I then belonged, forced the Electric Auto-Lite Company to recognize a new union but only after two deaths. For several days in May we fought the National Guard – bare-knuckle brawls mostly – but in the end the Guardsmen got panicky and shot into the crowd. But, Mr Fairley, sir, weren't you part of all that?'

In his deep, sonorous voice Fairley, who had been silent since his condemnation of southern politicians, roused himself to reply. 'I was, young man, but I had a double fight against the employers and against racism among working people who ought to have known better. Mainly, they thought we blacks were cheap labour and out to take their jobs. We had our greatest chance in 1932, Miss Browne,' he said, aware she might not know much about the Communist Party in America. 'We managed to put aside our squabbles and unite behind William Z. Foster and his running mate, James Ford, who was black.

The Party polled a hundred thousand votes – an all-time high – but that was against twenty-three million votes cast for Roosevelt.' He laughed wryly. 'After that we tore ourselves apart in the usual faction fighting – Trotskyists against Stalinists against socialists – I'm sure it was the same in your country.'

'Yes, but you won some fights,' Verity said, her eyes shining.

'Oh yes,' Forrest agreed, 'we won some fights, made our martyrs – in California, Detroit and in other cities – but, in the end, Roosevelt stole our clothes. He managed to identify himself with the worker and the union movement. The New Deal – you know about that, Miss Browne?'

'Yes. Public Works – getting people back to work?'

'Yep,' Forrest said. 'Men like our friend Senator Day hate the President's guts worse than they hate us union people. They call FDR a Communist but, of course, he's not that.'

Whether it was deliberate or not, Forrest had managed to make Day a representative of the oppressing class and depersonalized his insult to Fairley. He was saying, in effect, this man is the enemy personified and so his hatred is a compliment to all who stand against racism and brutal capitalism.

With dinner at an end, the party split up. The Captain went back to the bridge. Benyon excused himself saying that he was, after all, going back to his cabin to continue work on his lectures. Sam Forrest, Professor Dolmen and Warren Fairley went off with one of the ship's officers to explore the engine room while Edward and the ladies – under the Chief Steward's personal guidance – shuffled off towards the kitchens. Frank, with Benyon's permission, slipped off to find Philly.

Edward had been a little surprised that Verity had meekly agreed to be parted from the men in order to go and look at what might be called the distaff side of the ship. He didn't flatter himself that it was anything to do with wanting to be with him. She was friendly enough but kept her distance, either because she only had eyes for Sam Forrest or because she was preoccupied with what she was to do in the States. For anyone of her age and political persuasion, North America was of consuming interest. This was a country which had nailed its colours to the mast, so to speak, by inscribing Emma Lazarus's famous words on the Statue of Liberty – 'Give me your tired, your poor, your huddled masses yearning to breathe free.' But this was also the land of Henry Ford and Rockefeller – the country which had virtually invented capitalism. If Stalin's Soviet Union was one signpost to the future, was Roosevelt's America the other? And did one have to be the wrong way or could both be 'right'? At least these two philosophies offered alternatives to the evil of Fascism.

The Chief Steward, responsible for all the catering, was lecturing and his facts and figures were so many and so huge they were difficult to take in – twenty thousand pounds of poultry, seventeen thousand pounds of fish, fifty thousand pounds of vegetables, fifty thousand eggs, six thousand quarts of ice cream . . .

'So much ice cream?' Jane Barclay said dreamily. 'Sometimes in California, when the sun burns through to the bone, I imagine bathing in it.'

She had been very subdued since the dinner incident and Edward was glad to see her becoming more cheerful. Without thinking, he put an arm round her waist as they negotiated some narrow stairs and he saw Verity watching him. He withdrew his arm.

'Ah, well, I think you will be interested to see our cold rooms,' was all the Chief Steward would say.

The kitchens were situated immediately below the First Class restaurant and divided into the classes they serviced. It was a different world and, in their finery, they felt themselves an alien species compared with the bustling waiters, cooks and scullions. Verity felt rather embarrassed, as though she had sided with the enemy. It was ridiculous, she knew, and she tried to enjoy this insight into the ship's commissariat. It *was* fascinating and she tried to make mental notes of what she saw with a view to writing an article for the *New Gazette*. Only Doris Zinkeisen seemed quite at ease, stopping to chat with those still working. Although dinner was over and the dining-room closed, there was still a lot to do to clear up and prepare for the next day.

The Chief Steward continued to dazzle them with statistics and drew their attention to the fittings. They were shown electrically operated potato-peeling machines, ice cream freezers, automatic toasters, fruit juice extractors, silver-burnishing machines and many other ingenious labour-saving devices. They marvelled at the eight-oven cooking range, the grills, the bakery – there were three huge baking ovens and hundreds of oven tins. It was quite bewildering. Verity had a moment's vision of the *Titanic* lying at the bottom of the ocean. All her gleaming metal must now be rusted and rotten. She shivered. That was a quarter of a century ago and ships were much safer now, she told herself.

They had just about had enough when the Chief Steward asked again if they would like to look in the cold rooms.

'It's quite a sight,' he urged them. 'They have to be vast to store not only the beef and lamb carcasses but also the fruit and vegetables. Then there are separate chiller rooms for the fish, poultry and eggs – about forty-three thousand cubic feet in all. Each store room is for a different product and kept at a different temperature. There are eleven large freezer rooms in which the meat and fish are kept frozen. Look, I'll show you. It won't take a minute and then we'll go back.'

He was so proud of the ship's facilities it seemed churlish to disappoint him so they followed like obedient children through these vast catacombs. Edward was reminded of a visit he had paid to some caves in South Africa with prehistoric paintings on the walls. Would tourists one day look at the ruins of the *Queen Mary* in the same way?

Verity was reminded of something else when Jane Barclay used the word 'mausoleum'.

'That's right! I couldn't think what this reminded me of until you said that. Now I've got it! I was taken to see the Escurial outside Madrid – you know, where the Spanish kings are buried, each in their marble sarcophagus, one above the other, right round the walls. These steel freezer cabinets are just like that.'

She shivered again – partly because of the cold and partly from some idea that there was something sinister about all this shining steel.

'Now,' said the Chief Steward, pausing, 'Lord Edward, you may wish to come inside this room with me. It's the coldest of the rooms. I don't recommend the ladies enter without first returning to their cabins for coats. It's kept well below freezing

– approximately zero Fahrenheit – and no one could survive unprotected for more than an hour and, long before that, you would start suffering from hypothermia.'

'So how do the cooks – or whoever – manage?' Verity asked.

'The cooks don't come in here,' he explained. 'We have three butchers and they wear protective clothing, including masks, when they select the meat or fish to be unfrozen.'

Mrs Dolmen shivered and pulled her wrap over her shoulders. Verity, seeing that she was becoming uncomfortable, said, 'Well, get on with it then, Edward. We're beginning to freeze and we want to return to civilization.'

The Chief Steward ushered him in through the heavy door, pulling it shut behind them. 'We have to keep the temperature at the right level,' he explained as Edward looked behind him with some alarm. The place was illuminated by bright white lights which increased the feeling of being in some nightmare arctic country. He could see animal carcasses hanging in ranks from hooks on a rail in the ceiling.

'How do you move such great weights?' he inquired.

The Chief Steward pushed a button. Slowly, with much clanging and clanking, the carcasses began to move along the rail swinging slightly and looking for all the world like a procession of scarlet-robed prelates – except that through his steaming breath Edward could see that these were not hooded but headless.

Then he let out a cry of horror and pointed. 'What's that, for God's sake? Stop the machine.'

The Chief Steward pushed the button again and the swinging carcasses came to a halt. Hanging from one of the hooks was the body of a man. He was quite naked. There was a rope about his neck attached to one of the metal hooks. The two men stood almost literally frozen to the spot, mouths agape at the horror before them. Edward shouted, 'It's Tom Barrett,' and began to run, or rather stagger, towards the still swinging corpse. As he did so, the Chief Steward cried a warning. 'Don't touch! If you do, your hand may freeze to the metal. There's nothing we can do. Come outside and I'll summon the butcher.'

But the butcher had already been about his business.

5

Verity had taken Mrs Dolmen back to her cabin in a state of shock, crying hysterically and calling for her husband. Only when he and then the doctor arrived did she feel able to leave the distraught woman. She was clearly of a very nervous disposition and Verity wondered if she ought to sympathize with Professor Dolmen for having to put up with his wife's nerves or blame him for the state of them. Of course, it had been a great shock to all of them when they heard Edward's shout of horror and he and the Chief Steward had burst out of the cold room but it wasn't as if the ladies left outside had actually seen anything. The Chief Steward had gone off to fetch assistance and inform the Captain of what they had found. Edward had remained on guard outside and had at first refused to tell anyone what the matter was. At Verity's insistence, he had finally divulged that they had discovered the body of Tom Barrett but, to her fury, he resolutely refused to let her enter the room and view the corpse nor would he comment on whether the death had been an accident or something else.

'What are you afraid of?' she had said urgently. 'Do you think I am going to run off and telephone the *New Gazette* – headline: Murder on the *Queen Mary*?'

Edward made no answer and, with difficulty, she reined in her resentment. It occurred to her that she might indeed telephone a story to the paper, as soon as she knew what the story was. She had met Barrett only briefly but he had seemed a pleasant young man. What was Lord Benyon's valet doing dying in the *Queen Mary*'s cold storage? She bit her lip. She must give no promise to Edward or anyone else which would stop her doing her journalistic duty. Now she came to think about it, it was just the sort of story Joe Weaver liked and she felt the guilt that always crept up on her when she found herself turning someone's misfortune into 'entertainment' for the nation's breakfast tables.

Edward's expression was grim. He was horrified at what he had seen and he feared this death would not be the last. He was itching to get back to Lord Benyon and make sure he was safe. As soon as he had left the freezer room it had struck him that, if Barrett had been killed, it must be because he was Benyon's protector and that must mean Benyon himself was in grave danger – might, indeed, already be dead. When, at last, the doctor and several ship's officers arrived to relieve him, Edward raced up to A Deck, all the time chanting curses to himself. He had been given a job to do and, not twelve hours into the mission, he had already failed. It was with a sigh of relief that, entering Benyon's cabin, he saw his charge working peacefully at his desk, his pen in his hand and books and papers spread about him like feathers in a nest.

What he saw in Edward's face, however, made Benyon go pale. When he heard what had happened to Barrett, he took off his spectacles and buried his head in his hands.

'This is too awful. The poor boy! And I happen to know that he was engaged to be married.'

'But you're all right, that's the main thing,' Edward gasped.

'No,' Benyon said fiercely, 'that's not the main thing. The main thing is a young man has been butchered for my sake . . . protecting me. It should not have happened.'

Edward apologized. 'I did not mean to sound heartless. I would give anything to have prevented it. It was a horrible thing and I shall never forget what I have just seen, but your mission might help us win a war. Nothing can be more important than that.'

'I don't blame *you*, Edward. Don't think I was questioning your judgement. I just can't –'

At that moment Marcus Fern came in, looking scared. 'The Purser telephoned me and said something bad had happened and I was to come here. Thank God you're all right, Benyon. I thought you might have been taken ill.'

Edward gave him a concise account of the discovery of

70

Barrett's body. When he had finished, the three men looked at one another in consternation. Simultaneously, they recognized they were in a trap. The *Queen Mary* had seemed so safe. They had been cocooned in luxury, lulled into a false sense of security, but now they realized that, behind a veneer of civilization at its most artificial, there lurked very real danger. The worst of it was that, for the next few days, there was no escape . . . no turning back. It was feasible, Edward supposed, to have a warship rendezvous with them and take off Benyon but the logistics were daunting. He wasn't even sure exactly how someone was conveyed from one ship to another in mid-ocean. He had a vision of ropes and a man bobbing over the waves on some sort of boatswain's chair. He shuddered. In any case, the publicity of such a manoeuvre would be just what Benyon did not want. No, they must go on but never let their man out of sight.

'Thank God I brought my man, Fenton, with me. He's totally trustworthy and with your permission, Benyon, I'll have him sleep in my suite, in Barrett's bed.'

Benyon nodded so Edward went to the telephone and summoned Fenton. Verity arrived, accompanied, as always, by Sam Forrest. Edward was tempted to tell him this was no business of his and ask him to leave but he restrained himself.

'Verity, could you come into the next cabin for a moment. If you will forgive me, Benyon, there's just a couple of things I need to say to Verity in private.'

Reluctantly, she followed him into his cabin and he shut the door after them.

'What's this all about?' she said truculently. 'I suppose you want to shut me up.'

'How's Mrs Dolmen?' Edward asked, ignoring her question.

'The doctor's given her a sedative. Her husband's with her. By the way,' she said meaningfully, 'if you want to know, the doctor told me about finding the body on the meat rack. Tom Barrett was murdered. Presumably, that has something to do with his being Lord Benyon's valet. If that *is* what he was. There's no good you looking like that. It's much better that you are open with me. I haven't discussed this with anyone except Sam but rumours are flying round the ship. You can't keep this sort of thing secret.'

'Does that mean it's your duty to send a report through to the *New Gazette*? I suppose it would be quite a coup for you.'

'Damn you, Edward, I'll do what I think fit. Don't preach at me. I knew you wanted to put pressure on me to keep quiet. So far, you've given me no reason why I should. I'm not promising anything.'

'If I admitted to you that Barrett's death was, almost certainly, to do with Benyon because he wasn't just his valet but also his bodyguard, would that satisfy you?'

'Why does he need a bodyguard?'

'He is going to the States on business of national importance . . . to talk to the President. I can't tell you anything more.'

'I'd worked that out for myself,' she said shortly. 'Why else would he be killed? It has to be because of who he was with.'

'All right, but from now on anything I tell you about why Lord Benyon is going to America is confidential and not for publication.'

'I don't want to know why he's going to the States. Anything you tell me in confidence you'll never read in a newspaper I write for – you ought to know that by now – but the murder *will* be reported in newspapers on both sides of the Atlantic and I might as well report it as anyone else. At least I will be accurate.'

'As long as we understand each other because, of course, I want your help . . . yours and Sam's, but our investigation has to be confidential. Will you tell Sam the rules?'

She took this as an apology of sorts and decided she would be forgiving.

'I will.'

They shook hands on the deal, a little embarrassed but glad to have straightened things out.

They returned to Benyon's cabin to find Sam, Marcus Fern and Benyon still trying to come to terms with the death. Fenton had also joined them so the suite was beginning to look overcrowded.

'For it to be so ugly . . .' Fern was saying. 'Did it need to be so beastly?'

'It's obscene,' Sam said vehemently, hitting his fist against the wall. 'To kill him and then strip him and hang him on a rack of carcasses . . .!'

'Horrible!' Verity agreed. 'I saw bad things in Spain but over there you expect people to do awful things to each other. Not here . . . not on the *Queen Mary*.'

'Terrible wherever it happened,' Benyon murmured.

'But how do you know that's what did happen?' Marcus Fern said, surprisingly.

'What do you mean?'

'I mean, Miss Browne, how do you know the killer stripped Barrett *after* he had killed him and when did he hang him up? Was it some sort of awful joke? The murderer can't have thought the body would not be found. I'm sorry to sound callous but it may be important. It may tell us why the killer did what he did.'

'As you say, it was just a sick-making joke.' Despite the cabin being hot and stuffy, Verity shivered.

'Maybe, but perhaps he wanted to distract us from seeing something else,' Fern said, looking at Edward.

'The horror might blind us to something which could incriminate him?' Edward mused, interested. 'That's true. The doctor will be able to tell us how he died and whether he was dead before he was strung up. I'm sorry . . .' he said, seeing a look of disgust on Benyon's face. 'We must do all we can to catch this man, whoever it is, before he strikes again. Fern is right, we must try and understand him.'

Forrest said, 'I suppose his clothes might have been taken off him because they gave something away. Perhaps they had the murderer's blood on them?'

'But his underclothes? Why take them?' Verity demanded. 'That was just too beastly.'

'By taking all his clothes,' Forrest said gently, 'he hoped to confuse us.'

'I'm pretty certain he was killed by a blow to the head – or at least knocked unconscious – so he would not have known what else the killer did to him, if that makes it easier, Verity,' Edward said. 'There was very little blood but, of course, at such a low temperature that's hardly surprising. Still, there's one other thing we have to take into account. We have to assume that, along with his clothes, the killer took his gun.' Edward surveyed the cabin bleakly. 'We are up against a man with a .38 automatic.'

There was a knock on the door and the Purser and Captain appeared, the latter white-faced and clearly badly upset. First the insult to Warren Fairley and now this savage killing of the man charged with protecting Lord Benyon – this crossing was turning into a nightmare.

'I will put out an announcement in the ship's newspaper that there has been an accident and a man has died,' the Captain said. 'We'll have to hope that scotches any rumours of something worse. The freezer room's been sealed off and I have alerted the New York Police Department. They will board the ship as soon as we dock. In the meantime, the doctor is examining the body. We'll have his preliminary report in an hour or two. I suppose we must take it that this was an attack on you, Lord Benyon?' The tone of his voice was disapproving. 'I don't quite know what to do, short of imprisoning you in your cabin. If the storm comes upon us tomorrow, as is forecast, you will have every excuse to keep to your berth.'

Benyon looked as though he might burst into tears but said stoutly enough, 'I am not concerned with my own safety, Captain, but with this horrible murder . . . Is there anything we can do to apprehend the man? I suppose it was a man?'

'It must have been a man and a reasonably strong one too. The hooks come down from the rail on a wire and once the carcass is attached, it is winched up until the hook reaches the rail. Even so, one can't envisage a woman doing it – not without help.'

'We're up against someone quite ruthless then?'

'I fear so. Mr Fern . . . Lord Edward . . . I rely on you to see that Lord Benyon is never left alone.'

'Of course, Captain,' Fern said. 'Lord Edward and I will keep him safe.'

'We'll do our best, certainly. My man here, Fenton, is going to replace Tom Barrett, Captain Peel. He's thoroughly trustworthy and worth two of me in a scrap.'

The Captain looked at Fenton doubtfully. The latter returned his stare but said nothing.

'I promise you, he's a sound man and with Mr Forrest's aid – if he's willing to help . . .'

'Count me in, Corinth.'

'Good! As I was saying, with Mr Forrest's help and Mr Fern

and my nephew Frank, we ought to be all right. By the way, where is that boy? Purser, do you think you could run him to ground for me? I would guess he's drooling over the Roosevelt girl.'

'Certainly, my lord. If you'll excuse me, I'll do that and then go about my duties. It's important everything should appear normal as far as is possible.'

'Yes,' the Captain said. 'I must go to the bridge. We'll talk again tomorrow morning, gentlemen.'

'Captain. I must get in touch with the authorities in London and report what has happened. Is it safe to use the telephone in my cabin? Is it secure?'

'Secure? Ah, I see what you mean. Perhaps it will be better if you come to the bridge with me. I too must put in my report. The chairman will want to be informed. Dear me, this is a terrible business. Goodnight, all of you, and I hope you are able to sleep tonight. I confess, I am not sure I will.'

All this time, Frank was blissfully unaware that his employer was in need of his support and assistance. As his uncle had suspected, he was in the Verandah Grill which, after dinner, turned into a nightclub. It had a small, sycamore dance floor surrounded by candlelit tables at which couples could sit out, watch the dancers, drink wine or cocktails and gaze into each other's eyes. Behind a balustrade there was a raised floor with tables at which one could eat à la carte if one wanted a change from the restaurant. On a fine night, the windows – twenty-two in all – might be thrown open. The sills were heated to maintain the temperature in the room and the views over the darkened sea were guaranteed to engender romance.

It had been an unexpected but delightful release for Frank when, at the end of dinner, Lord Benyon had decided to go back to his cabin to work and not join the tour of the engine room. Frank had asked permission to 'go and explore' and Benyon, who knew what it was like to be infatuated with a girl, told him 'to make himself scarce.' Like a puppy let off its lead, he went running off in search of Philly. He found her at last in the bar, perched on a stool, her long legs swinging idly, a cigarette in her mouth. She was practising making smoke rings and flirting with Roger, the bar steward. She wore more of a silver sheath than a dress, by Mainbocher – a name Frank might have been tempted to mention in his prayers had he ever heard it. It was quite unlike anything he had seen on an English girl and showed her boyish figure to perfection. Her shoulders were bare – the dress was strapless – and around her neck was a pearl choker and on her hands, long white gloves.

'Oh there you are, Philly.' He scowled at the barman who shrugged and started polishing glasses. 'Come and dance, will you? They say there may be a storm tomorrow so this could be our last chance for a bit.'

'Oughtn't you to be sitting by your master?' she said nastily, not liking to be ordered about.

Frank flushed. 'I've got an hour or two. Please, Philly, don't be awkward.'

'Shan't!'

'Please, Philly, don't tease.'

'Beg my pardon for being a horrid bully.'

'What? Oh, yes, all right. Beg pardon, m'lady.' He bowed ironically.

She stubbed out her cigarette. He held out his hand and she put hers in his, waving at Roger with the other. 'See you,' she said, as though apologizing.

When they had left the bar, Frank said, 'I wish you wouldn't flirt with the barman. It's not the done thing, you know.'

'Not the done thing,' she mimicked. She tugged at him to make him stop. 'But it is the "done thing" to fool around with me?'

'What do you mean, Philly?' Frank said, looking at her with surprise.

'Well, I just mean . . . Oh, I don't know what I mean. Come on then.'

She kissed him lightly on the lips. 'Let's fool around. Why not? As you say, we may not have much time.'

Frank had no idea what she meant, unless she was referring to the coming storm, but, with the taste of her lips on his, he wasn't capable of thinking clearly.

When they reached the dance floor, Frank saw it as some enchanted place. It was bathed by coloured lights reflecting off a glass ball spinning high above the dancers and leaving pools of darkness, deep enough for lovers to drown in. There were two or three other couples on the floor, each in their own little world, ignoring anything and anyone else. When the girl wrapped her bare arms around his neck and put her cheek against his, Frank found he could float. He knew he ought to be surprised but with this girl nothing surprised him. The scent of her made him almost swoon and, when she raised her head, and invited his kisses, her breath stole his away. They had been dancing for the best part of an hour before Frank realized that one of the other couples consisted of Perry Roosevelt glued to some girl he had never seen before.

At last they sat down and a waiter brought them champagne. Frank wanted to say something interesting to impress Philly. He wanted to be witty and compliment her on her dress and ask her about herself but he was tongue-tied. She put her hand on his cheek and stroked it. 'Almost a man,' she said with a sigh.

'What's that supposed to mean?' Frank said, indignation giving him back the power of speech.

'Nothing, only . . .'

'Only what? I suppose you are going to say I'm too young to know what it means to be in love but that's poppycock. I know I love you, Philly. You're the loveliest girl I ever met and . . .'

She put a finger against his lips. 'Hush now. We've only known each other a few hours. Much too soon to be using big little words like love.'

'Only a few hours but I feel as if I have known you all my life. Please, Philly, don't –'

He was interrupted by Perry who dragged up a chair and sat down, demanding a drink.

'You're bottled already,' Philly told him.

'No I'm not.' His elbow slipped off the edge of the table and his head jerked.

'Where's your girl, anyway?' she said crossly.

'I ditched her. She bored me. Waiter! Whiskey sour! I can't drink this muck. It gives me a headache.'

'Perry!' Frank said in exasperation. 'Can't you see, you're butting in. We don't want you.'

'Well, you've got me, so there. I think you're being beastly, both of you. I told you, Philly. I found him first. You always take my things. It's not fair.'

'Oh, do stop bleating, Perry. Be a dear and go and find Mother.'

'She's lying down with one of her "heads", so there. I can't go back to the cabin.'

'I'm not a "thing", anyway,' said Frank, annoyed and by now a little drunk himself.

'What are you then? A person? You can't be a real person. You haven't even got a name. What *do* you call yourself? You're a lord, I know that. But are you Duke something? Or maybe a dukelet – a duke in training.'

'Call me what you like,' Frank said crossly, taking Philly's hand. 'Dance?'

'Not yet, Frank, I'm pooped out. Perry, don't be a bore. What have you done with that girl of yours?'

'I told you. She bored me. Everything bores me except you and Frank . . . No, I'm serious, Frank. What's your name? It's ridiculous not knowing what to call you.'

Frank sighed. 'I'm called Lord Corinth, if you must know, until my father dies and then I become the Duke of Mersham. But I don't want to be a duke. I'm going to give it up – renounce it – if they'll let me. I'm a Communist and we don't believe in having an aristocracy.'

'Oh, that's bullshit, Frank. You love being an aristocrat just like I love being a Roosevelt – even if it's only a minor one.' Perry prodded him with the spite of the envious drunk.

Frank might have had some difficulty replying politely but at this moment the Purser appeared and asked him to go to Lord Benyon's cabin where he was needed. Guiltily, he sprang to his feet, knocking over his champagne glass, said a perfunctory 'goodbye' to the twins and hurried back to his employer. Philly, rather put out at his abrupt departure – she wasn't used to men leaving her on the dance floor – shrugged and said, 'I guess, Perry my sweet, if you're not too drunk to dance, I'll have to make do with you after all.'

Appropriately, the band struck up 'Dancing with Tears in my Eyes' and, by the time they reached 'Stormy Weather', Perry and Philly were entwined like lovers, consoling each other for life's disappointments as they had done ever since childhood.

When he was told how Tom Barrett's corpse had been found hanging from a hook in the cold room, Frank blanched.

'That's horrible ... disgusting. These people ... will they stop at nothing?' He shuddered. 'First, they shoot at us – hoping the car will smash and kill us all – and now they kill poor Barrett. But I don't understand. Why was he naked and why didn't they just toss his body overboard?'

'To answer your second question first,' Edward said, returning to the cabin after making his report to London, 'pushing a body overboard is not so easy. A lifeless body is very heavy to manoeuvre and the *Queen Mary* isn't some little tramp steamer. There's always someone about on deck and the guard-rails are mostly very high. You might be able to jump overboard without anyone noticing, if you were determined to commit suicide, but to throw someone over, dead or alive, would be almost impossible without being seen.'

'But why was he killed?' Frank persisted. 'Why not kill Lord Benyon? I'm sorry, sir, but you know what I mean. You were alone in here working and there for the taking.'

'Thank you very much,' Benyon said with a grimace. 'That makes me feel very relaxed.'

'But Frank's right,' Verity chimed in. 'Why kill Barrett and put us all on our guard?'

'Well, I can think of three reasons,' Edward said. 'First, he was the strong man in our party, trained to deal with trouble and armed, so to have him out of the way must make the murderer feel much safer. Second, as I say, Barrett was armed. His clothes, his wallet, are missing and so is his gun. I've searched the cabin – no sign of it.'

'That was so horrible – that he should be naked,' Verity said. 'Why did they do that to him? To humiliate him? It is too awful.'

'I don't know why they did that,' Edward said sombrely. 'I've been trying to work out what he was wearing. I think he was wearing that blue jacket and blue linen trousers.'

'Yes, and those yachting shoes he liked. Said they gave him grip,' Forrest added.

'And don't forget the tie. Was it regimental?' Verity added.

'No, not regimental. It was bright pink ... I know, it was a Leander tie! I'm sure, now I think of it, he said he rowed. Well,' he continued grimly, 'if we see any of those clothes on somebody, there's our murderer but I don't suppose that's likely. I expect they were thrown over the side.'

'Except the gun,' Benyon suggested. 'I can see why the murderer or murderers – there may be more than one – took the gun but why the clothes?'

'I don't know. Perhaps there was something on them – blood possibly – which the murderer didn't want us to see.'

'You said there was a third reason, Uncle, why Barrett was killed.'

'He might have recognized his murderer.'

'You mean among the passengers?' Verity asked.

'Or crew, I suppose.'

They looked at each other uncomfortably. At last Sam Forrest said, 'I guess we'll have to keep a twenty-four-hour watch.'

Edward looked at him gratefully. 'Is that an offer to be one of the watchers?'

'Sure is. I guess my President don't want his guests picked off by some Nazi. There's five of us –'

'Six,' Verity insisted, 'or else I can't count. Mr Fern, Edward, Fenton, Frank, Sam and me. Do we have a gun among us?'

They all looked at Verity and then at Edward. 'If Verity says she's going to do something, she does it,' he said.

She looked at him and smiled. She couldn't help thinking that this was a very different man from the one she had met two years before who regarded all women as delicate objects to be kept on a pedestal and worshipped but never allowed to *do* anything.

'That's settled then. But no gun?' she said.

'I'm afraid not,' Edward said.

'I've got this little piece,' Forrest drawled, sliding a revolver out of his pocket. 'Never without it. Mine's a rough world and so I carry this.'

They all looked at him in amazement and, in Verity's case, awe.

'Well, that's comforting,' Marcus Fern said, 'though I don't suppose we can draw a gun on the *Queen Mary*. Could we ask the Captain to lend us one of the crew to add to our forces?'

'In an emergency,' Edward said, 'but I think there's enough of us. There are only three more days, after all . . .'

But, early the next morning, the wind began to blow.

6

At eight thirty, when Edward and Frank went down to the dining-room for breakfast, they found they were almost alone. It was Sunday so perhaps it was not surprising but, as the movement of the ship grew increasingly unsettling, the late risers became 'missing, believed seasick'. Uncle and nephew were both good sailors but the roll of the ship was very much greater than they had anticipated. It wasn't just a normal roll but an alarming, corkscrew motion which made it very difficult to walk.

The waiter, mopping up the spilled coffee – it was almost impossible to drink from a cup without it spilling – informed them that they had met a fifty-five mile an hour gale and that the next twelve hours were going to be very unpleasant. 'They've reduced speed to fifteen knots,' he told them, with grim satisfaction. 'It's the first real storm the *Queen*'s had to weather.'

'I thought they'd designed this ship to be the most stable of any great liner. It certainly doesn't feel like it,' Frank said fretfully.

They soon gave up their meal and went on deck but found the absence of hand-rails in the corridors – which were much wider than those in most liners – made even walking dangerous. In the lounge, the unanchored furniture was sliding across the floor and stewards were having to corral armchairs, like heifers, inside rope barriers.

When they at last got on deck the wind and rain took their breath away. The seas were mountainous and the great ship seemed to slide down the side of one wave with no thought of ever rising up the slope of the next. Edward asked a passing crew member if the storm was worse than expected but he pretended not to hear.

The altar had not been set up in the lounge so there was no chance of praying for calm. The Sunday service, the Purser informed them, had been postponed so they staggered back to Benyon's suite to find him lying in his berth feeling very unwell. Fenton, who seemed unaffected by the motion of the ship, said, 'I called the doctor and he's promised to be here in the next hour but apparently there are some seriously ill passengers. There have been several accidents and he said someone's broken their leg falling downstairs.'

Verity was sitting on the bed wiping Benyon's forehead with a cold flannel but she was looking rather green and her skin was clammy.

'You'd better go and lie down,' Edward told her.

'Oh, don't fuss. I'm all right.' No sooner had she uttered the words than a particularly fearsome wallow made her go a deeper shade of green and she only just made the lavatory in time. Edward wanted to help but she waved him away. 'It's nothing,' she gasped. 'Go and see Mr Fern. He's suffering too.'

Fern was in bed looking pale and wan. He said he had been trying to read but had given it up. 'All I can do now is just pray for it to stop. Do you think it will *ever* stop?' he inquired mournfully.

Frank wandered off to see if he could find the twins. They weren't in any of the public rooms, as far as he could see, and a steward directed him to their cabin on A Deck.

He knocked and there was a muffled 'Come in.'

'Oh, it's you,' Philly said faintly. She was wearing a silk dressing-gown and her hair was mussed and uncombed. Her white, almost transparent, skin looked even more like tightly drawn muslin than usual. 'It's Mother. She's not good at sea and she only came on the *Queen Mary* because they told her it wouldn't roll – but it's worse than the *Normandie*.'

'Can I do anything?'

'Come and see her. I've told her all about you. Maybe you can distract her.'

'I'll do my best.'

Mrs Roosevelt was indeed in a bad way. She had vomited

up everything she could and was now retching in that painful way which is more like hiccups than anything else.

'How are you, Mrs Roosevelt?' Frank said, with some embarrassment. As a first encounter, this was probably not the best time for small talk and he wondered if the poor woman would really want him to see her prostrated.

'Ma, this is Lord Corinth – Frank – who we were telling you about.'

'Lord Corinth, I'm so pleased to . . .' She made an attempt to raise her head from the pillow but fell back.

'Please don't move, Mrs Roosevelt. Is there anything I can get to make you more comfortable?'

'No . . . no, thank you. Forgive me . . . could you get my eau de Cologne from the shelf over the basin in the bathroom?'

Frank went in to the bathroom to find that all the little bottles which had been on the shelf were rolling about on the floor. He got down on his knees, gathered as many as he could see and put them in the wash basin which was the only available place where they would not roll straight back on to the floor. There seemed to be an armamentarium of drugs. He picked up one bottle but it was not the eau de Cologne. When he finally identified it, he gathered it up with another bottle and, without thinking, read the label: 'Arsenic trioxide. Danger – take as directed.'

He wondered why she should be taking arsenic but, at that moment, Philly appeared in the bathroom and Frank passed the scent bottle to her.

'I think I'd better go,' he whispered. 'If you feel up to it, come up on deck later. The storm is something you should . . . you know, witness . . . to tell your grandchildren.'

She looked at him as though he were mad and then said in a low voice, 'I'll try. Go now. Thank you for coming.'

On the way back to his own cabin, he met Bernard Hunt, who seemed quite untroubled by the ship's motion. He grasped Frank by the arm and pulled him into the cocktail lounge. 'Have a drink, my boy. It will steady you.'

'I don't think I could but you go ahead.'

'Well, I will then. I know it's only ten o'clock but a small brandy, Roger, please.'

He took out a cigarette and put it in his mouth before remembering his manners. 'You don't smoke, do you? Disgusting habit – always meant to give it up.'

Frank looked at the man curiously. He was almost sure he was drunk but he wasn't quite experienced enough to be certain. Hunt put a hand on his knee. It was casual enough but Frank had no wish to be mauled by those yellow fingers with their bitten nails. He slid down on a sofa but Hunt pursued him. A particularly violent plunge, which seemed to set the *Queen Mary* on her side, gave Frank an excuse to struggle to his feet.

'I don't like this at all,' he said, not certain whether he referred to Hunt's groping or the ship's motion. 'Did it do this on the maiden voyage?'

'Did *she* do this, you mean. Ships are feminine. No, but it amuses me, this bucking and twisting. She's showing her feminine side. Know what I mean?'

He smiled, showing yellow, equine teeth. 'But that's not what I wanted to talk to you about.' Frank was now sure the man was drunk – at ten o'clock in the morning – and he tried to be amused but was inwardly rather revolted. 'I hear you were in Spain. Good show and all that. Meet a man there called Griffiths-Jones? A Party worker – one of the best.'

'No, but I've heard Verity – Miss Browne – talk about him. He's a big shot, isn't he? But how do you know him? You're not a Communist, are you?'

It seemed to Frank inconceivable that this unpleasant creature – an art historian and, he now had to believe, a homosexual – should be a Party member. Though why Communists *shouldn't* be interested in art he couldn't have said.

'Not a Party member. I carry no card – wouldn't be wise, old man, not in my position.' He rubbed the side of his nose with the roguish exaggeration of the drunk. 'But in every sense a "fellow-traveller".' He sniggered. 'It's not about me – it's about *you* I want to talk. I'm seriously impressed. The son of a duke and a fully paid-up member of the Party! That's . . . that's spiffing.'

This was getting worse, worse even than Perry Roosevelt asking him all those questions. Why couldn't people leave him alone? And why was it even Communists seemed *pleased* he was an aristocrat? It was what he had joined the Party to get away from.

'And you ran away from school! Good for you. I was at Marlborough. Hated the place. That was why I took to art – to escape! It didn't always work but . . . that fagging! I was always being beaten because I hadn't cleaned my fagmaster's footer boots, or some such rot! And the food – bread and margarine. We had a bad time of it . . . the war, you know. I was always cold. And the lavatories . . . so insanitary. A double row of doorless compartments – no privacy, not even there. The other boys would send down rafts of burning paper to singe my bottom. They hated me because I didn't like footer . . .'

The pain and contempt with which he spoke the word 'footer' made Frank stare. Behind this languid, asthenic man was something very hard – a ball of hatred which most of the time he kept well hidden – but because of the drink and the storm, and because this boy attracted him and had himself hated school, he was revealing parts of himself he usually kept secret.

'It was a bestial place . . .' Hunt shuddered, 'and so cold. So damn cold . . . and those bloody, boring practical jokes. Perhaps it was different at Eton. They called me a pansy and did things to me . . . horrible things.'

'But you loved art . . .?' Frank said, interested despite himself.

'Yes, my father was in Paris for the Peace Conference. He was a diplomat. I almost *lived* in the Louvre during the holidays. I'd started a magazine at school – *The Aesthete* we called it. It was against everything I hated, especially footer. I started writing about art then and I never stopped.'

'I started a magazine at Eton,' Frank chimed in, but Hunt was not listening. He was remembering. 'Cambridge was better.'

'Did you know my uncle?'

'No, I wasn't at Trinity. I had my own set. My friends were at King's. Morgan Forster . . . heard of him?' Frank hadn't, not being a reader of novels. 'I was frightfully keen on Picasso and Blake, and a boy called . . .' He sniggered again. 'Never mind that.'

86

'But were you converted to Communism?' Frank asked.

'Sh!' Hunt said, with exaggerated alarm. 'Mustn't say that. I told you, I'm not a Communist. Shouldn't really have said anything. But you're safe, aren't you?'

'I can keep a secret, if that's what you mean.'

'I knew you could. I went to the Soviet Union in '32 . . . to look at the pictures. I wanted to see the Hermitage.'

'And was it wonderful?' Frank asked, excited at last.

'So wonderful . . . the Poussins . . .'

'No, no. I mean the Soviet Union. Was it utopia?'

Hunt smiled crookedly. 'Not what I call utopia. The lavatories were worse than at school – unbelievably filthy. The food was bad and there wasn't much of it. I refused to tour all those beastly factories but we were impressed. A group of us went. We could see they had done wonderful things. They had industrialized very fast but you couldn't judge it by normal Western standards. They had come so far in so short a time. It was natural there were still problems.'

'But that was where you became . . . what you said you're not?'

'I suppose so,' Hunt conceded. 'Mind you, they thought I was "decadent" – the Party, I mean. They wouldn't give me my card; said I was more use *outside* the Party. They sent me to the States and it was there I met that man, Senator Day.'

'You know Day?' Frank exclaimed.

'He made it his business to investigate people like me . . . like Warren Fairley, too. He made our lives difficult. I was offered a research job in the National Gallery in Washington but Day, damn him, heard about it and discovered I'd been to the Soviet Union and had the offer withdrawn. All for the good in the end but I'll never forgive him . . . never!'

At that moment they were interrupted by Edward. He nodded to Hunt and then, holding on to a convenient pillar to support himself against the ship's dipping and diving, signalled to his nephew.

'Sorry to disturb you,' he said with sarcasm, 'but it's your turn on duty. Report to Benyon's cabin and relieve Mr Fern, will you? Damn this ship,' he gasped as a particularly violent heave sent the crockery flying and the furniture not fixed to the floor slipping and sliding across the room. 'I really can't believe this is acceptable in this so-called modern miracle of engineering. It is quite frightening on deck and the Captain has had to cut our speed by a half so God knows when we'll reach New York. There have been at least two nasty accidents already. An elderly woman in Tourist Class was badly hurt when she tried to go through a swing door and it swung back and knocked her off her feet. Someone else fell and broke an arm in one of the corridors. There ought to be rails to hold on to but, apparently, they thought the ship was too stable to need them!'

'What's happened about Tom Barrett? Do we know how he died yet?' Frank asked.

'The doctor says he was knocked on the head by a club or metal bar but we haven't found any sign of it. The Captain has announced that there was a fatal accident – quite understandable in these conditions, I should think. Most people won't realize it happened before the storm. There will be a short church service tomorrow or whenever the storm abates.'

'Gosh, will there be a burial at sea? I wouldn't mind being buried at sea.'

'No, certainly not. The body will be taken home for his relatives to bury. At the moment, it's in cold storage – I mean, not where we found it but ... you know what I mean. The police will want to have a proper post mortem, I imagine. Now, be a good chap and get along to Benyon. What was Hunt talking to you about so earnestly – art appreciation? He looks rather drunk but it's hard to tell when everyone's falling about like Laurel and Hardy.'

'He put his hand on my knee and told me he was a "fellow-traveller",' Frank said, making off before his uncle could reply.

'What, another queer pinko?' Edward said in disgust. He looked over at the sofa where Hunt was fast asleep, his mouth open and his brandy glass empty in his lap.

Frank found Marcus Fern looking very green about the gills and sent him off to his cabin to lie on his bunk for which he was suitably grateful.

'Lord Benyon's sleeping, I think. He's got his eyes shut, anyway. Lock the door after me. Your uncle's man – what's his name? – Fenton, will relieve you in a couple of hours.'

Frank went into Benyon's bedroom and found him asleep, as Fern had said, so he returned to the outer room and threw himself into a chair. The ship was plunging ever deeper and seemed ever more reluctant to raise her bows before the next great wave. For the first time, Frank really began to think the *Queen Mary* had some basic design fault. It couldn't be right – even in these heavy seas – for such a great ship to roll in such an odd corkscrew motion and it occurred to him that it was possible she might sink. It seemed absurd but there was the fate of *Titanic* to consider. They had called her unsinkable.

Fortunately, his rather morbid imaginings were interrupted by a feeble call from the bedroom. Frank went in to find Benyon in a pitiable state. He had nothing left to vomit but was wretchedly weak and a very odd colour.

'Are you all right, sir?' he inquired fatuously.

'Frank, is that you?' Benyon said faintly, putting out a hand. Frank wasn't used to holding hands with men he hardly knew but the appeal went to his heart and he grasped it. He was disturbed to find it dry and papery. He had expected it to be damp and hot.

'Should I call the doctor, sir?'

'No, no thank you, my boy. He can do nothing. I was praying we would have a smooth crossing but God had other ideas. Perhaps the storm has been whipped up by our enemies. What do you think?' The little joke seemed to revive him and he went on, 'At first I thought I was going to die but now I've reached the stage where I fear I may not. Do you think we are going to sink?'

'No, of course not,' Frank answered firmly. 'Have a little water. I think you may be dehydrated.'

' "Water, water everywhere nor any drop to drink," ' Benyon quoted and, rather pleased with himself, managed to raise his head from the bed and sip from the glass Frank held for him. He sank back wearily but his eyes were open and he was obviously thinking about something other than his physical condition because he said, 'They say you're a Communist, Frank. Is that right?'

'I am indeed, sir. It's the only thing to be – you must see that.' Frank, realizing he might have sounded hectoring, added, 'At least, that's how it seems to me.'

'Tell me.'

'Oh, you don't want to hear my views on life.'

'But I do. It would help take my mind off this infernal seasickness.'

'Well, I don't pretend to be very original. I just think it's all obvious. Everything is moving so fast now – science, technology, the way society works. It's quite different from your generation. Sorry, sir, I didn't intend to be rude but you know what I mean.'

'Go on. So what makes Communism the philosophy suited to this new, fast-moving world?'

'Everyone should have an equal start in life. That goes without saying. Money and titles – it's all bosh and it gets in the way of progress. And all our industries should be state-owned. Why should men like Henry Ford make millions at our expense? And all those war profiteers who made fortunes out of supplying boots or biscuits to the army, let alone arms. Why should Lord Londonderry be one of the richest men in the world because he happens to own land with coal under it? It's iniquitous.'

'State ownership has been tried but it fails because it stifles the innovator and the entrepreneur. You say society is changing so fast – that's because people can make money out of their inventions and enjoy the fruits of their hard work.'

'The experiment in the Soviet Union proves it can work.'

'Have you seen it?' Benyon asked drily.

'No, but I've talked to people who have. Anyway, money isn't the only stimulus to bring out the best in man. There's patriotism and honour.'

Benyon said gently, 'I agree. That's why I'm sailing this dangerous sea. It's certainly not for my own profit. But –'

'That's right! Honour – the respect of your fellow citizens – that's stimulus enough, surely? It's harnessing the competitive instinct to honour rather than money.'

'I don't agree. I wish I did.'

'It doesn't matter now. The people will take what is theirs as they have in the Soviet Union.'

Benyon sighed. 'When you talk about the people taking what is theirs, my heart sinks. Do you really think the weak, the hungry and the poor will get their share?'

'You think it's all rot, sir, but look at Spain. People . . . even people like Verity who know . . . talk about the war as if it were the first battle against Fascism but it's not. Or it wasn't when it started, at any rate.'

'What was it then?'

'It was the spontaneous uprising of the workers to take what was theirs from the landowners and the exploiters. They formed communes and workers' co-operatives . . .'

'But now they are the puppets of ideologues and are manipulated by bigots who don't care who they have to trample over to get the society they want . . .'

There was more strength in Benyon's voice and Frank had to smile. 'You're feeling better, sir?'

Benyon laughed. 'I do believe I am. Tell me, do you think men like Senator Day will join the revolution?'

'No, they will be eliminated. Men like Day – racists and anti-Semites – must be disposed of.'

He spoke so coldly and with such determination that Lord Benyon felt a chill run down his spine. 'You don't mean that, Frank. You're very young . . .'

'But that just means I haven't been corrupted yet.'

'And you would kill anyone who disagreed with you?'

'I don't know. I suppose I would try to re-educate them first . . .'

'It's odd,' Verity was saying, 'I thought boats were all about feeling the wind in your hair and the spray in your face, particularly when there's a storm, but here we are on a sofa in a room like the Ritz only it happens to be swaying about worse than an earthquake.'

'Have you ever been to the Ritz?' Sam Forrest asked.

'As a matter of fact, I have. Purely for research purposes, you understand. "Know your enemy" and all that. But what I mean is the ship's so huge that it's a world of its own and one looks inward, not out to sea.'

'I guess, and yet the only thing between us and a watery grave is an eggshell.'

'Oh yeah? Some eggshell!'

They were seated in an almost empty room, staring at a

rather vulgar mural of some 'mythical goings-on', as Verity put it, which involved a swan and a near-naked lady.

'You know,' Sam said, 'that painting gives me ideas. You see that swan – don't you think it looks a bit like me?'

'It's got a rather stupid, greedy face so I don't think it does,' she replied tactfully. 'But if you feel like what I've heard Edward describe, in his dear, old-fashioned way, as spooning, then I have to say I don't feel quite up to it. If we stay like this I don't think I'm going to be sick, but any attempt to walk could be fatal.'

'Right then,' Sam replied philosophically, 'let's talk. I'm puzzled by this murder.'

'Hush,' Verity urged him. 'We promised not to spread rumours.'

'Come on, this place is as empty as Washington in August. Your friend Lord Corinth or whatever I'm supposed to call him –.'

'You mean Edward or Frank?'

'Edward, and may I add – in parenthesis – are you aware that he's stuck on you like –?'

'Not for discussion, Sam. Sorry, but I don't know you well enough.'

'That can be attended to . . .' Seeing a look on her face which, had he known it, had also on occasion made Edward pause, he changed tack. 'He says, though he wraps it up in all sorts of circumlocutions, that Mr Barrett wasn't just Lord Benyon's valet but also his "heavy". In passing, may I say that – being a good, blue-collar worker – until this last week I'd never met a lord and now I'm drowning in them.' The ship gave a particularly violent jerk and he added, 'And maybe drowning *with* them. I thought you English could build ships?'

'So someone wants to stop Lord Benyon meeting your President. That's clear. But why kill Tom Barrett and not Benyon? Whatever we do to try and protect him, we could hardly defend him against a man with a gun.'

'Lord Edward told you why. Barrett must have recognized this man – perhaps he followed him into the bowels of the ship and got hit on the head.'

'Yes, that must be it and we'll never know who. There are –

what? – at least two thousand souls on board. Could be any one of them.'

'Not true. It has to be either a member of the crew – and not an ordinary seaman, I mean a steward or officer, someone who wouldn't attract any attention in First Class – or one of the First Class passengers. The stewards keep a lookout for interlopers from the other classes. It makes me very uneasy. I realize now I ought to be in Tourist but there we are . . .'

'You know, Sam, you said you were drowning in lords? Well, I don't agree. There are a few celebrities – like Warren Fairley – but there aren't many what I would call aristocrats on board, or even diplomats. They're mostly rich Americans.'

'It's obvious, isn't it? Who has money since the Depression? Not dukes and earls but Americans whose shares are beginning to pay dividends at last.'

'Right. That was why I was quite surprised by Major Cranton and his wife.'

'Who?'

'You know – that English couple with a cabin next to Frank's. How can they afford to be travelling First Class to the States on the *Queen Mary*?'

'You should ask them.'

'I think I will,' Verity said meditatively. 'I'm such a curious cat. It must be why I'm such a good journalist.'

'Sure, and you're real smart, no question,' Sam responded, but his agreement made Verity uneasy. What had been a little joke now sounded like bragging. She found herself thinking that Edward would not have let her get away with it.

'Edward's with Lord Benyon, isn't he? Let's go and relieve him,' she said abruptly.

As they staggered from one pillar to another, clutching at each other to remain upright, Sam said, 'This would be a dandy time and place to murder someone. In a ship in a storm, any sort of accident is possible and who could say if a man who broke his neck falling down a gangway was pushed?'

'But it makes it harder if the victim never leaves his cabin because of seasickness,' Verity pointed out.

* * *

Edward was sitting beside Benyon's bed reading him Dr Johnson.

'Where's Fenton?' Verity inquired.

'I sent him off to sleuth among the crew but I doubt he'll turn up anything interesting.'

'Why are you boring the invalid with Dr Johnson?' Verity asked, leaning over Edward's shoulder.

'He's a favourite of mine,' Benyon explained, 'and so wise and rational I thought he would be an antidote to stormy seas.'

'Does he have anything to say about ships?' Verity inquired, looking anxiously at Benyon's bright, feverish eyes. She put her hand on his forehead and it was clammy.

Reading her mind, he said with a wan smile, 'Don't worry, my dear, though at this particular moment I would give anything to be dead, I have, paradoxically, no intention of dying. Make sense of that if you can.'

Edward was thumbing through his book. 'Dr Johnson doesn't say much about ships. He says somewhere that men who have never been soldiers or sailors feel as though they are not quite men.'

'Nonsense!' Benyon mumbled but, overcome with a desire to retch, was unable to expatiate on why it was nonsense.

Verity mopped his brow with a damp sponge and, when he gave her his hand like a sick child, she held it until he was calm again.

'Oh, and listen to this,' Edward said turning over a page. 'The good doctor also says that being in a ship is like being in gaol, with the chance of being drowned. Rather good, eh?'

At that moment, Marcus Fern put his head round the door. 'Are you all right, Benyon?'

It was a silly question but Benyon managed a smile. 'In that case, could I borrow Lord Edward for a moment?'

'Yes, you go and get some air,' Verity said. 'Sam and I will keep an eye on the patient.'

With a grateful glance at her and a slightly suspicious look at Forrest, Edward got up. He stretched himself and almost tipped over as the ship tilted alarmingly.

'Won't this ever end?' The cry, wrung out of the sick man, made all three of them look at one another in consternation.

'I'll go and ask the Captain,' Edward said. 'I'm sure the worst must be over.'

When they had gone, Verity and Forrest left Benyon to try and sleep and went to sit in the outer cabin. In a low voice, so as not to disturb the patient, Sam said, 'It seems real bad we can do nothing to find who killed Tom Barrett.'

'I know,' Verity agreed. 'That's just what I've been thinking. We are on guard and on the defensive. I was wondering if there was something we could do to get him to reveal himself. What we need is a beater.'

'How's that?'

'You know, someone who beats the game towards the guns. Surely you have that sort of thing in the States?'

'Not in my city, you don't, but I guess I know what you mean.'

'Or,' Verity continued meditatively, 'we could hang out a dead goat and see if the smell of blood flushes him out.'

'Hey! What a bloodthirsty little thing you are.'

'Don't call me "little",' she snapped at him.

'I was only admiring your get-up-and-go.' Sam tried to retrieve the situation. 'I meant no offence.' He hurried on, 'So who's volunteering to be the carcass which will attract the murderer?'

'It has to be Lord Benyon himself,' Verity said more calmly. 'We need to plan an ambush. We leave the cabin unguarded as obviously as possible, hide round the corner and then . . .'

'We catch him in the act.'

'Before the act,' Verity corrected him. 'The idea, dunderhead, is to stop Lord Benyon being killed, not facilitate it.'

'Dunderhead? I've never been called that before. Is it worse than me calling you . . .?' He registered her expression and decided not to pursue this line of defence but capitulate gracefully. 'When shall we try it?'

Verity went over to the connecting door and peered at the patient. 'He seems to be asleep. Why don't we try now?'

'But what if the enemy doesn't notice the room's unguarded?'

'We try again later.'

Sam looked dubious. 'I don't know. Shouldn't we check first with Corinth? We said we'd protect Benyon, not tie him to a stake.'

'What possible harm can there be? Look, I noticed there was a little cupboard or something just round the corner. I saw a maid open it and put something in.'

'Won't it be locked?'

'It shouldn't be. I slipped a wedge in the door to stop it closing properly. Go and see.'

'You're amazing! So this isn't some idea you've just cooked up? You've planned it.'

'Sure have, pardner,' Verity said, in a feeble attempt at an American accent. She was pleased with herself. What a coup it would be if she – if they, she corrected herself – could capture the big bad wolf while Edward did nothing but sit around waiting for something to happen. 'I think I shall call you Peter.' Sam looked puzzled. 'Like Peter and the wolf.'

He smiled uncomprehendingly and slipped out of the cabin, returning a moment later.

'Yep, the cupboard door's open. Shall we try it?'

'We have to be obvious but not obviously obvious, if you get me,' she said, taking command.

As noisily as they dared – not wishing to wake Benyon but trying to advertise their departure – they left the cabin joking and laughing. Turning the corner into the small passage between the cabins and finding the coast clear, they slipped into the cupboard. It was a tight squeeze and the only light came through the slightly open door.

After about a minute, although it seemed very much longer, Verity said, 'It's just like sardines, isn't it?'

'Sardines?'

'You must have played sardines when you were a child. Sort of like hide-and-seek. You hid in a cupboard or under the stairs with some nice boy and hoped for a kiss before you were found.'

Realizing what she had said, she added hurriedly, 'Not now, of course. I didn't mean . . .'

Sam Forrest, appreciating that this invitation was not going to be repeated, took Verity in his arms and kissed her on the mouth. She struggled, more for convention's sake than in genuine surprise, and then gave herself up to the pleasure of the kiss. It went through her mind that it had been some time since she had been kissed – not since she and Edward had gone to Spain to search for Frank. As they kissed, she found herself wondering why Edward had not tried to kiss her in that horrible little hotel outside Madrid where they had spent two nights while passes and other papers were prepared for them. It was true he was worried – they both were – but might it not have been comforting . . .?

Suddenly she noticed that it was quite dark. The cupboard door had closed. She released herself from Sam's embrace by standing on his toes.

'Ouch. Why did you do that? I was sort of enjoying myself.'

'I couldn't get your attention any other way. Open the door, will you? We won't see anyone creeping around if we're stuck in here.'

It was pitch dark now and, swearing, Sam felt around for a door catch.

'Damn it, I can't see what I'm doing. Have you got a match?'

'Of course not, you oaf. Sorry, I'm just panicking. I'm the oaf. I didn't bring my bag with me. Here, let me . . .' They fumbled around but there was no catch or knob on the inside of the cupboard door. 'Gosh, I'm going to write such a stinker to the chairman of Cunard about the design of their cupboards when I get out of here.'

'Oh yes?' whispered Sam. 'And how are you going to explain how you discovered the defect? Have you noticed, it's getting very hot in here?'

They were both very uncomfortable now and worried that, while they were locked in the cupboard in this absurd way, their charge might be being butchered.

'Break it open,' Verity commanded.

'But how will we explain . . . I must have been nuts to go along with this crazy –'

'Just get on with it, will you?'

Sam put his shoulder to the door but in the confined space it was difficult to get any purchase. He huffed and puffed while Verity became more and more irritable.

'Don't get sore with me, lady. This was all your stupid idea. I should have known better than to –'

'There was nothing wrong with the plan if you had kept your foot in the door.'

'Do you think someone closed the door on us deliberately?'

he said, suddenly alarmed. 'I don't see how it could have shut by itself.'

'Of course it could with the ship rolling like this. Look, you'd better get us out. I'm beginning to feel rather sick and there isn't much room to be sick in here.'

'Oh Christ!' he cried and slammed himself against the door with as much force as he could muster. As he did so and – as Verity remarked later – with all the timing of an Aldwych farce, the door was opened from the outside and Forrest fell into the arms of Edward Corinth. Both men collapsed on to the floor and a particularly violent roll led them to embrace each other with something like fervour.

A cabin door opened gingerly and a face appeared. It belonged to Senator Day.

'Could you gentlemen be a little quieter?' he inquired mildly. 'Marlene ain't full weight right now, on account of her stomach bein' shrunk up. The doc says she's real sick and needs her rest.'

Apologizing profusely, the two men disentangled themselves and found Benyon standing at the door of his cabin in his pyjamas. It was not an edifying spectacle, as Lord Benyon said in mild reproof when they had regained the cabin. 'I don't doubt your motives,' he said, with a kindly pat on Verity's back, 'but next time do tell me what you're planning so I can come and get you out of trouble.'

7

By the following morning the storm had abated although the seas were still huge, at least to Verity's eyes, and the *Queen Mary* was still wallowing and rolling like an angry hippopotamus.

'I am so disappointed,' Edward was saying. They were sitting on deck, the lifeboats hanging from davits above them. 'I was convinced, if there were a storm, we would hardly notice it but this is far worse than the *Normandie*. They will have to do something about it. The Captain was apologetic but, of course, it's the design which is at fault. It's nothing he can do anything about.'

'I'm getting my sea legs,' Verity said. 'I had some breakfast and I'm still feeling all right. Long may it last.'

There was silence as they stared out over the grey-green sea – bleak below the heavy black clouds through which no ray of sunshine could pass.

'That fracas last night. That was silly,' Verity said at last.

'It was rather,' Edward agreed. 'You're quite soft on Sam Forrest, aren't you?'

'I like him,' she admitted, defensively. 'His views and mine coincide on most things.'

'Unlike yours and mine,' he said bitterly. 'I had thought we might have had some time together but you seem so taken up with him.'

'That's not fair, Edward. Sam and I are just friends ... colleagues.'

'And am I just a friend?'

'A friend, yes. A close friend. I'm very fond of you but ...'

'We can never be more . . . Is that it?'

'No . . . yes. I mean, I really care for you. You know that and I wouldn't say it if I didn't mean it . . .'

'But . . .?'

'But we're so different. We look at the world through different spectacles. You know how I annoy you.'

'You don't annoy me . . . Well, you do but that's part of the reason I . . .' he hesitated, 'I love you. I want you to be my wife. There, laugh if you want but at least I've said it.'

'Oh, Edward. I . . . I'm glad you've said it. I really am. I'm flattered . . . honoured but . . .'

' "But" again? How I hate that word. Henceforth, I shall never use it.'

'But I'm not made for love and marriage. I just wouldn't be good at it. I like racketing around the world, taking what fate has to offer. I'm not made for nesting. You need someone who can bring you peace and give you children and the unconditional love you deserve.'

'So that means "no", does it?' he said moodily, scowling at the sea which at least had the grace to reflect his mood. He watched with satisfaction as a man turned green and leant over the rail. It was only right that other people should be as unhappy as he was.

'I'm afraid it does,' she said sadly. 'I do love you in my way and you're the first person I turn to when I need someone . . . when I'm in trouble.' She touched his arm and he didn't shake her off. 'But I'm so unstable. I think it's something to do with never having had a mother. I've never had an example to follow. Do you understand?'

He turned and grasped her by the hand. Further along the promenade deck, an elderly man looked at them with regret, taking them for lovers. 'Please, Verity . . . I don't want a conventional wife with good teeth, pearls round her neck and an ability to produce four children and run a household. I'm not advertising for a cook/housekeeper, you know.'

She laughed, without meaning to. 'That's one job I couldn't do!'

Edward went on remorselessly, determined now to have his say, come what may. 'It's wrong of you to think I can't deal with someone . . . different. You've taught me not to try and

100

dominate. I don't expect you . . . I don't want you to share my views on politics or life in general. You keep me alive by showing me how differently we can look at things.'

'I know . . . I'm not accusing you of being boring.'

'Well, that's what it sounded like,' he said, beginning to sulk. He let go her hand but she took his back.

'Edward, please. Don't let's quarrel. I do love you and if you wanted me . . .'

He looked up. 'Of course I want you.'

'Well then . . . oh dear! This isn't how it is in books.'

'What books?'

'Romantic novels . . . Ethel M. Dell.'

'You've never read a romance in your life. That's one of the things I love about you. You're a realist.'

'Well, *you* ought to be a realist,' she countered. 'What would the Duke say if you told him you were marrying me? He'd have apoplexy.'

'You do him an injustice,' he said, coldly.

'Sex but not marriage, then. Take it or leave it. You say yourself there's a war coming. Who knows what the world will be like when it's over. I can't tie myself down until the last battle has been won.'

'There never is a last battle,' he said, despairingly. 'But thank you for saying what you did . . . about loving me. It means –'

'Not butting in, am I?' Sam Forrest, breezy, good-natured, unsuspecting of the nature of the scene he had interrupted, patted Edward on the back. 'What about a game of deck quoits?'

'Not for me, but I am sure Miss Browne would like you to entertain her,' he replied brusquely, striding off as if he had somewhere to go.

'Ouch!' Sam said. 'He bites.'

By midday, the sun was struggling to break through the clouds and occasionally succeeding, lightening everyone's spirits. The sea, too, looked more at ease with itself and the ship, though still bucking, as Sam put it, 'like a steer on its way to the stockyard', permitted deck games and allowed unskilful players to blame the elements for their inadequacies.

101

Edward ceased his pacing and sighed. In the distance, he could see Verity and Sam playing an energetic game of shuttlecock. He sat down heavily on a long chair and tried to turn his mind to what Fern had told him after they had left Lord Benyon's cabin the previous day. He had seen someone who wasn't what they pretended to be. Edward had already made the same identification but they agreed to do nothing for the moment – or at least until Edward had spoken to Major Ferguson by telephone.

His gloom deepened. It was all turning into the most awful mess. He had dished his chances with Verity. His proposal had been awkward, ill timed, absurd. He punched a fist into the palm of his other hand. The worst thing was he couldn't run away and bury his head in some convenient sand. The ship, which had seemed so large, had narrowed to the width of a cell. What was it Dr Johnson had said? Being on a ship is being in gaol with the chance of being drowned? Something like that and, as so often, he had been right. Edward snorted and then pulled himself together. He hated wallowing in self-pity. It was unmanly and he was suddenly ashamed of himself. Was Verity not right to say she was unsuited to marriage? Could he really imagine her changing nappies? For that matter, wasn't *he* too old for children? Verity and he growing old together like Darby and Joan! He had to smile. He was maudlin and he hated that. He was *not* old he told himself firmly.

The sight of passengers, wrapped in rugs against the chill, reading or dozing in the long chairs which lined the sun deck, proclaimed that the worst of the bad weather was over. Stewards ran about serving drinks and even a little food which proved that stomachs were coming to terms with this endlessly moving world. Edward was surprised to see Senator Day and his wife and even more surprised when the Senator waved to him. Had he been forgiven for writhing around on the floor outside his cabin with Sam Forrest? Good manners prevented him from pretending not to see them. Reluctantly, he went over and perched on a stool at the lady's feet.

'I am glad to see you up, Mrs Day,' he said courteously. 'I gather, like so many of us, you were badly affected by the storm.'

'Yes indeed, I was afflicted . . . about to give out, as we say

102

down south but George . . .' she indicated the Senator, 'was quite unaffected. He is a most remarkable man, Lord Edward. You know, he never takes any exercise. I've told him time and time again to take exercise. I dread he may have a heart attack. He's not as strong as he looks and his position in society . . . his responsibilities . . . the worries. I want him to learn to swim or play golf but he won't.'

Day held up a hand in pretend protest. 'Marlene, hush your mouth. Lord Edward doesn't want to hear about me.' He was clearly pleased to have his wife speak of him with such warmth to this English aristocrat.

There was nothing forced about Mrs Day's words and Edward wondered if, after all, she did love her husband and was not the put-upon wretch they had all taken pleasure in pitying at the Captain's table on their first night. He certainly had not expected her to be so voluble. It must be relief at surviving the storm, he supposed.

'My wife tells me I behaved badly at dinner the other night . . . "ain't fit to roll with a pig", as she put it.' The Senator sounded a little less confident than usual. 'Do you think I insulted the Captain and, if so, should I apologize?'

'It's not for me to say,' Edward replied, 'but I suppose, confined as we are for these few days, we ought to tolerate each other's foibles.'

'That's just what I was telling him,' Mrs Day said. 'I told him, you wouldn't find English lords being . . . plumb uncouth . . . there's no other word for it. Sometimes he ain't got a grain of sense.' She smiled and put a hand on her husband's.

'Oh, I don't know . . .' Edward began, wondering if this English lord had not just been 'uncouth' to Verity and Sam Forrest.

'The trouble is,' the Senator said confidentially, 'I just have a prejudice against sitting down with coloured folk . . . can't abide them. Now, I guess that may make me old-fashioned but there it is. It's the way I've been brought up. But he ain't got no call accusin' me,' he added, beginning to work himself up again.

'Mr Fairley is a remarkable man, Senator, and I would be proud to sit with him at any table.'

'Would you now?' Day said, in what might have been

genuine amazement. 'I'd never have credited it. And what sticks in my gullet, I have to say, is him being married to a white girl. I recall the words of our great President, John Quincy Adams. "Black and white blood cannot intermingle in marriage without gross outrage upon the law of nature."'

'But that was a hundred years ago! Surely –'

'I believe the President had just attended a performance of the play *Othello* by William Shakespeare,' the Senator continued remorselessly. 'If my memory serves me right, he went on to say, "Who in real life would have Desdemona for his sister, daughter or wife?"'

'I am sorry,' Edward said, suddenly disgusted with Day and with himself for listening, 'I cannot hear any more of this. I would be proud to call Mr Fairley my friend and I find your remarks repellent. Good day to you.'

He tipped his hat to Mrs Day and went off, wondering if he were a prig but deciding he had no obligation to stay and listen to more of the man's repulsive views on miscegenation. He shook his head. It surely promised ill for the United States if the Senator represented any significant body of opinion. He was well aware that in Britain, too, there was prejudice against foreigners and anyone with a different coloured skin or shape of eye. Words like 'dago' and 'wop' were used unthinkingly about Spanish and Italians but were they not almost affectionate? Or at least humorous, like calling a Welshman 'Taffy' or a Scot 'Jock'? He must ask Verity about it.

Then he remembered that he was not keen on hearing her views on anything at the moment and was hit by a soggy feeling in the pit of his stomach. It came to him that, after so many months, he had at last nerved himself to propose marriage to the woman he loved and he had been rejected. Damn and blast! He would put her right out of his mind and he would never ask her to marry him again even if she came to him on bended knee. He smiled at the very idea of Verity on bended knee and felt momentarily more cheerful.

Frank and Perry Roosevelt were so engrossed in a fierce game of deck tennis that Edward did not like to disturb them, so he stopped beside the slim girl with whom Frank was obviously smitten. As he looked at her, it struck him that there was something ethereal about her and it crossed his mind that she might be ill. When he raised his hat and asked permission to sit beside her, she looked at him with vivid blue eyes – or not blue exactly, he decided, but aquamarine. They watched the game in companionable silence for two or three minutes. Then she said, 'You are Frank's uncle, Lord Edward Corinth?'

'I have that honour,' he agreed, smiling. 'He's a fine boy and I'm proud of him but – I'm sure he will have told you – he can get carried away.'

'Oh yes, he's told us all about running away from school and going to fight in Spain.'

Edward hadn't quite meant that.

'It's so romantic.' She sighed. 'He's very handsome, isn't he?'

Edward shot her a glance. Was she teasing him? He couldn't tell. A line from *Othello* came into his head. 'And often did beguile her of her tears, when I did speak of some distressful stroke, that my youth suffered.' Had this girl been beguiled by Frank's tales of derring-do?

Philly looked into the middle distance, holding her hat against the wind. It was straw, with a blue band round it and, against her white dress, seemed to emphasize her fragility. He thought what a graceful pose it was – a woman with her hand arched above her head, securing a wayward hat – and wished he were a painter.

'And your twin . . . he is your twin, is he not?'

'He is.'

'He and Frank have become great friends.'

'Shipboard intimacy – nothing more, I think. I like your nephew a lot, Lord Edward, but experience has taught me that these friendships, particularly if they have to be sustained by letter over an ocean, seldom survive.'

'Well, I hope this proves an exception. It is very important for England to have as many friends as possible in the United States, with war looming . . .'

'Particularly if their name is Roosevelt?'

'Particularly so,' Edward agreed. On an impulse, he added, 'Had you met Senator Day . . . before this trip, I mean?'

'We met him in London, at a reception at the embassy,' she said vaguely.

'Oh, did you? He's no friend to Britain, I understand?'

'I didn't know that. Mr and Mrs Fairley were there too. I remember because they had "words". Isn't that what you English say?'

'That's what we say.' He smiled. 'Frank probably told you about the Senator calling Mr Fairley a ... well, something I'm not going to repeat, at the Captain's table. It was quite embarrassing.'

'Yes, he told us. But didn't I just see you conversing with Senator and Mrs Day? I thought they must be friends of yours.' She sounded rather accusing.

'I was merely being polite but when he started ... you know ... to air his opinions, I left them. I don't think you would call us friends.'

The girl looked at him, perhaps quizzically. He could not read her expression. She stood up. 'Please forgive me, Lord Edward, but I must go see my mother. She is still in her cabin. It is taking her a long time to find her "sea legs".'

'Of course,' Edward said also rising. 'Perhaps you and your mother and your brother, of course, would care to join us for dinner in the Verandah Grill this evening?'

She hesitated. 'That is very kind of you but doesn't the Captain demand your presence?'

'Oh no. He has a lot of passengers to keep happy so he extends the compliment of an invitation to his table to as many as possible during the crossing. I've heard the food in the Verandah Grill is better than in the restaurant,' he added as an inducement.

'I am sure, if my mother is well enough, we would be delighted to accept your invitation,' the girl said formally and made a little bow which Edward felt held a hint of mockery. She was enchanting, he had to agree with his nephew, and her presence made it easier to forget his snubbing by Verity.

The two boys stopped playing, Perry claiming victory. Despite the wind, both were sweating and Perry suggested they should try out the Turkish bath. Not waiting to be formally introduced to Edward, he said, 'What about you, sir? Will you come?'

Edward was about to refuse but then thought, Why not? It

was ridiculous not to make use of the ship's facilities and it might help him slough off his depression.

'If it wouldn't be a bore, I would like to. By the way, I don't think we have been properly introduced. I'm Edward Corinth, but I expect you had worked that out. I have just asked your sister if you and your mother would dine with us tonight.'

'Indeed, sir. That's very kind of you.' Playfully, he banged Frank on the shoulder. 'Frank speaks very well of you, sir, which is more than I would of my uncle.'

Edward was pleased but tried not to show it. 'Elderly relatives usually put a damper on the pleasures of their younger kinsfolk, eh Frank? But please don't keep calling me "sir". That does make me feel my age.'

'What shall I call you?'

'How about Edward?' he found himself saying. It was usually many months before he invited this sort of intimacy and he saw Frank glance at him in surprise. There was something charming about these two young Americans which made them hard to resist. Was it just good manners or some natural gift – a grace with which you are either born or not?

'For goodness sake, Uncle, you sound like some Edwardian roué. Though to be honest, I'm not sure what a roué has to do to become one.'

Abashed, Edward retreated but Frank took him by the arm, which he squeezed companionably. 'Of course we'd like you to come with us and try out the *hammam*. Who knows, we may need a chaperon.'

Edward looked at the two boys doubtfully but their invitation seemed genuine so together they trooped down to the swimming-bath on C Deck.

Edward lay prostrate upon the stainless-steel massage slab, like a body in the morgue, considering the strangeness of it all. Here he was, in the middle of the Atlantic, being pummelled by a masseur with hands like pistons, but always aware of the sway of the great ship slicing through the water. His muscles were relaxed and he felt all the strains of the past few days falling away. When he got back to London, he told himself, he must use the gym regularly. He had, not so many years ago, been fit enough to run a hundred yards not much over the four minute mark. Now, he thought ruefully, he was sinking into middle age and its attendant physical deterioration.

He opened one eye and saw, on two adjoining slabs, his nephew and the young American, both semi-comatose in the hands of their masseurs. He could not help noticing that, while Frank had the strength and animal physicality of a young man reaching his natural peak, Perry Roosevelt had the airy grace of the athlete. Not as heavily muscled as Frank, he was wiry and, Edward thought, might make up in speed what he lacked in endurance.

Apart from the slap of flesh on flesh and the occasional shout from someone in the swimming-pool, there was silence. Without thinking about it, he said, 'You boys ought to race each other. The Purser was telling me that, on the *Queen Mary's* maiden voyage, Lord Burghley ran just over four hundred yards round the promenade deck, in full evening dress, in under sixty seconds. Of course, he's an Olympic runner but it would be interesting to see if you could get near his time.'

Frank, his eyes still closed, said, 'Sounds like hard work to me.'

'But think how you would impress Philly,' Perry urged him. 'I'm game if you are.'

'I'm much more likely to make a fool of myself than impress anyone.'

'You're not yellow, are you?' Perry goaded. 'Think of the interest: England versus America. I can see myself attracting a lot of money.'

'Betting? Here, I say!' Edward said in alarm. 'I don't think that's on.'

'I tell you what, Uncle, I'll do it if you will.'

'Race you? I'd say not. I would look the most awful idiot. They'd think I was trying to prove something.'

'Why not? Why not prove you're not an antique quite yet?'

At that moment they heard a strange noise which made the masseurs stop and listen. There it was again – a stifled scream.

'Is there anyone else down here?' Edward demanded of his masseur.

'Only Miss Barclay, sir, in the steam room.'

With one accord, Edward and the two boys rose from their slabs and, followed by the masseurs, went through the door into the tepidarium. There was no one there so they continued through into the steam room. Through the steam, which swirled about them like a miasma, they could just make out the figure of a woman. As Edward approached, he recognized the bottle-blonde hair. Jane Barclay, dressed in nothing but a swim-suit, lay on her back on a wooden bench. Her head was twisted, as if she had lost consciousness seeking air. The room tempera-ture was almost unbearable and the steam scalding. There was a strip of white linen on the floor beside the bench.

'Turn off the steam! Quick, man,' Edward shouted at his masseur as he stared unbelieving at the body laid out in front of him.

The masseur left the room and the others helped Frank lift the girl and carry her out.

'Gently, gently!' Edward said. 'Lay her on one of the massage slabs.' When they had done so, he put his hand on her wrist and then his ear to her chest.

'Is she alive?' Frank asked, his eyes wide with alarm.

'Perry, run and call the doctor, will you? There's a telephone beside the swimming-pool with the emergency number on it. She's still alive but her pulse is very weak, so hurry.' Still in his bathing trunks with a bathrobe thrown over his shoulders, the boy disappeared to get help.

Frank looked at his uncle. 'A nasty accident. I wonder how it could have happened.'

Edward looked at him curiously. 'What makes you think it was an accident?'

'What else could it be?'

'Go and look at the temperature controls. They're in a box over there, do you see?' He pointed to a corner cupboard and Frank went over and opened it. There were a series of gauges and switches marked with the different rooms they controlled. There were six rooms in all: the massage room, the tepidarium, the steam room in which Jane Barclay had almost scalded herself to death, the calidarium, the laconicum and an attend-ant's room.

Edward turned to his masseur. 'This is the only control panel?'

'Yes, my lord.'

'Did you notice the setting for the steam room before you switched it off?'

'It was on red – maximum heat and steam.'

'Shouldn't the control box be kept locked?' Frank asked.

The masseur looked troubled. 'We thought there was no need to lock it when the rooms are in use. There's always at least one of us present and, if the box was locked, it might be difficult to alter the temperature of any of the rooms quickly. We keep adjusting them so the rooms are kept at the regulation temperature. You see here, sir? The temperature norm is clearly marked on each dial.'

'How could the temperature in the steam room have fluctuated to such an extreme degree?'

'I don't know. We will have it thoroughly checked when we reach New York, my lord, but I don't see how it is possible. It's never happened before. Someone must have been playing with the controls.'

The doctor arrived with a nurse and Edward was happy to see some signs of the girl reviving. She had had a narrow escape. He found he was shivering so he put on a bathrobe and prepared to go back to his cabin and change.

As he was leaving, he asked the masseur, 'How long would it take for the steam room to reach the temperature we found it at?'

'About twenty or thirty minutes I would think, my lord. The fact is we've never had it that high so I can't be sure.'

Reaching the door, Edward was met by a distraught Warren Fairley. Brushing Edward aside, he ran over to the slab on which his wife lay. Taking no notice of the doctor and nurse, he picked her up and cradled her against his chest. He bowed his head over her and began to kiss her forehead and then her lips. Then, with a howl of anguish, he looked for the first time at the others. 'Who has done this thing?' he roared. 'Tell me, for God's sake, who has done this?'

'We don't know,' Edward said. 'It may have been an accident. We heard a scream and went into the steam room and found your wife . . .'

It came to Edward that they were acting out a scene from *Othello*. The noble Moor weeping over the body of his Desdemona as the Venetian nobles looked on. Only this time, thank God, Desdemona was not quite dead. She opened her eyes and the doctor gently took her from her husband and laid her back on the slab with a towel over her.

'She'll be all right,' he said to Fairley. 'Let her rest for a minute or two and then we'll take her to the sick-bay.'

Aware that there was nothing more he could do, and not wishing to intrude on so private a grief, Edward took Frank by the arm.

'Mr Fairley, we're going to get dressed and then, if there is anything we can do . . .'

But Fairley was not listening. There could be no doubt about one thing, at least. Warren Fairley might be something of a womanizer but his love for his wife was genuine enough.

8

The Captain looked at Edward in consternation. 'You're not trying to tell me, Lord Edward, that this terrible accident wasn't an accident?'

'I don't see how it can have been. There appears to be nothing wrong with the controls to the steam room – though, of course, they will have to be thoroughly tested after we dock in New York. Someone altered the temperature control to asphyxiate or scald to death Jane Barclay.'

'That's unbelievable! Who on earth would want to do a thing like that?'

'It's not for me to speculate,' Edward said, infuriatingly.

'Well, I think it's absolute nonsense.'

The Captain's nerves were being tested to the limit. He had seen the barometer drop five millibars in three hours, revealing serious deficiencies in the ship's stabilizers. Several people had been hurt falling down companionways and, in one case, out of bed. The propellers were noisy and the vibration so severe he had to face the fact that they would probably have to be replaced. That might mean – horror of horrors – three months in dry dock. There had been a host of complaints and three passengers – of whom Senator Day was the most aggressive – were threatening to sue Cunard. Then there had been the unexplained murder of the fellow guarding their most import- ant passenger, Lord Benyon, and now this! The potential for bad publicity and subsequent loss of revenue was enormous and he, as Captain, carried the responsibility.

'You must give me your word, Lord Edward, that you will

repeat none of this . . . speculation to anyone else. You understand that we must not alarm the passengers?'

Edward looked at him critically. 'I understand the difficulty
you are in, Captain Peel, but you must realize that there is a
murderer on board. The death of Tom Barrett proves it even if
we persuade ourselves that Miss Barclay's life was put in
danger by faulty temperature contols. Don't look so glum,
Captain. The company can hardly be blamed for the presence
of a murderer but it is open to claims for negligence if, indeed,
Miss Barclay's life was threatened by malfunctioning steam
controls.' The Captain went grey. His mouth worked but no
words came out. 'Either way,' Edward went on inexorably, 'if
we fail to take any action, the police may accuse us of playing
fast and loose with the lives of innocent people.'

'By "us", you mean me.'

'No. I too am charged with the protection of one passenger,
Lord Benyon.' He sighed and relented a little. 'Nevertheless, I
agree with you that there is no point in alarming the passengers
unnecessarily. The situation won't be improved by having a lot
of frightened people imagining things.'

The Captain's brow cleared. 'Then we are agreed in calling
Miss Barclay's . . . accident . . . an accident?'

'Yes, but you should insist on taking witness-statements
from all those involved, myself included. That would show the
authorities that you hadn't taken the matter lightly.'

'Yes, indeed . . . witness-statements.'

'You will put something in the *Ocean Times*?' This was the
ship's newspaper which was delivered to every cabin each
morning.

'Yes. I will say that, owing to a technical fault, the Turkish
bath will be closed but massages, ultra-violet, infra-red and
diathermic treatments can still be booked.'

Edward nodded. 'I will leave you, Captain. I know how
much you have to do and I wish you did not have to deal with
this as well. By the way, I thought it might help to take people's
minds off things if we staged a race tonight before dinner.'

'A race?'

'Yes. You remember Lord Burghley ran round the ship in
some extraordinary time on the maiden voyage. I have wagered
my nephew and his young friend, Perry Roosevelt, they can't

113

better it. The boys have agreed to take a shot at it and, much against my better judgement, they have persuaded me to run too . . . on behalf of the antiques, don't you know.'

'Very good! I am most grateful to you for thinking of such a thing. You may be certain, Lord Edward, that my report to the chairman, Sir Percy Bates, will emphasize the manner in which you have put yourself out to help us. Will you dine with me tonight after the race?'

'That's very kind of you, Captain, but we have decided to try out the Verandah Grill this evening and admire Miss Zinkeisen's mural.'

'Excellent! A race! What a good idea. I shall tell the Purser to make quite a thing of it. A prize . . . yes, we shall give a prize. It will lift all our spirits and encourage people to mingle. We English are so bad at talking to strangers. The Americans are much more friendly.'

Edward laughed. 'I fear there are unfriendly people aboard but whether they are English or not we cannot tell.'

'Do you think, Lord Edward, there can be any connection between . . . you know . . . Miss Barclay's "accident" and Mr Barrett's killing?'

'I wish I knew, Captain. I wish I knew.'

'We must be vigilant.' Captain Peel pressed Edward's hand. 'I feel reassured that you are keeping watch – our Cerberus.' He smiled but his smile never reached his eyes.

Edward found Frank deep in conversation with Verity and Sam Forrest. They were on the sun deck just below the Verandah Grill where they were to eat that evening. Somehow, Jane Barclay's accident made it easier for him to meet Verity, as if his offer of marriage and her rejection had never happened. The steward had brought tea in a 'silver' pot and there were scones and little cakes.

'I haven't had tea like this for years,' Verity said with her mouth full. 'It must be the English in me. However far I wander,' she continued, waving her arms for dramatic emphasis, 'my heart belongs to –'

'The Cockpit at Eton,' Frank finished the sentence for her.

'Don't you remember? We had tea there last year when you were investigating –'

She cut him short. 'Of course. Ah, there you are, Edward. What did the Captain say?'

The truth was Verity didn't want Sam to think she hung around Eton having tea with the sons of dukes. Her Communist credentials had already been weakened by travelling First Class on the *Queen Mary*. She told herself she must start acting like the revolutionary she had imagined herself to be when she joined the Party to celebrate her twenty-first birthday.

'He's in a state about the bad publicity all this could bring Cunard. I promised him we would be discreet. He wants to believe Jane Barclay's ordeal in the steam room was an accident.'

'Huh!' Verity ejaculated. 'And what about poor Tom Barrett? I suppose he was killed by a carcass of frozen beef.'

'Verity!' Sam exclaimed. 'You sound as if it's all a joke.'

'I don't mean to,' she said, looking at him earnestly, cream on her lips and a scone in mid-air. 'I didn't know Mr Barrett but he was killed protecting Lord Benyon and that makes it very much our business, doesn't it, Edward? Look, here he is!'

For a moment, Edward expected to see the ghost of Tom Barrett but it was Benyon . . . looking like a ghost. Accompanied by Fenton, holding rugs and a bottle of pills, he was walking gingerly along the deck. Although the sea had calmed considerably in the last hour or two, Benyon still found the motion unpleasant. He was very pale but was at least able to leave his cabin without feeling he was about to vomit.

'You must have thought I had died,' he said, rather unfortunately in view of the conversation he had interrupted, 'but I have survived. The Purser says it will be quite calm by tonight. He tells me that you two are going to race round the deck with some young American called Roosevelt?'

'Yes, indeed, sir! Very sporting of Uncle Ned.'

It was clear Benyon did not know about Jane Barclay and it was tacitly agreed that nothing should be said to him about it until he was in better spirits.

'I am determined to go back on one of the new airships – the *Hindenburg*, perhaps. I really don't think I could face another day like yesterday. It's that feeling you are never going to be on dry land again that is so awful.' He shuddered. 'Do you know, I think I could manage a cup of tea and a scone. That must mean I'm better, mustn't it?'

Verity poured him a cup and they asked the ever-attentive steward to bring them more scones.

'I think an airship can sway about,' Sam said. 'That's what I've been told, anyway.'

'But they must be the future, surely?' Benyon insisted.

'There's always that outside chance of fire,' Frank ventured.

'No, you can put that out of your mind,' Sam said confidently. 'This friend of mine says they're so safe now, they even have a smoking-room.'

The Roosevelt twins came by – it was the nature of their environment that you could never *not* see someone for more than half an hour if they left their cabin. Frank introduced them to Benyon and he was charmed by them, particularly Philly whose pale beauty was almost an aura which set her apart from her more mundane brother.

'We thought we'd shove one of those thingamabobs about the deck, you know, shovelboard or whatever it's called. Why don't you come, Lord Benyon? It's not energetic.'

'No thank you, my boy. Perhaps tomorrow when I'm feeling stronger.'

'Well, you'll come, Frank, won't you?' Philly said, touching the boy's hand. He looked wildly about him as if he had been energized by some alien force.

'Would that be all right, sir?'

'You run along. I'll be all right with Fenton. He has been quite wonderful. If your master ever displeases you, Fenton, I hope you will come and work for me.'

'That's very kind of you, my lord,' Fenton said, flattered.

The rather stooped figure of the elderly German who had dined with them on the first night at the Captain's table appeared in front of them and addressed Benyon. 'Forgive me, my lord. May I speak with you one minute . . . in private?'

'Of course. It's Professor Dolmen, isn't it? Let's walk a little. I think it will do me good.'

116

'This sea! But you are better, sir?'

'Much better thank you, Professor Dolmen, but may I take your arm? I'm still unsteady on my feet.'

'*Natürlich!* And I only just since have known who you are, my lord. You must please pardon my English tongue. I practise for America but I am still not so good, I think.'

'Your English is very good. I apologize that my German is bad but my French is better.'

'No, it is good I practise English. You will correct me, please, if I am wrong.'

'It is an honour to meet so distinguished a scientist.'

'That is very kind of you to tell me, my lord, but the truth is I am not so – how did you say? – "distinguished". I may still be refused entry to the United States.'

'You are emigrating?'

'With great regret,' he said bitterly. 'The Nazis! You see, I am a Jew.'

'I thought you might be when I heard you refusing meat and shellfish at dinner with the Captain.'

'Ah, you noticed. You have a sharp eye.'

'But there's a kosher kitchen on board.'

'So I have been told but, I must tell you, we were trying not to – how must I say? – advertise my race.'

'There is no prejudice against Jews in the United States. You have no need to worry and, as an aeronautical engineer, I am certain you will be most welcome.'

'That is what I had hoped but I was recognized by Senator Day. He has much influence with the government and he hates Jews, and me in particular.'

'Good heavens! Why?'

'I do not know why he hates Jews as a race but so many do today. He hates me more than other Jews because, when he came to Germany to meet the Führer before he went on to London, I refused to do what he wanted.'

'What was that?'

'He has interests in an American aircraft company and he wanted me to hand over to him information about the new fighter I was working on. Reichsmarshal Goering is depending on it to win the war. If I tell you it has jet engines, does that mean anything to you?'

117

'A little. We too have been experimenting. But how near to production is this new fighter?'

'Not so near, my friend. Perhaps four years. The Reichsmarshal hopes the war will not come until 1941 when the Luftwaffe will be much superior to your Royal Air Force.'

It was absurd but also quite understandable, Benyon thought, that Dolmen should speak with pride of his work for a regime which was rejecting him and which threatened all his people.

'The Führer has been told this by the Reichsmarshal,' Dolmen went on, 'but has chosen to ignore our work because he believes the war will be soon – next year perhaps – and so the jet engines will not be ready. He is making a big mistake, I think.'

'So, when you refused to give the Senator the information he asked for, you were just being patriotic?'

'That is so. But then, only four weeks later, I was told my life was in danger if I did not leave. As a Jew, you understand, I think the Senator made trouble for me.'

'But he cannot prevent you entering the States, particularly with all you have to offer.'

'He will try. You see, I did a foolish thing. In order to be allowed to work, I joined the Party.'

'The Communist Party?'

'No, no! The National Socialists – the Nazi Party. It was 1935 and I can only say I did not truly understand what these people were doing. And I was afraid. To be out of a job and a Jew! I thought I could protect myself.'

'So Senator Day knows this and will inform the immigration people?'

'Yes. He has told me he will do it.'

'How can I help?'

'Please, my lord, when we land in New York, speak to the immigration authority for me. You are going to meet the President, I understand? You can, perhaps, ask him to help me?'

'My meeting with the President is supposed to be a secret but it seems everyone knows. Not that it matters,' Benyon added hurriedly, not wanting Dolmen to think such a meeting was of any particular significance. 'I shall do my best, Professor Dolmen. You must not worry. The Senator may believe he is all-powerful but, in reality, I doubt he can do what he threatens.'

'That is so good of you, my lord,' Dolmen said, seizing his benefactor by the arm. 'I knew, as an English gentleman, you would come to my aid. The Herr Senator is not a gentleman. He is a . . .' The English words escaped him. '*Ich hasse das schwein*,' he ended and the look of fury which convulsed his face shocked Benyon. This determined little man was not an enemy to be underestimated.

'I say, old boy, mind if I join you? I used to be rather good at this.'

The distraction caused Frank to miss his shot and Philly laughed heartily.

'Damn boat! Why can't it keep still?' he said crossly.

'Sorry, old boy, did I put you off your stroke? Didn't mean to and all that rot. Major Cranton's the name, what?'

He put out his hand and held it outstretched until, reluctantly, Frank had to take it. From his ramrod-straight back, watery blue eyes and small moustache cut to a bristle, to the heavy brogues on his feet, there could be no mistaking Major Cranton. Everything about him said ex-Army and his sallow complexion suggested some years in India. He only needed a swagger stick to complete the picture.

'Or am I *de trop*, as the froggies say?'

There was something a little desperate in his attempt to be seen as a 'good fellow' and Frank softened. 'Of course not, sir. By all means join us, Major Cranton. We were only fooling around. By the way, my name's Frank Corinth. This young idiot is Perry Roosevelt and this is his sister, Philly.'

After hands were shaken, Cranton took hold of a shovel and soon proved himself adept at the game. After ten minutes, Frank threw down his shovel. 'You're too good for us, Major. What about a drink?'

They collapsed in deck chairs and the steward brought them fruit juices.

119

'You have the cabin next to mine, don't you, Major?'

'I do. And may I ask whether you are going to America on holiday?'

'I'm working for Lord Benyon,' Frank said, importantly.

'Lord Benyon? Is that who it is? I thought I recognized his face. In distinguished company, what? Reminds me of when I was in India. The Viceroy was visiting my chief and I was parading the guard of honour. Dash it, do you know, I failed to recognize the blighter. Felt the most awful ass and the CO didn't half tear me off a strip. Deserved it, too, I dare say . . .'

The Major went on to tell a long and involved story of a scandal in Poona twenty years before and Frank's attention wandered. He wondered how he was to detach Philly from her twin long enough to impress on her that she was the love of his life. He had heard that moonlight was good for that sort of thing and, with the skies clearing, perhaps tonight he might be able to lure her on deck. He had started rehearsing speeches he might make when suddenly he realized Major Cranton had stopped talking and was watching him with interest.

'I was just saying, I met your father once. Very fine man, the Duke. Do give him my regards when next you see him.'

There was something banal yet rather odd about the Major's chatter. It was as if he was determined to rub it in that he was a typical ex-Army bore but there was something in his face which made Frank suspect it must be an act. He had certainly been in the Army – no doubt about that – but what was he doing in a First Class cabin on the *Queen Mary* and, without wishing to sound snobbish, where had he met the Duke of Mersham?

Before he could ask any probing questions, however, they were joined by Verity and Sam Forrest and the Major made a surprisingly speedy exit.

'Who the hell was that guy?' Sam inquired.

'A Major Cranton. He has the cabin next to mine.'

'I thought there was something fishy about him,' Philly said.

'I know what you mean,' Frank agreed.

Edward knocked on the door of Warren Fairley's cabin and heard a muttering – almost a cooing – which persuaded him

120

that his visit was inopportune but, as he turned away, the door opened and Fairley appeared. In the doorway, he looked enormous and his face threatening but, when he saw who it was, his expression softened and he bade Edward enter.

'My wife owes her life to you.' His voice resonated bizarrely in the enclosed space.

'Oh, it was nothing at all. The main thing is she's all right. She *is* all right, I trust?'

'She's sleeping now,' Fairley replied, indicating the inner cabin. 'But, Lord Edward, I say again, we owe you so much. If there is anything . . .'

'Please, Mr Fairley –'

'You will call me Warren, I hope.'

'Yes, of course, thank you. But all three of us heard your wife's cries and we all – including the masseurs – went to see what was wrong. You mustn't think it was I alone . . . She's not badly scalded? The steam was lethal.'

'Thank God, no, but she is weak and the doctor has given her a sedative. But tell me, Lord Edward, could it have been an accident?'

'It might have been,' Edward said slowly.

'But you don't think it was?'

'I don't see how it could have been. Someone had twisted the knob controlling the heat. It would be hard to do that accidentally. Have you spoken to the Captain?'

'He has been to visit us and he is very concerned. He has instructed the door to the control panel in the Turkish bath to be locked and the key to be held by the senior masseur on duty. Locking the door after the horse has bolted, I fear. I agree with you: I don't believe it was an accident.'

'Does she remember what happened?'

'Not much. She says she must have fallen asleep and not noticed the rise in temperature.'

'I picked this up from beside your wife when we found her.' Edward held out a strip of linen. 'Smell it. There is just the hint of chloroform.'

'You think Jane was put to sleep by whoever turned up the temperature?'

'It looks that way but, fortunately, she can't have been deeply unconscious or she would not have screamed. I think

121

she must have regained consciousness, screamed and then fainted. But who would wish to harm Miss Barclay?'

'That, of course, is the question. It may be that they wished to hurt me by hurting Jane. I have many enemies and I don't know the faces of all of them.'

'We live in evil days, Mr Fairley . . . Warren. It seems no one is safe. Perhaps it is as well that I tell you, in the strictest confidence, that the death of Mr Barrett, Lord Benyon's valet, may not have been an accident. In fact, it was murder. It is important that we do not alarm passengers so – at least until we reach New York – the Captain has ascribed his death to the ship's violent movements in the storm – a tragic fall. Though, as you know, his body was discovered before the weather worsened.'

'I see,' Fairley said, sombrely. 'And you think Mr Barrett's death and the attack on my wife are connected?'

'I don't know how, but it is possible.'

'And what should I do?'

'There is nothing to do except watch and wait. I very much hope that now we are on the alert for danger, our murderer will go to ground. Or wherever it is you go on a ship to avoid detection,' he added, trying not to sound too alarmist.

'But you don't think so?' Fairley said, shrewdly. 'You don't think the murderer, whoever he is, *will* "go to ground"?'

'No.' There was a noise from the inner cabin. Edward said, 'I will go now but if there is anything I can do or if you see anything suspicious, you will please tell me – or the Captain, of course, but he has so much else to worry about. This storm has shown up some inadequacies in the stabilizers and the propellers may need replacing, I understand. All of which is making the Captain lose sleep, without unexplained sudden death adding to his burden.'

With the seas now calm, anxious passengers hauled themselves out of their berths determined to get their money's worth from all the facilities the *Queen Mary* had to offer. The hairdressers, who had been sitting around filing their nails and discussing what they would do when they reached New York, were suddenly too busy to chatter. The massage room was full and there were complaints that the steam room had been sealed off pending a visit from the safety inspectors and the police in New York.

The swimming-bath was packed with shrieking children and energetic young men and women showing off to each other. In the gymnasium, much huffing and puffing indicated that gentlemen wished to be at their physical peak when they reached the New World. On the promenade decks, less energetic passengers paraded, stopping to chat with one another as though trapped in some never-ending cocktail party. The storm provided a topic of conversation for everyone and interesting injuries were a passport to social intercourse. Soon complete strangers were swapping seasick cures and showing each other bruises gained when, unable to find a hand-rail in the passageways, they had been tossed around 'like rag dolls'. It was rumoured that a stowaway had been apprehended in the engine room, more dead than alive. And there was Tom Barrett's death and Jane Barclay's 'accident' in the steam room to discuss.

The Purser and his assistants were organizing all sorts of entertainments from deck sports to Lotto, and a Mrs Pillman won £833 in the auction pool with a guess of 747 miles for the ship's noon-to-noon run, which reflected a highly satisfactory speed of twenty-eight knots. But the main topic of conversation was the race between Perry Roosevelt, Lord Edward Corinth and his nephew. It was to take place at seven o'clock with the participants in full evening dress. To the disappointment of many, the Captain had ruled that it was too dangerous for them to race the four hundred yards round the promenade deck together. There had been enough accidents and he was not going to risk another. Each would run alone, timed by the Purser on his massive stop-watch. Lots were drawn and Edward was to go first, Frank second and Perry last.

Verity had urged Sam Forrest to take part but he had refused on the grounds that – strong as he was – he was no athlete and, in any case, to butt in on a private challenge would not be good manners.

'But then there's no one to represent the workers,' she protested.

'Don't get mad at me,' he said, in mock fear at her scowling face. 'This isn't a political contest. You're still feeling sore because you think we ought to be travelling in steerage. Isn't that right?'

'No, certainly not,' she replied uncertainly. 'I don't care who wins these stupid games but it would be nice if Edward had a bit of competition. That's all.'

'Young Frank was telling me that Lord Edward was something of an athlete at school and university. Cricket and ... what was the other? ... yes, I remember ... rackets. Frank had to tell me about that. I'd never heard of it. Frank says it's a fast version of squash.'

'Oh, who cares! He's middle-aged now and that was all a long time ago.'

'Hey, honey, what's eating you? I guess the poor sap's got under your skin. What did he do? Ask you to marry him?'

Verity was so stunned that Sam had guessed the source of her irritation that she was silent but her face told him everything.

'So, that's it! He asked you to marry him. You said no, and now you're regretting it.'

'I'm not regretting it,' she said through gritted teeth. 'And don't call me "honey". I'm nobody's sweet-little-thing. As for Edward, it's against my principles to marry into the aristocracy and I told him so. In fact, it's against my principles to marry anyone.'

'So why the bad temper?'

'I'm not in a bad temper,' she said crossly.

'I'm sorry,' he said, becoming serious. 'I didn't mean to tease but, from what I've seen of him, he's a good man. Perhaps you *should* marry him.'

'Not you, too! I'm fed up with people telling me what a "good chap" Edward is. I know he's a good chap and I like him – I even love him, if you must know – but I don't want to marry him. Is that a crime? Sex, maybe, but marriage ... only over my dead body.'

Sam Forrest prided himself on being broad-minded but he had never heard a respectable woman talk this way. He had certainly never heard a lady say she preferred sex to marriage and he tried not to feel shocked.

'Stop looking shocked,' Verity said sharply. 'You're all a lot

124

of schoolgirls.' After this rather inappropriate rebuke – she knew better than anyone just how frank schoolgirls could be in private talk – she stalked off.

Sam whistled, took out a cigarette, lit it and leaned against the deck rail looking out to sea. There was nothing in view except endless waves rolling blue-green against the blue backdrop of sky. It was five o'clock but the sun still glared as though hoping to make up for the storm clouds of the previous day. It was borne in on him that Verity was very different from the girls he knew back home. Politics, where he came from, were left to the men and the unions were all-male organizations. The idea that a woman could play a man's role in the world was new to him. Edward had told him something of what Verity had seen and suffered in Spain and Sam wondered if her experiences had coarsened her, and then was ashamed of himself. This was, after all, 1937 and, if there were to be a war, women would have to take on men's jobs in many spheres and occupations, as they had done in the previous conflict.

He thought he would follow her down to her cabin. If he were honest with himself – which he was trying not to be – there was just the thought in the back of his mind that he might get Verity into bed and that was certainly something he would be happy to engineer. To his dismay, he literally bumped into Senator Day, a man whose views he abhorred and whom he found physically repulsive.

'I was lookin' for you, young man, and – having found you – I would be grateful for a moment of your time.' Sam opened his mouth to make his excuses when Day forestalled him. 'Now don't deny me this courtesy. You and I don't see eye to eye particularly – never have, never will – but I have something to tell you which I guess you'll thank me for.'

Without causing a row, it was hard for Sam to refuse and, in any case, his curiosity was aroused. What could this odious man possibly have to tell him?

'Sure, shall we talk here or in the bar?'

'In my cabin, if you please. Some people have long ears and I'd as soon say what I have to say away from prying eyes.'

When the Senator had closed the door behind them, Sam said, 'Well, then, what is it you have to say to me?'

'I'm not sure whether you are aware of this, Mr Forrest, but

I have business interests in South Carolina, my own state, and also in Tennessee.'

'I did not know, Senator, and I have no idea why you should think I would want to know.'

The Senator ignored the interruption. 'Three years ago we – myself and several other businessmen – established in that great state of Tennessee what I am proud to say is the largest electricity generating station in the USA. Our work will bring light and power to many thousands of our citizens who have, up to the present time, had to rely on the strength of their arms to warm their bodies. As the Prophet Isaiah says in the Good Book, "The people that walked in darkness have seen a great light."'

'You must think me dumb, Senator, but I still don't understand what you are driving at.'

'I merely wished you to rejoice with me that we are doing good work in our great country.'

'Right. You are doing great work and no doubt hope to be rewarded for it.'

'Not on this earth,' sighed the Senator unconvincingly. 'If I thought that, I'd be whistling Dixie. However – and this is where you can help me – I also invest in coal and copper mines in Tennessee. Once again my aim – and it's an honourable aim – is to bring wealth and power to our southern states. Unfortunately, just lately, we have had threats and intimidation from your union – from your friend Mr John L. Lewis to be precise – who wishes to infiltrate Communists and Jews into our mines.'

'You mean your mineworkers want to join the union?'

'The Negro is not like us,' the Senator said, attempting to put his arm round Sam's shoulders but failing. 'The black man has no head for business. He's nothing but a child in business and that's the way we look after him – like he's ours – and he don't need unions to be high in hog heaven.'

Sam looked at him with contempt. 'Let me get this straight. You want me to use my influence – such as it is – to discourage our people from unionizing your mines? From what I've heard, your mineworkers are treated little better than slaves.'

'Now that is a slander, Mr Forrest, and I am surprised at you for giving it credence. As the psalmist says, "I have not seen the righteous forsaken nor his seed begging bread."'

126

'Senator Day, I am going to pretend this conversation never took place. I will not hear another word from you.'

'You won't help me with my little problem?' he inquired mildly.

'I will not.'

'And if I were to tell the authorities you have been consorting with known Communists – sleeping with the enemy of our great nation –'

'Is this some sort of clumsy blackmail attempt?' Sam cut in, suddenly angrier than he had ever been in his life.

'Not blackmail – just a warning. You know how it is – you got to ride the herd. Things can get out however hard you try to keep them to your bosom. Take Miss Browne, for instance –'

'Leave Miss Browne out of this.'

'Does Miss Browne know that you have a wife and child back home? No, I thought not. And how puzzled your friends in the union would be to know that you travel First Class on this great ship and mingle with the British aristocracy. Would your reputation be enhanced, I wonder?'

More than anything in the world, Sam wanted to punch this man in the face but he retained enough control over himself to know that this was just what the devil wanted. He was hoping for a scandal which would be interpreted and misinterpreted back home as an unprovoked attack on a member of the Senate. There would be talk of some shady deal and his reputation would be lost for ever.

'If you slander me, Senator Day, I will not rest until you go to gaol.'

It was not quite what he had meant to say and he felt the weakness of his words but he was too angry to think straight. Then he remembered something from his childhood study of the Bible. 'The psalmist also says, if I remember rightly, "Ethiopia shall soon stretch out her hand to God," which I interpret as meaning the black man *will* have justice.'

As Sam stumbled out of the cabin, he found he was sweating and finding it hard to catch his breath. He decided he must go on deck and get some fresh air. He had forgotten all about the race and was bewildered, when he reached the promenade deck, to find himself coralled behind a rope along with many other passengers. As he raised his eyes, he met Verity's on the other side of the deck, similarly cordoned off. He half raised his hand but either she did not see or she was ignoring him. He experienced a sinking feeling in his stomach. Was everything about to go wrong?

Edward was to run first. After discussion with the Purser, he was permitted to remove his jacket and loosen his collar. It was a sprint – and this gave him confidence. He doubted, aged thirty-six, whether he could have run a mile with any credit but four hundred yards he could manage. At Eton, he had once done a mile in four minutes ten but that was twenty-odd years ago. He took up his position and the Purser gave him ready, steady, go. The difficult moment was the sharp turn round the Verandah Grill and, predictably, it was there he slipped. Had his pumps been rubber-soled, no doubt his grip would have held but they weren't and it didn't. With a cry of anguish, he fell on the knee which he had damaged in a car accident eighteen months earlier. He was helped to his feet by sympathetic passengers and laid to rest, as it were, on one of the long chairs. The doctor came to minister to him but there was nothing for him to do but rest the leg as much as he could. Fenton brought a cold compress and spread it gently over his knee.

'May I offer my commiserations, my lord. The Purser tells me you were making very good time.'

'Damn and blast! How irresponsible of me. As a cripple, how will I be able to prevent anyone doing their worst to Lord Benyon? What a fool I was to think I was still a boy.'

At that moment Verity came up with Frank.

'Oh, stuff,' Verity said firmly. 'It was just an accident. Could have happened to anyone. I thought it was jolly plucky of you to have a go and the Purser said you were breaking all sorts of records.'

'Yes, that was ripping! I'm most awfully proud of you and all that but, I say, do you think I ought to pull out, Uncle Ned? I mean, would people say I was being heartless if I ran?'

'No, everyone's expecting you to run. They would be disappointed if you pulled out. Just be careful on the turn.'

Frank's run was a very respectable one minute ten seconds and he was fairly mobbed when he reached the finishing post.

Edward, left alone but for Fenton, on his chair of suffering, smiled wryly to himself – to the victor, the spoils.

The Purser called on the stewards to clear the deck. The slim, almost frail figure of Perry Roosevelt was hunched over the start line. At the word 'go', he leapt off the mark and was round the Verandah Grill in a flash. As he burst over the finishing line and collapsed on the deck, the Purser declared fifty-nine seconds. Perry had broken Lord Burghley's one minute spurt and he, of course, was an Olympic sprinter. The first to congratulate him was his sister who appeared from below decks like a jack-in-the-box. She was concerned that he had exhausted himself and insisted he walk slowly up and down, leaning on her shoulder, until the air had returned to his lungs and he could talk.

Frank came up to his friend and clapped him on the back. 'That was an amazing feat, old boy. Many congrats. The champagne's on me tonight – or rather on Uncle Ned.'

He turned to see Edward waving at him. 'What is it, Uncle?' the boy said, seeing how agitated he was.

'Can you see Benyon anywhere? He said he was going to be here. I've sent Fenton down to the cabin to make sure he's all right. I can't go myself. This damn leg is going to drive me mad.'

'Don't worry, Uncle. I can't see Mr Fern either. I expect they are working and forgot to come up on deck.'

'I expect so,' Edward agreed, but he felt uneasy all the same.

When Fenton reappeared, he leant over Edward in order not to be heard by anyone nearby.

'What is it, Fenton? Tell me Lord Benyon is all right.'

'He is quite well, my lord. He is working in his cabin.'

'Then what is it? Clearly something's wrong.'

'It's Mr Fern, my lord. He wanted me to inform you that he has found Senator Day in the swimming-pool.'

'But he can't swim. His wife told me so.'

'He was fully dressed, my lord, lying at the bottom of the pool.'

'Good heavens! Are you trying to tell me the Senator's dead? Drowned?'

'That is correct, my lord.'

129

'What was it? An accident?'

'Mr Fern informs me that he was knocked unconscious and pushed in the water, my lord. He wondered if you would care to join him at the swimming-pool. He thought you might wish to view the body.'

9

'Damn my damn knee! Here, get me a stick or something, will you, Fenton? Hey! Frank, come over here a moment.'

His nephew, who had been laughing at something Philly had said to him, came over, fixing his collar. Edward lowered his voice. 'Fenton's just been telling me the most extraordinary thing. Apparently, Fern has found Senator Day drowned . . . in the swimming-bath.'

'Good Lord! An accident?'

'Fenton says not. He says it's murder.'

Fenton returned with two sticks. 'Fenton, why is Mr Fern sure it was murder?' Frank asked.

'He tells me Senator Day had been hit over the head with what I believe is called a "blunt instrument" before he went into the water.'

'Well, that sounds fairly conclusive,' Edward said. 'No sign of the blunt instrument, I suppose?'

'No, my lord, I understand the murder weapon has not yet been located.'

'What a surprise. Come with me, will you, Frank? I might need some help with the stairs.'

'I wouldn't miss it for the world, Uncle. I suppose I ought to be upset, or at least surprised, but he was such an awful man. I say, there's Verity. Verity! Come over here. They've found –'

'Keep your voice down, Frank. We don't want the whole world to know.'

'I don't see how you can stop them. I mean, soon there won't be any of the ship's facilities left open. I wouldn't wonder if Cunard get complaints on that score. And really, even without counting storm injuries, the casualty list is becoming rather long. One spends five hundred pounds, or more, only to risk having one's head bashed in. I say, Verity, have you heard what has happened?'

'Frank, it's not a joke. A man has been killed. It might have been Lord Benyon but even Senator Day didn't deserve this.'

'I think he did,' Frank said, stubbornly. 'I'm sorry, Uncle. I didn't mean to be flippant.'

'Edward! What's happened?' Verity demanded, wide-eyed. 'Has someone else been murdered?'

'Seems like it,' he said. 'Ow! Watch it, Frank!'

On either side of Edward, they made their way, painfully slowly, down the stairs, Frank telling Verity what they knew of Day's death.

'Gosh, I see what you mean, Frank. The *Queen Mary* is supposed to be a luxury hotel on water, not a battlefield. There's poor Tom Barrett – found frozen. Then Jane Barclay –'

'Poached . . .' Frank added, unnecessarily.

'And now the beastly Senator Day has been drowned. Do you think we are at the mercy of a deranged chef?'

'I don't know. It might be a mad masseur,' Frank said, rather wittily he thought.

'Stop it, you two. I mean it. It's not a joke. Whatever we think . . . thought . . . of Senator Day, he didn't deserve to be murdered.'

'I'm afraid you'll find that's a minority view, Uncle Ned. Almost everyone I can think of hated his guts. There'll be several people only too relieved to discover someone has done the job for them.'

They met Fern just outside the swimming-pool.

'What's happened to you?' Fern asked. 'Have you hurt your leg?'

'Don't worry about me,' Edward said irascibly. 'Tell us what happened?'

'Well, Benyon and I were working and then he remembered your race. He said he wanted to finish what he was doing but I ought to go up and watch it.'

'But surely,' Verity said, 'the swimming-pool wasn't on your way?'

'No. I made a detour. I had time. I'd never seen the pool so I thought I would give it a look.'

'And . . .?' Edward prompted.

'There was no one there. I suppose everyone was up on deck for the race. I went to the edge of the bath and peered over. It's very pretty – cream bricks with green guide lines to keep you straight when you're swimming. That was when I saw the body. It was face down. At first I thought it was just some old clothes but then I saw what was left of his head. It was disgusting. There was a sort of red scum round it – blood, I suppose.'

'Then what did you do?'

'Well, for a second I thought I ought to dive in and rescue whoever it was but then I thought I wouldn't. He was so very dead and there was no way I could do anything. I would never have been able to drag the body out of the water. And, to be honest, I didn't want to go anywhere near it.'

'So what *did* you do?' Edward pressed him.

'I'd noticed the emergency telephone. It was red, you see. So I picked it up and two men came very quickly . . . from the gymnasium, I think.'

'What men?'

'They were dressed in white. I think they worked there. They started dragging the body out of the water.'

'And then?'

'And then I was sick. Ugh! It's still on my shoes.'

Verity said, 'How soon did you know it was Senator Day?'

'The clothes looked familiar. Then I saw the tie floating beneath him. At first I thought one of the green lines on the bottom of the pool was crooked but then I realized what it was and who it must be. Corinth, you remember that horrible iridescent green tie he wore all the time?'

'I remember.' A line of Francis Bacon's came into his mind. 'A man that studieth revenge keeps his own wounds green.' A thin smile shaped his mouth.

Edward rolled the wine around in his mouth, savouring what was, in his view, the greatest of all red Burgundies – Musigny

1919 from de Vogüé. In a splurge of self-indulgence, he summoned the sommelier and ordered a bottle of 1921 Château
d'Yquem to drink with dessert. If he was to die, then he would
at least do so with nectar on his lips. It seemed heartless, but
what else was there to do? Captain Peel had begged everyone
to carry on as though nothing had happened. Of course, they
could not do this. Everyone in First Class – and, for all he
knew, throughout the ship – could talk of nothing else but
Senator Day's murder.

In a vain attempt to distract the company, Edward asked the
voluble Doris Zinkeisen to tell them about her mural. It wasn't
that he could have missed it but the artist took such delight in
having it admired, it would have been a sin not to have let her
lecture him.

'I wanted colour and movement, Lord Edward. See how I
have captured the carnival atmosphere. The ringmaster with
his whip, the monkey dressed in a tutu on the back of the
donkey, the lion and the lion tamer . . . Do say you like it.'

Edward was torn. It was gaudy, rather vulgar, reminding
him of the frieze round a child's bedroom. On the other hand,
there was something a little sinister about the cavorting figures.
The lion tamer seemed to be whipping his animal unnecessarily
viciously and the half-naked black girl was rather embarrassing. However, it had a certain vigour which was welcome after
Vanessa Bell's over-polite garden scenes which decorated the
restaurant on C Deck.

'I love it,' he said firmly, and was rewarded by Doris's smile
of pure pleasure. He knew how brave an artist had to be to
take on a commission for a public work of art. The philistine
press could be brutal in its jeering incomprehension of 'modern
art' but, what was worse, most people ignored the art around
them. What was 'wallpaper' to the average passenger was the
work of many weeks of anxious effort on the part of the artist.

'And that horrible man – he was so rude.'

'Which man?'

'Senator Day. He asked me to show him this and then stood
in front of it and sneered. He said it was . . . "barbaric". He said
there was too much naked flesh and I should have left out my
black girl. And that coming from a man renowned for being a
licentious hypocrite. He said . . . well, it doesn't matter what

else he said but it was hurtful. I am not afraid to admit to you, dear Lord Edward, that he made me cry. I'm glad he's dead.'

She said this with such vehemence that Edward was startled. 'No one seemed to have liked him, I'm afraid, except his poor wife.'

'And he treated her abominably,' Doris said, clutching at his arm. 'I don't talk scandal, as you know, but he was so full of "religion". When he was telling me off, he quoted Scripture at me – I don't know what exactly but it had to do with the sins of the flesh. And this was a man who could not keep his hands off the girls. His wife was always finding him groping some little actress who couldn't defend herself.'

'How do you mean: "couldn't defend herself"?'

'Oh, perhaps you don't know. He managed to get himself in the Hay's Office. Do you know what that is?'

'It's the self-censorship code of the film industry in Hollywood, isn't it?'

'That's right. The government thought people were being corrupted by the movies. Three years ago, Joseph Breen was given the job of cleaning out the Augean stables. No more lustful kissing. No more naked flesh on display. Even when a love scene was being filmed and two actors were on a bed, one of them had to keep a foot on the ground so they didn't go too far and actually start . . . you know . . . enjoying themselves.'

'How did Day get involved with Hollywood? He knew nothing about films, did he?'

'No, of course not. He was a chum of Breen's. There must have been money involved. There always is but the point is it gave him terrific power over writers, directors, actors and, above all, actresses. If he had an actor or actress put on the black list, they had no chance of getting a job.'

'And Day used this power . . . for his own ends?'

'You bet he did. It was quite a scandal when I was last in Hollywood but what could anyone do?'

'Couldn't they report him?'

'To whom? He had all the politicians sewn up. Still, I did hear FDR was going to try to do something about it.'

'How do you mean?'

'Well, of course, technically the Hay's Code is operated within the industry. It isn't a government department but Day

135

was a politician – one of Roosevelt's bitterest enemies. FDR was determined to get him out. That was one of the reasons Day was doing what he could to become ambassador in London. To get him out of the way, FDR might have pushed him upstairs, so to speak.'

'You're very well informed, Doris.'

'I am. I have friends throughout the business. I have to know who's up, who's down, who's in, who's out, who's sleeping with whom.'

Frank had been right – the Senator had been universally disliked and his passing went unmourned. There was sympathy for the widow and, rather surprisingly, Mrs Dolmen proved the most sympathetic. She had gone to sit with the poor woman and, in her fractured English, had tried to bring her some little comfort. Perhaps she, too, knew what it was like to be married to a demanding and ambitious husband.

Edward put down his wine glass and wiped his mouth with the linen napkin. He looked around the table. It was odd, he thought, how quickly cliques were formed – alliances made and enmities shared. Those with whom he had dined at the Captain's table on that first night were present, with the exception of Mrs Dolmen who was still on duty in the Days' cabin. There was Lord Benyon, Marcus Fern, Frank, of course, Verity and Sam Forrest, Professor Dolmen, Warren Fairley and Jane Barclay, who seemed to have recovered from her ordeal remarkably quickly.

In addition there were the Roosevelts – the twins, Philly and Perry, and their mother, a charming, highly nervous woman in her fifties, still beautiful like a rose in September which threatened to be blown away in the next storm. It was a pleasure to see the way the twins treated her – teasing, affectionate and loving but always in control. Edward was inclined to think he agreed with the Duke of Windsor on one thing – but only one – that in America children exercised authority over their parents.

Idly, he began to view each of them as possible suspects. As soon as he realized what he was doing he felt guilty, but that did not stop him. First, who to exclude? He could hardly suspect Lord Benyon. It was true he was one of the few people not on deck watching the race but it was preposterous to think this distinguished man would murder a fellow passenger even if he had a motive – which, as far as Edward knew, he did not. Frank and Perry had been racing and he was pretty sure Philly had been watching on deck the whole time, but he could not swear to it.

Much as she disliked the Senator, he could hardly imagine Verity killing him. He smiled and caught her eye. If she knew what he was thinking! On the other hand, Sam Forrest, now looking at her with sheep's eyes, was a suspect. He had appeared on deck just as the race began, looking pale and rather fuddled, by no means the cheerful young man – seemingly without a care in the world – he had been half an hour earlier. But, as far as Edward was aware, Forrest did not know the Senator and, though he might dislike his political views, that was hardly a motive for murder.

Professor Dolmen was looking happy. He knew Dolmen had had a conversation with Lord Benyon after which he seemed very much more at his ease and Edward wondered what Benyon had said to him. That left Warren Fairley who, on the face of it, had the best motive for wanting Day out of the way. He had made no secret of his enmity. Day personified all he hated about his country and the South in particular. Day was a bigot and had put every obstacle he could in the way of Fairley as he pursued his career and fought the great fight against racism. Perhaps the Senator had threatened or insulted him once too often. Physically, he was the most powerful man at the table and would have had no problem in knocking Day unconscious. Might it not have been a terrible accident – a moment of madness, not a deliberate attempt at murder? Fairley was calm enough now but, of course, he was an actor by profession.

Seeing Edward's eyes on him, Fairley leant over the table. ' "Who from my cabin tempted me to walk? . . . Methought that Gloucester stumbled; and, in falling, struck me, that thought to stay him, overboard, into the tumbling billows of the main. Lord, Lord! methought what pain it was to drown . . ." '

'Richard III?'

'Yes. I never played it.'

'Of course not!'

'Why do you say that, Lord Edward? White men "black-up" to play Othello.'

'Yes, but you could hardly "white-up"!'

'I should not need to,' Fairley said with disdain. 'Shakespeare calls on the imagination of all of us in the audience. "On your imaginary forces work . . ." '

'I had never thought like that but, of course, you are right.'

'But you cannot see the audience accepting a black Henry V?'

'No.'

'Nor I, not in our lifetime anyway, but one day . . .'

' "The perilous narrow ocean parts asunder",' Edward quoted.

'I see you know your *Henry V*,' Fairley said approvingly, 'and 'tis true, the ocean is perilous. Are you trying to decide if I murdered Senator Day?'

Edward, taken aback by this shrewd guess, said hurriedly, 'That would be absurd.'

'Not totally, I hated him and wanted him dead. He was my enemy. This Senate Committee he was setting up with his friend, Senator Dies, to root out un-American activities is aimed at me and people like me.'

Edward looked at him searchingly. 'But you didn't kill him?'

'I didn't, but someone did . . . someone who will also deny it.'

'But he will be a liar, and I don't believe you are a liar.'

'Thank you, Lord Edward,' Fairley said in amusement. 'But remember, actors are liars by profession.'

Edward shook himself mentally. What on earth was he thinking about? Senator Day might have been killed by anyone in First Class. There was no reason to pick on one of the passengers he happened to know. Anyone could have slipped away from watching the race – or, like Lord Benyon, not bothered to come up on deck – and done the deed. At least Major Cranton was not in the frame. He had been very much in evidence before and during the race, making loud, would-be jocular remarks abut the contestants. Marcus Fern had discovered the body so he was, by definition, the main suspect but a clever man would hardly be found with the corpse – unless it was some sort of double bluff.

Edward had been studying the passenger list Ferguson had given him and there was one particular passenger who interested him. But, what did it matter? Edward had to remind himself that his purpose was not to track down Day's killer but to keep Lord Benyon safe. His only interest in finding the Senator's murderer was if the killer also had Benyon on his list. On the face of it, he didn't think it likely. There was nothing to tie the two men together. Physically, they were chalk and cheese. It was impossible for the Senator to have been mistaken for Benyon. Day was a shambling bear of a man and Benyon a frail wisp by comparison. He sighed. There was one thing he did mean to do: telephone Major Ferguson and give him a brief, if necessarily guarded, account of what had happened to Senator Day. The storm had made communication with the outside world virtually impossible but, with the Captain's permission, he ought now to be able to speak to London.

When dinner ended – a much better meal than they had had in the main dining-room – they went their separate ways. Edward was on duty and he accompanied Benyon back to the cabin and put him to bed. He was still exhausted by the storm and his violent seasickness. Edward's knee was hurting. He cursed himself for being a fool – pitting himself against youth – but the damage had been done and he knew he needed to rest it if he was to be able to walk properly when they reached New York. The doctor had given him anti-inflammatory pills and there was nothing else anyone could do for him. Inevitably, Frank went off with the twins to put their mother to bed – she was complaining of one of her headaches – and then, no doubt, to dance the night away. He admired the boy's energy but wondered if it had really been worth bringing him if all he did was philander with the first pretty girl he saw.

Verity and Sam Forrest went off together, to do what Edward did not know nor care to imagine. It was annoying, though, because he wanted to talk things over with her. In the past, her caustic wit and down-to-earth assessment of the facts had been of considerable help to him when he was trying to puzzle something out but tonight she had other priorities.

'By the way,' Sam said, as they got up from dinner, 'I've got some brandy in my cabin. Why don't we . . .?'

Verity looked at him suspiciously but his face was as innocent as a babe's. She was on the point of saying she didn't drink brandy when – for no reason other than that she was bored and rather depressed – she said, 'All right, just a nightcap.'

Sam lay sprawled on the bed, his toothglass – half-full of brandy – cupped in his hands. He had taken off his jacket and loosened his collar. Verity was slumped in the armchair, looking at him intently. She had thought she knew him but now decided she didn't. She knew certain things about him. He was a good-looking American boy with all the optimism and charm of youth. He was a good speaker – she had heard him turn potentially ugly meetings into enthusiastic support for Anglo-American labour unity. Despite his youth, he was the chosen representative of one of the most powerful labour leaders in the United States. He had a great future and she liked men with drive. But . . . there was a 'but' . . . he did not quite have Edward's intelligence and certainly not his education. There was something a little callow about him, she decided.

'What do you think about all this?' Sam asked.

'The murder?'

'Yes – the murder. What else?'

'Good riddance, I suppose. He had enemies. He seemed to *like* having enemies.'

'I was one, you know.'

'He hated Communists and unions, so no doubt he hated you.'

'That's so, but me in particular.'

'What had you ever done to him?'

'It was what I wouldn't do. He had interests in Tennessee – mines, power . . . he had a finger in many pies. He asked me to use my influence with my union to see there were no strikes.'

'But that's absurd! Why should he think you would do that?'

'He tried to blackmail me.'

140

'But you can't be blackmailed if you haven't done anything wrong.'

Sam bit his lip. 'He said he would tell the authorities I was a Communist.'

'But you're not a Communist.'

'No, but they know I "consort" with Communists.'

'And that's so bad?'

'It would mark me for life. In my country, being a Communist makes you an outcast. It's like being a member of a particular religion. You have to be prepared to give up everything for the cause.'

'That's what it's like in England.'

'Not as bad,' he said flatly. 'He said I slept with Communists – or at least with one Communist.'

Verity narrowed her eyes. 'But you don't.'

'No, I don't, but I would like to.'

Verity was silent for a moment and took a sip of her brandy. 'Well, I suppose if you are going to be accused of sleeping with the enemy, then you better had.'

She got up from her chair, put the glass down on the dressing-table and began to unzip her dress – a little black dress which rode high on her legs and which she knew made her look rather taller than she actually was. In Spain, her face had become almost gaunt but, since her return, she had put on a little flesh and the weariness had gone out of her. Her skin glowed – the sea air seemed to do it good – and the black marks beneath her eyes had vanished. Sam watched from the bed, unmoving, as she kicked off her shoes and stepped out of her dress. It was hot in the cabin and bead marks of sweat stood out on her forehead and upper lip.

'Well, do I have to do this all on my own?'

Sam came to life, getting off the bed, upsetting a little of his brandy as he did so. He took the girl in his arms and kissed her as he had imagined kissing her all those weeks they had trailed round English provincial towns together. He released her and took off his shirt, studs bursting in all directions. Then he took off his shoes and socks.

'Why do men look so ridiculous in their socks?' he said, trying to sound relaxed but failing.

'And girls in camiknickers?'

Sam gulped and found himself at a loss for words. After a minute or two standing in the middle of the cabin kissing, Verity said, 'Have you got a . . . you know?'

'What? Oh, one of those. I believe I have.'

It was so difficult for the man, he thought. It didn't do to look calculating but without a French letter . . . He opened the drawer of the table beside his bed and, over his shoulder, Verity saw a photograph with the Durex on top of it.

'Whose photo is it?'

'Just a snapshot,' he said hurriedly.

There was something in his voice which made Verity reach over and take it before he could shut the drawer. 'You don't mind me looking, do you?'

The camera had caught the pretty girl in her gingham dress looking at the baby in her arms with that combination of bewilderment and ecstasy which marks out a young mother with her firstborn.

'It's your wife and baby, isn't it?'

'I . . . yes, but . . .'

Verity raised her hand and slapped him hard on the side of his face.

'But you never asked me,' he said miserably. And it was true. In all the weeks she had known him, she had never asked if he were married. Somehow, she had assumed he was unattached. He had certainly never mentioned a wife. She felt the greatest fool. Of course a man like Sam Forrest would be married. Wasn't every man she had ever desired married?

Not quite, she reminded herself. Not quite . . .

10

The next morning the sun shone, the sea was lapis lazuli and the long chairs were soon filled with women coating themselves in Nurona sun-tan cream. Even Lord Benyon ventured on to the sun deck and sat, shrouded in a rug, alongside Marcus Fern. The two men were discussing the speech he was to make to the New York business community.

Verity could not resist interrupting them to ask what he was going to say about the state of Britain. 'Will you talk about the way in which our industry is owned by the rich, worked by the poor and profits the shareholder? Will you tell them how the armaments manufacturers are getting fat on selling arms to the Fascists? Will you tell them about the stinking poverty of our great cities? Will you tell them how our great banks are run by men who think only of profit and never of principle? I imagine not.'

'No, I will not, my dear, because to do so would make us look as though we were still living in Dickens' England. Besides, it isn't true – not all of it, anyway. I will tell them I travelled across the Atlantic in one of the greatest ships ever built, and built in England. I will tell them they must open their markets to our goods and invest in our industry. I will tell them we need their economic aid to keep the peace in troubled times.'

'All very well,' Verity said belligerently, folding her hands over her chest, 'but you know as well as I do that, until industry is state-owned, we will always be at the mercy of the money-men and the profiteers.'

Keeping his temper, Benyon replied, 'I agree with you that

the state should have a role in industry. It should ensure our coal mines and our steel works are properly managed and the workers properly rewarded for their work. It should see that profits are fairly distributed but government has neither the expertise nor the personnel to run industry. You may not know it but, in Russia, state-owned industry is proving a catastrophe. Bureaucracy and corruption are ruining it.'

'Why corruption?'

'Because the desire to make money is universal and, if the state tries to stifle that urge, it will find another outlet – corruption, back-street profit, fiddles and bribes.'

'I don't believe you. Show me your evidence.'

'And the collective farms are leading the Soviet Union towards a famine of unimaginable horror.'

'I don't believe you,' Verity repeated. 'At least Stalin has given his country full employment.' It was all she could manage before stumping off in a worse temper than before.

'Miss Browne seems upset,' Marcus Fern said, as the two men resumed their work. 'I am almost sad that the young are so serious. In my day, they would be interested only in dancing and the pleasures of flirtation.'

'Marcus! I wouldn't have believed you were ever flirtatious.'

'Stop it, Benyon! Now, what were we saying . . .'

Benyon took up his pen and, poised to return to his notes, said with a smile, 'In any case, I think Miss Browne's bad temper is derived from exactly that – love or disappointment in love. Have you not noticed? Mr Forrest looks almost as down in the dumps as Miss Browne. I would surmise a lovers' tiff.'

Edward, too, had noticed that Sam and Verity were no longer on speaking terms and he rebuked himself for being pleased. He was curious as to what had happened to make them quarrel but too wise to make any direct inquiries. He was leaning over the rail, smoking a gasper and resting his bad leg, when he became aware of some sort of commotion further down the deck. Being one of those people constitutionally unable to ignore a rumpus, he hobbled towards it, leaning on a crutch the doctor had lent him. He saw that it was Doris Zinkeisen and she was screaming at the Purser.

As she saw Edward approaching, she turned her attention to him. 'My picture ... the mural ... it's been attacked ... vandalized.'

She was weeping and her mascara had smudged her eyes so she looked both absurd and pathetic. Edward took her by the arm and said, 'Someone has damaged your picture? How frightful. Who would do such a thing? Show me ... please.'

To the Purser's relief, Edward's obvious concern calmed her and the three of them made their way to the Verandah Grill. They were joined by Verity and Bernard Hunt who, when they heard what had happened, were as outraged as Edward and this, too, seemed to comfort the artist.

Standing in front of the mural, Verity expressed Edward's own thought. 'If Senator Day wasn't dead, I might have thought this was his work.'

Someone had thrown black paint over the mural, obscuring much of the carnival scene. The lion tamer had disappeared and so had the dancing girls. As he peered at the damage Edward let out a cry. The bare-breasted black girl cavorting behind the lion had been cut with some sort of knife. It was a savage attack and all of them standing in front of the picture were shocked into silence.

'How disgusting!' Bernard Hunt exclaimed, clutching one of Doris's hands. 'I am so sorry, my dear. It's too horrible but ...' he went close to the mural to examine the damage, 'it's mostly superficial. I have a friend in New York who restores pictures for the National Gallery in Washington. I will get him to look at this as soon as we dock. My poor darling, this is an attack on all of us who love art.'

Doris's sobbing began to abate.

'This is the work of an unbalanced mind. I'm sorry, Miss Zinkeisen, but there can be no doubt about it: the attack on your picture is a sort of mad censorship. Someone among us feels threatened by bare female flesh and this black girl in particular. It's quite horrible, as Hunt says, but let's hope he's right and it can be repaired. What we have to hope is that whoever did it doesn't attack the real thing.'

145

'What do you mean, Edward?' Verity said. 'There are no black women on board, as far as I know.'

'No, but there is a black man and there are plenty of women. I don't like it. I don't like it at all.'

The Purser had gone off to report this latest disaster to Captain Peel. As Edward continued to examine the painting, he arrived and, pushing Edward to one side almost rudely, he stared at it uncomprehendingly.

Edward asked the Purser who had discovered the damage.

'The cleaners at six o'clock this morning. As you know, the Verandah turns itself into a nightclub after dinner. At one o'clock it closes and the waiters do some basic tidying up. Then the cleaners come very early to do all the public rooms before seven thirty.'

'I see. Is the Verandah Grill locked at night?'

'No. None of the public rooms are locked at night.'

In exasperation the Captain said, 'There's no question of shutting the Grill.' He turned to the Purser. 'You had better get the carpenters to board over the damage. Miss Zinkeisen,' the Captain went on, 'I am horrified by what has been done to your work and I promise you it will be repaired as soon as possible.'

'Thank you, Captain.' She was calmer now. 'Bernard ... Mr Hunt says he will arrange to have an expert restorer come on board at New York and, of course, I can repaint where I have to. But who could do such a thing?'

'It seems there must be a madman among us,' was all the Captain could say.

'V, have you got a moment? I'd like to talk this over if you have time.'

Verity was pleased to have something to occupy her. She was determined, as far as possible, to keep out of Sam's way and a confabulation with Edward was a legitimate excuse to absent herself a while. It was awkward Sam having the cabin next to hers. She would keep on bumping into him and, really, there was nothing she wanted to say to him. She had been a fool. She had believed that he was unattached – a carefree young man, very much to her taste, sharing many of her interests and concerns. Suddenly, he had revealed himself to be a cheat and a liar – just like all the other men she had ever slept with – all two of them. She smiled inwardly. She didn't see why she should blame herself. She wasn't promiscuous. There had been David Griffiths-Jones – her first lover – and Ben Belasco, the novelist, whom she had met in Spain. That was all. After all, she was twenty-six – soon to be twenty-seven. Damn it, she was almost a virgin. Now Edward, he had . . .

Her ruminations were interrupted by the sound of Edward's voice. He sounded irritable.

'Are you listening? I said, did you see, when we were looking at the mural, there's a panel in it about three-foot square which can be taken out – an inspection hatch? Doris told me about it but I had forgotten. They had to be able to get at the clock on the next deck down or something. V! Oh, I give up.'

'Sorry, I was miles away. What clock?'

'It doesn't matter. Come to my cabin in fifteen minutes. I want to get Frank. He was dancing with the Roosevelt girl in here last night. Perhaps he saw something. Ouch! Blast this leg.'

'I'll fetch Frank. You go and rest your leg. You oughtn't to be hopping around on it, at least until the swelling subsides.'

They left Doris with Bernard Hunt. He was being unexpectedly sympathetic – perhaps because he cared more about art than about people, Edward thought unkindly. The Captain, with a shrug of his shoulders, had returned to the bridge and the Purser went off to find someone to board over the damage. He had, however, imparted one important piece of information before he left. Apparently, one of the engineers checking the heating system in the Turkish bath had discovered that his toolbox, which he had left near the control panel, was missing a hammer.

Verity found Frank still in bed, complaining of a hangover. When he heard what had occurred he said he would join them 'in two ticks'. As Verity left his cabin she bumped into the Dolmens who had already heard about the attack on the mural.

'This is not correct what is happening on this ship,' the Professor said plaintively. 'It would not be permitted on a German ship. *Es gefällt mir nicht.*'

147

Verity agreed, it certainly wasn't right.

Before going to his cabin, Edward decided to check on his charge. He was satisfied to find Benyon on a long chair talking to Fern. He could hardly be safer. He greeted the two men and told them about the attack on Doris's mural. Benyon was horrified.

'Good Lord, that's too bad. I'll go and find out if there is anything I can do.'

'Hunt has been very kind. He says he has a tame picture restorer in New York who he will get on board to repair the mural.'

'Good. I have to admit I don't like the mural but the whole thing is bizarre and sinister. I mean, one could argue it's healthy art can still arouse such passion but the viciousness of it . . . With the artist here to see it. Poor Miss Zinkeisen! It's clearly a personal attack on her. There is too much hatred on this ship. I will be very glad to be back on dry land.'

Not as glad as I will be! Edward thought ruefully. What ought to have been a pleasant four or five days in a floating luxury hotel had turned into a succession of highly unpleasant incidents, most horrible of all, of course, Tom Barrett's murder. He couldn't put it out of his mind: the corpse swinging naked among the carcasses and the thought that, if Benyon was right, there was a girl back home who loved him and whom he had planned to marry.

Benyon was speaking again. 'Could it have anything to do with Professor Dolmen, I wonder? No, I don't see how it could. It's ironic that such a very German German should be exiled by those to whom he was so loyal.'

'Whatever do you mean, Benyon?'

'Didn't I tell you? No, of course I didn't because it was confidential but I don't see it matters now that awful man Day is dead.'

He proceeded to tell Edward how Dolmen had asked him to intercede for him with the immigration authorities if Senator Day had carried out his threat and laid information against him.

'A Jew and a Nazi!' Edward exclaimed.

'It's not as odd as you might suppose,' Fern said. 'I know through my business contacts that a number of Jews joined the Nazi Party in the hope of influencing Hitler and ingratiating themselves with the Party. For a man like Dolmen, who feels himself to be a German first and a Jew a long way after, the idea of not being allowed to work would have seemed too awful to contemplate. While the Nazis needed him, they wouldn't have bothered him but then, for some reason, they must have decided to use his race against him. He was probably lucky to be allowed to emigrate. Knowing what he does about the Luftwaffe and the development of the jet engine, I'm surprised they didn't just shoot him.'

Back in his cabin, Edward lay down on his bed and lit a cigarette. He blew a smoke ring and watched it float lazily up to the ceiling. He needed to make sense of all that had happened on the *Queen Mary* since he had come on board three days ago. It was not very long but it seemed an age. He had a feeling he had missed some vital clue which would make what was opaline translucent.

There was a knock on the door and Verity arrived, with Frank hard on her heels. 'What's this?' Frank asked. 'A council of war?'

He perched himself on the end of the bed and Verity collapsed into the armchair. No one said anything about asking Sam Forrest to join them.

'That's right – we need to thrash things out. Fenton will be here in a second. Ah, here he is. Take a pew, will you, Fenton. We need your counsel. I feel I am floundering and if we don't look sharp, someone will have a go at Benyon and perhaps we won't be there to stop him, but I'm convinced, if we pool our knowledge, we might be able to make sense of all the beastly things which have been happening. Frank, have you heard? Poor Miss Zinkeisen's mural was vandalized during the night. I suppose you didn't notice anything or anyone acting suspiciously before you went to bed?'

'Verity just told me. Was it badly damaged?'

'It had black paint thrown on it and the figure of the black girl was cut with a knife. A vicious attack.'

'How horrible! No, I'm afraid I noticed nothing. As far as I know, it was all right when I went to bed. I admit I didn't look at it but I'm sure I would have noticed if it had been attacked.'

'I didn't expect you to have seen anything. It must have been done in the middle of the night or very early in the morning before the cleaners arrived. Now, to more serious matters. I am only interested in Day's murder in so far as it relates to our job which is to deliver Benyon safe and well to FBI Agent Fawcett in New York and, which amounts to the same thing, establish who killed Tom Barrett. It sounds cold-hearted, I know, but if we don't focus on Benyon we may miss something vital.'

'But surely we can't ignore Day's murder?' Verity put in.

'No. I am not saying we should ignore it but we only need to know who murdered him to be sure he isn't going to go on and kill Lord Benyon.'

Frank whistled. 'I suppose you're right. So what do we do?'

'Let's begin with Tom Barrett. I think we have to assume that he was killed because he was guarding Benyon. Does anyone disagree?'

'None of us really knew him,' Frank pointed out, 'but I can't imagine there could be any other reason. That was why he was on board.'

'Right,' Verity said, 'and I think that suggests whoever killed him knew about Benyon and what he is going to do in the States – not, of course, that Edward has told us what that is but we know it's pretty important.'

'Which means,' Frank concluded, 'that the killer is a passenger on the ship for that one reason.'

'It's a pity we can't discover which passengers booked their tickets after Benyon made his reservation. That might narrow it down'. Verity lit another cigarette, contributing to the blue haze which hung over them. She coughed and waved her hand in front of her face. 'Open a window or whatever you call it, will you, Frank?'

'The same thought had occurred to me,' Edward said. 'I telephoned Barrett's boss back in London and asked him to do some digging. I hope to get some answers soon. I was given a list of the First Class passengers but it doesn't say when their reservations were made. And I'll ask Benyon to tell me exactly when he or his staff made the booking.'

'My lord, could Mr Barrett's killer be a member of the crew or one of the servants?'

'It's possible, Fenton, but I doubt it unless you have noticed anything which might suggest otherwise. There are relatively few crew members who are free to wander about First Class without a good reason. There's the Purser, of course, the bartender – Roger, isn't it? – and various waiters and so on. I think, Fenton, you could make it your job to see if any of them are exhibiting signs of wanting to murder the passengers. As for the ladies' maids and the valets – again, I'll have to leave that to you to investigate.'

'Very good, my lord. I will attend to it.'

'Are we looking for a man?' Verity inquired.

'As far as Tom Barrett is concerned, the answer is yes. Even with the winch, there is no way a woman could have lifted his body on to the hook. And the blow to his head was very heavy.'

'Is it significant that Barrett and Day were both hit on the head with a blunt instrument?'

'It may be but, until the police forensic bods examine the bodies, we have no way of knowing whether it was the same blunt instrument. It's not very likely even if both killings were by the same person. He would hardly hold on to some – no doubt bloodied – truncheon or hammer after killing Tom. He would bung it overboard. There's never any shortage of blunt instruments.'

'Ugh!' Verity exclaimed. 'What a horrible picture you paint of some madman going around battering people to death.'

'I think it's most unlikely the two killings are related,' Edward said.

'I agree,' Frank chipped in. 'Day had lots of enemies but they weren't Barrett's enemies.'

'Well,' Verity said, stubbing out her half-smoked cigarette, 'let's concentrate on Day's death for a moment.' She waved her finger at Edward, 'I know you said "only so far as it sheds light on Barrett" but still we cannot ignore it. I mean, two unconnected murders on one Atlantic crossing...? How likely is that? Do we know if Day was dead before he hit the water?'

'The doctor thinks not. He drowned. There was water in his lungs.'

'Oh, how awful! I have always hated the thought of drowning. But doesn't that suggest it might *not* have been a man who knocked him on the head? All it needed was a light blow, just enough to unsteady him and tip him into the pool.'

Frank reached for his uncle's gold cigarette case which lay on the bed but Edward grabbed his arm.

'Uncle! Don't be an ass. I'm sorry but I don't see why I shouldn't smoke. You two puff away like Stephenson's Rocket. Anyway, look at this packet.' He held up Verity's packet of Camels. 'It says Camels soothe the throat and my throat needs soothing.'

'Oh all right then, if you must!' Edward surrendered. 'Fenton?'

'No thank you, my lord. Might I suggest, my lord, it might help if we make a list of the Senator's known enemies?'

'Good idea,' Frank said. 'Day had plenty of people gunning for him. Will you take notes, Fenton?' He counted off on his fingers. 'Warren Fairley has to be top of the list. He hated Day and never pretended otherwise. They were political enemies and Day was doing his best to prevent Warren performing in the States. You heard what he said about this new committee to investigate – what did he call it? – un-American activities – whatever that means.'

'And Sam hated him too,' Verity put in, her voice sounding rather choked.

'Oh?' Edward encouraged her as non-committally as he could.

'Yes. Day thought he was a Communist and Sam told me he had tried to blackmail him to help deal with some industrial dispute – I don't know quite what. Anyway, Sam wasn't having any of it. Still,' she could not prevent herself from adding, 'I can't imagine Sam murdering anyone, even if he is a bit of a heel.'

There was a silence. Frank and Edward tried not to look expectant but failed. Verity wrestled with herself. She did not quite know why she owed Edward an explanation of her recent ill-temper. It was none of his business. On the other hand she liked honesty, hated muddle and misunderstanding. 'I suppose I had better tell you – though it has nothing to do with anything – he rather misled me into thinking he was unmarried but in fact he *is* married.'

152

No one wished to make any comment. Edward said, 'Benyon has just told me Professor Dolmen has a motive as well. Apparently Day was going to try and prevent his being allowed to enter the United States. It turns out he is or was a Nazi – believe it or not – even though he's a Jew. But Dolmen is a scientist. He wanted above all to be allowed to work and he couldn't work if he did not join the Party.' As he said this, it flashed through Edward's mind that he could imagine the mirror image of this situation occurring in Stalin's Soviet Union. Would the Communist Party allow anyone to have a government job without joining the Party? He doubted it. He wondered if there would come a time when Verity might understand the nature of the beast to which she had attached herself. 'Anyway,' he went on, 'Day was planning to use this against him – or so Dolmen believed.'

'Gosh!' Verity exclaimed. 'That's extraordinary. Some people are just so naive.'

Edward grinned wryly to himself.

'Everyone hated Day,' Frank said. 'The Roosevelts couldn't stand him. Oh God, if we went through the First Class passengers we could probably find a hundred who'd have been quite happy to see the end of that man.'

'Why did the Roosevelts hate him?' Edward asked.

'Oh, let me think . . . I don't really know. Perry must have said something . . . I suppose I could ask him?'

'No, leave that to me. It might be embarrassing for you,' Edward told him.

'Who had the opportunity to kill Day?' Verity asked.

'Put it the other way, V. Who wasn't at the race? I did a list but, of course, the murderer might be someone quite different . . .'

'Like Major Cranton, for instance,' Frank said, puffing at his cigarette. 'There's something wrong about him. And there's Doris Zinkeisen although she's not my idea of a murderer. I rather like her, despite the clothes she wears and the stories she tells, but she is Jewish and makes her living working in Hollywood. She might easily have made an enemy of Day.'

'I know,' Edward agreed, 'and, if the attack on her mural had happened before Day was killed, she would certainly be a prime suspect . . .'

'And anyway, as you say, she doesn't look like a murderer – whatever a murderer looks like. She's too ... too fey,' Verity said.

'Cranton was very much in evidence during the race. We can dismiss any idea of his being Day's killer.' Edward spoke a trifle regretfully.

'There's Bernard Hunt,' Frank put in. 'I told you the dirty old man put a hand on my knee.'

'Gosh, no, really?'

'I don't see why you are so surprised, V. Some people think I'm rather good-looking. Just joking,' he added, as Verity threw a cushion at him.

'Now, children,' Edward rebuked them, 'this is serious. Mind you, we've all noticed the girl – Philly. She seems to think you're handsome.'

Frank blushed. 'Tommy rot! Still, what about Philly's mother? Do you know she has arsenic beside her bed?'

'Mrs Roosevelt has arsenic?' Edward exclaimed.

'Yes, in a bottle. I saw it when I went to her cabin during the storm to see how she was.'

'Perhaps that's why she has so many headaches?' Verity suggested.

Edward looked as though he was going to say something but in the end kept silent.

'There was one odd thing about Philly,' Verity said pensively. 'She went down below deck just before the race and when she reappeared she was wearing a different dress.'

'Very good, V! That's just the sort of thing a woman sees and a man doesn't.'

'But – haven't you noticed? Philly's as clean as a cat.' Frank was eager in her defence. 'She's always changing her clothes and washing ... she washes all the time. It's a sort of phobia. Still, you can't really think Philly killed anyone? It's ridiculous. Day was a bear of a man. He could have broken her with a flick of his finger. She couldn't have killed him.' There was silence and Frank went on in panic. 'Are you suggesting Philly had to change her dress because she had blood on it?'

'I'm not suggesting anything, Frank. I'm just saying what I saw.'

'And women don't kill men. Or, if they do, they poison them,' he said, suddenly remembering that Lord Weaver's stepdaughter had poisoned old General Craig, or so his uncle had told him, over a fine port one evening at Mersham Castle.

'But going back to Hunt,' Verity continued, 'he may be a homosexual but that doesn't mean he's a murderer.'

'No,' Frank agreed, 'but he also told me – when he was drunk in the storm – that he was a "fellow-traveller".'

'"Fellow-traveller"! Horrible jargon! Do you have to use it?'

'I just mean, Uncle, that he's not a Party member but he thinks along the same lines as us.'

'I know what it means but it's such a . . . Oh, I suppose I'm old-fashioned.'

'But we love you,' Very said jokingly and then wished she had not. She hurried on, 'We haven't mentioned the attack on Jane Barclay. It's not much fun being poached to death. I suppose that's related to everything else in some way?'

'I've got an idea about that,' Edward interjected, 'but I don't want to say anything for the moment,' he added irritatingly. 'I'm probably wrong. In fact, I thought I might totter along and have a word with her. While I do that, Fenton, will you pursue your investigations into any of the crew with access to First Class and among the passengers' servants? Verity, will you have a talk to Bernard Hunt? As he's a fellow what-do-y'-call-it and you are a full-blown "traveller", you may have something in common. No, better not get into politics. Ask him for some advice on a picture . . . say you are thinking of commissioning Doris Zinkeisen to do a portrait for you.'

'Of whom?'

'How do I know? Me, perhaps. It would be a nice gesture.'

'Huh!'

'What shall I do?' Frank asked.

'Well, I think you should talk to Perry Roosevelt.'

'But you said you'd ask him about –'

'Not about why he didn't like Day. Just try and find out something about the Roosevelts as a family – their background and so on. You really know nothing.'

'I do. When we first met, we had a sort of mutual catechism. He asked me about my family and I asked him about his. Not that it really amounted to much, I suppose,' he added, wrink-

155

ling his brow. 'But I didn't like it at the time. I hate talking about my people.'

'We *do* embarrass you, I realize,' Edward smiled, 'but that's the purpose of relations.' Frank opened his mouth to protest but Edward had something else to say. 'I think you will find there's something important he hasn't told you, Frank.'

'What sort of thing?'

'About Philly.'

'About Philly?' Frank echoed.

'Your inamorata,' Edward said drily.

Frank looked at his uncle in dismay.

As Edward limped off to find Jane Barclay he met the Purser, who said the Captain would be grateful for a word and asked him to go on to the bridge.

By the time he had negotiated the various steps and stairs to the wheelhouse, Edward's gammy leg was hurting badly and he was cursing under his breath with a fluency and command of the vernacular which might have impressed his nephew, had he heard him. However, the effort was worthwhile. Standing on the bridge of the *Queen Mary*, surrounded by smartly uniformed officers, was, he imagined, rather like being with the gods on top of Mount Olympus. The views were vast and his eye, having nowhere to rest except on wave after wave cresting in lacy foam as the great ship cleaved the water, reverted to the shining equipment directly in front of him. There were all sorts of dials and wheels, mostly cased in brass, and he suddenly felt what it must be like to be an illiterate. He knew roughly what he was looking at but none of it made any sense to him.

As he watched, fascinated and humbled by the complexity of the gadgets and dials which were being operated with so much confidence and efficiency, he realized how cushioned the passengers were against the reality of their environment. They were little more aware of what it means to be at sea than babies in a perambulator. The Captain was deep in conversation with his first officer but, catching sight of Edward, he came over with a smile at his evident awe.

'It is remarkable, isn't it, Lord Edward? The engines are, of course, the beating heart of our great ship but the wheelhouse

156

is the eyes and ears. You see this,' he said, pointing to a fan-shaped instrument on a metal trunk. 'We have a gyro compass and a gyro pilot. The gyro compass provides a permanent indication of true north and is unaffected by the movement of the ship. Then these, on each side of the bridge, are steering repeaters. They "repeat" the master compass. This one,' he said, tapping the dial, 'is operated in conjunction with a wireless direction-finding installation. There's also a thirty-day continuous course-recording instrument – you see, over here – in which all changes of course and the time of their occurrence are automatically registered.'

'I see, or rather I don't see,' Edward said, unable to take it all in. 'It's good to know you can't get lost in this trackless waste. Is this the steering gear?'

'Yes, but it's not just your ordinary helm. It detects any variation of course and determines the amount of helm required to correct it.'

'And those, over there?'

'Searchlights. High intensity arc lights. Come up to the bridge again tonight and you can see the way they illumine the ocean. It's pretty impressive. Do you want to hold the helm? It's quite something to say you've steered the *Queen Mary*.'

Edward grasped a little wheel fitted to the main steering apparatus. 'Does this really steer the ship?' he asked in amazement.

'It allows ordinary hand steering but, for most of the time, she's on automatic.'

'No chance of meeting any icebergs then?' Edward bit his tongue. What on earth had made him say it? It must be the pain in his knee.

The Captain smiled grimly. 'On this crossing, anything's possible. By the way, this came for you. It had to be decoded so it couldn't go direct to you.' He handed Edward a slip of paper folded in half.

Edward read it and then pocketed it. 'It's just as I supposed.'

'Can you deal with it?'

'Yes, thank you, Captain. I'll let you know if I need assistance.'

* * *

157

'Frank tells me you are a "fellow-traveller",' Verity said conversationally.

Bernard Hunt looked nervously over his shoulder. 'Oh no. Did he say that? It must have been the storm. I . . . I wouldn't want it known. I'm an art dealer, not a politician.'

'I'm afraid the Nazis have made it impossible to distinguish between politics and our private life. *Are* you a member of the Party?'

Hunt squirmed in his seat, his horse-like face a mask of melancholy. 'Not a Party member – a sympathizer, as the boy told you – that's all. Please, I don't want to discuss it.'

'Do you think there's such a thing as Communist art?' Verity was genuinely interested.

Hunt put on his lecturing voice and Verity, who was used to being talked at by Comrades, sat back and listened. 'Artists have always put into their work something of their attitude towards life. That doesn't mean all art has to be as directly propagandist as Goya's *Third of May*, Delacroix's *Liberty on the Barricades* or David's *Death of Marat* but, even in paintings which, at first sight, seem not to present any definite attitude towards life, such a view is latent. A painter of historical scenes will be attracted by those that tally with his own outlook and a portrait painter will be making some statement about the sitter.'

'So all paintings are a kind of propaganda?'

'Of course! The spectator is always going to be affected by the subject matter – whether it's an apple or a woman. What could be more fatal for art than cutting it off from the serious activities of life?'

'But surely that means the difference between good art and bad art is simply how effective it is as propaganda?'

'No. An artist may be competent or incompetent but art which does not contribute to the public good is bad art. Lenin, quoting Lurçat, says: "*L'art n'est plus un jeu gratuit; c'est une activité offensive.*" '

'But here, on the *Queen Mary*, the art you have chosen is bourgeois art?' Verity waved her hand at a painting of a bunch of flowers to make her point.

'Art today is in a mess, I grant you. It's all a matter of the status of the artist. Pre-capitalism, in the Middle Ages, the artist was a servant of the community with a definite status in

158

society. Now he's a servant of the leisured class. And, what's worse, he thinks he's not a craftsman but imagines he's someone special. He's gradually isolated himself from the working class. But there is hope. I wanted to commission Diego Rivera to do a mural in the New Realist style but Cunard wouldn't have it, so I had to put up with Doris Zinkeisen.'

'Don't you like her art?'

'It's all right but compared with Rivera . . .' He left the rest unsaid. 'At least it provoked a response in one spectator and proved Lenin's point that art *is* an act of aggression.'

'Who do you think killed Senator Day?' Verity said, abruptly changing the subject.

'You know that,' Hunt replied, looking surprised.

'How do you mean?'

'Surely it was your friend Sam Forrest? That's what everyone thinks. He was being blackmailed by that awful man so he tapped him on the head and put him in the pool. We saw him when he came on deck. He looked frightful and then we heard about Day being killed. It didn't take Einstein to work out who did it.'

'Except for the murderer, Sam was the last person to see him alive,' Verity said slowly, 'but he didn't do it. I'm sure of it.'

Hunt looked at her pityingly and seemed about to say something but checked himself.

'Well,' Verity said unhappily, 'you can't think he attacked Jane Barclay or damaged Miss Zinkeisen's mural.'

'Not the mural. That was Major Cranton. I more or less saw him do it.'

'Good heavens!'

'I saw him walking out of the Verandah Grill with an ice bucket. I followed him up on deck and watched him throw it over the side.'

'What . . . iced water?'

'No, the ice bucket was full of black paint.'

'When was this?'

'About five o'clock this morning. I woke up early and went for a stroll. The ship's wonderful when it's empty of people.'

'But what did you do? You must have been horrified to see a work of art you had commissioned being vandalized?'

'At the time, I had no idea what he was doing walking about with a pail of black stuff.'

'You didn't ask him?'

'I thought about it, even walked up to him and opened my mouth to speak but he gave me such a look I'm afraid I turned tail. I admit it, I was frightened. I'm not physically courageous, you understand, Miss Browne.'

'But you're telling me now. Aren't you afraid of what he might do when he discovers you've told me?'

'I'm not sure I really care any more. Anyway, I thought if you told that nice Lord Edward Corinth he would know what to do without involving me.'

'But I don't understand. Why don't you care any more?'

'I've just been on the telephone to my friend in New York. He's my business partner, you understand. I sent over a painting I had bought cheaply in London which I was convinced was by Poussin. The world authority on Poussin is a man called Ray Parish. He's attached to the Metropolitan. Anyway, Parish says it's not a Poussin after all so I'm effectively broke.' He saw that Verity had no idea who Poussin was. 'Not heard of Poussin? One of the world's greatest artists? Nicolas Poussin, French, born 1594, died 1665? Ah well, *sic transit* and so on.'

'Of course I've heard of Poussin,' she countered, unconvincingly.

'I gambled and lost. I was certain but it seems I was wrong.'

'But you said you bought it cheap?'

'Cheap, but it still used all the money I could scrape together.'

'Can't you just sell it on for what it is?'

'Maybe, but now it's certain it's not a Poussin, I won't get very much for it.'

'I'm sorry. Is it a beautiful painting?'

'As a matter of fact it is – the Holy Family with St John.'

'A religious painting?'

'Naturally. Why, does it shock you?'

'Surprised, that's all, after what you said about Communist painting. But I see I'm just being silly.'

'Yes, you are and, anyway, why are you sorry? It's nothing to do with you. I'm going to drown my sorrows with Roger at the bar. Coming?'

'A bit early for me, I'm afraid.'

'Well then . . .' He shrugged and strolled off, whistling under his breath.

'You've got to tell me.'

'Tell you what?' Perry sounded bored.

'My uncle says there's something I don't know . . . something I ought to know.'

'But what don't you know?'

'If I knew that, I wouldn't have to ask.'

'You're making my head spin. I didn't sleep so well last night. Come and see my mother. She likes you. Maybe she can tell you what you want to know.'

'Those headaches your mother seems to have so often . . . is she ill? I mean seriously ill?'

'*She's* not ill,' Perry said, his voice neutral.

'But someone else is?'

'Stop asking me questions. I told you, it makes my head hurt.'

'Perry, I need to know. We're friends, aren't we? My uncle wouldn't have said what he did if there wasn't something to know.'

'Your uncle's smarter than he looks.' Perry hesitated. 'Well, I suppose you will have to know sometime, but don't tell Philly I told you.'

'Philly? It's got to do with her?'

'I thought you would have guessed. Didn't you see the arsenic in my mother's cabin? I thought Philly saw you pick it up off the floor.'

'Yes, I thought it odd. What does it mean? Is someone taking poison?'

'You could say that.' Perry smiled wryly. 'Philly has leukaemia. It's a kind of cancer . . . of the blood. Arsenic trioxide is what she has to take – medicine, you understand – but I don't think it's making any difference. Did you think we were poisoning someone?'

'Leukaemia! I . . . I can't believe it. She looks so well . . . so beautiful!'

'You mean the way her skin looks transparent sometimes . . .

161

as though you could look right through her? That's her illness, so the doctors say.'

'Is she . . . is she going to die?'

'We're all going to die.'

'Don't joke, Perry. I don't see how you can joke about it.'

'Is there anything else to do but laugh in the face of death? I don't know when she will die,' he said roughly. 'It could be tomorrow, next week or even next year. God knows. At least, if he exists, he must.'

'Oh my God!' Frank was aware of how inadequate his words were. He was fascinated by the girl . . . a finger's breadth away from loving her . . . and now this. He felt bewildered, sick in the stomach, unable to take it in. He wanted to rush to her side but, if he did, what would he say? 'Spend the rest of your life with me, however short a time that is.' She would laugh at him.

Perry, understanding his confusion continued, more gently, 'I didn't want to tell you because she's happy with you. She enjoys feeling beautiful . . . being courted. She wanted to have you as her last lover and she has. Now I'm afraid she'll sense you know and all that will be over. You'll be kind to her and she won't be able to bear it.'

'I swear I won't. I mean I'll be kind to her . . . of course I will! But I won't let her know I know.'

'Try not to, anyway,' Perry said, sounding as serious as he ever could.

'So that's what's making your mother so ill . . . watching Philly . . .?'

'Die? That and worrying about me.'

'About you?'

'We're twins, remember.'

'Of course! It must be terrible for you seeing your twin . . . seeing her . . .'

'Not only that. The doc says I have to face it . . . I may develop the same thing.'

Frank looked at him with dawning comprehension. 'Perry, I didn't think. I . . .'

In a spontaneous gesture which his father, the Duke, would have considered un-English, the boy put his arms around his friend and hugged him. Perry, surprised, at first resisted and

162

then returned his embrace. 'You're a bloody fool, Frank', he said in his ear. 'This was all I ever wanted but you have given it to me like this so it means something else.'

'What do you mean?' Frank said, pushing him away but still holding him by both arms.

'It doesn't matter,' Perry said wearily.

'Tell me.'

'You know . . . you must know . . . I love you.' He shook himself free. 'I love you . . . damn you, and now I disgust you. I disgust myself. Goodbye, don't follow me. I'm just going to find a conveniently empty part of the deck and throw myself over the side. Hey, don't look like that. I'm only joking. Go and find Philly. Make her happy.'

11

That evening, there was to be a fancy-dress ball. Every night there was dancing but this was different. The Purser announced that he had chests full of costumes which passengers were welcome to pick over if they had nothing of their own to wear. But, before that, there was to be a brief service for Tom Barrett and Senator Day. The funerals would, of course, wait on the wishes of the two men's families but Captain Peel did not feel it right that their violent deaths should go unmarked, even if it did make some passengers uneasy. He had been relieved that there had been no panic following the murder of Senator Day. It was as though even passengers who had never met the man knew his reputation and were unsurprised that one of their number had chosen to do away with him. How terrible, Captain Peel thought, to be murdered and for no one to be surprised. Irritation at the inconvenience of having the swimming-pool closed seemed the nearest there was to grief at the man's passing.

At three o'clock, a small group of passengers repaired to the library where the altar had been erected and several rows of seats set up in front of it. Verity refused to attend on principle. She was, being a Communist, an atheist and, as she said, although she occasionally attended a religious service out of respect for other people's feelings, she had not liked Day and his views on race had appalled her. Sam Forrest, too, absolutely refused to attend. 'It would be like gloating,' he said brusquely when Verity had asked him. Rather surprisingly, Warren Fairley was there. Glancing ruefully at Edward, he whispered that, much as he had disliked the Senator, he did not approve of murder and was there in silent protest.

As there would also be prayers for Tom Barrett, Lord Benyon, Marcus Fern, Edward and Frank sat themselves down in the front row. Edward buried his face in his hands and tried to pray for Barrett, whom he had hardly known but had liked and sincerely mourned. The trouble was that, however hard he tried to bring to mind Barrett's pleasant, boyish face, the Senator's unpleasant mask, twisted by hatred of his fellow man, insisted on taking its place. Whether the Senator had in life been quite so repellent he could not now say but, in his mind's eye, the man looked grotesquely evil.

Mrs Dolmen was there supporting Mrs Day and Edward could not help but wonder why the two women had found such solace in each other's company. Was it because, in their different ways, both their husbands were bullies? On reflection, Edward was inclined to think that it was more than this. Was there an unconscious triumph for Mrs Dolmen in being able to succour Mrs Day, the widow of the man who had threatened to keep her husband and herself out of the promised land? She certainly seemed to have added an inch to her stature as she helped the widow into a chair in the front row. Edward chided himself for his cynicism.

Professor Dolmen had chosen not to attend, which was no surprise, but Jane Barclay – white as the linen cloth on the altar – was there, clutching her husband's arm.

The Captain spoke a few words, expressing his shock and horror at the death of the two men, and then the service started. It was led by the *Queen Mary's* own clergyman. The whole thing lasted no more than forty minutes but Edward was glad it had been held. Death, he thought, ought never to be shuffled to one side as a minor inconvenience for those left behind. They owed it, too, to Day's widow who seemed genuinely grief-stricken. Perhaps, he mused, a familiar monster was better than no monster at all. He meditated on the unpredictability of fate. For all the Senator's religion – his quoting of Scripture on every possible occasion – he had not been what he would call a God-fearing man. The God of the southern states was not his God. Day's God had been a dark, revengeful God, wielding a two-edged sword. Edward tried to pray.

What human instrument of such a God had finally caught up with the Senator? Had Death made an appointment with him on this ship, sailing across the Atlantic, as a grim joke? To die on an ocean of water ... in a swimming-pool! Did God have a macabre sense of humour? Or did God not come into it? The murderer ... what if he ... or she ...? If she ... who? Why? Edward's experience, limited though it was, suggested that a man might, with his superior strength, kill a woman on impulse but for a woman to kill a man ... that required effort and planning ... premeditation, and premeditation meant the hangman's rope or the electric chair. It was a barbarism, he believed, to hang a woman but where was the logic of his partiality? Was not all killing wrong, even if it was the law's decree? Too many questions getting him nowhere. A woman could be as evil as a man ... but, more often than not, she was driven to kill by a malevolent man. Few women killed compared to men and to do so they had to have a very good reason. Nemesis seemed too melodramatic a word but certainly evil went wherever men went, even on the *Queen Mary*.

His musings were interrupted by the priest's final dismissal. To go in peace ... if only that proved possible. As the little congregation disbanded, Edward was approached by Jane Barclay. 'I guess I ought to thank you for saving my life back in that steam room. If you ... you and your nephew ... hadn't heard ...'

'No need to thank me,' Edward said lightly. 'I'm glad to see you up and about. Are you well enough to join me for a drink before lunch?'

'Sure, why not? Warren's got to rehearse.'

'Rehearse?'

'Yes, the Captain's asked him if he would sing at the ball tonight. He never says no,' she added, a little wearily.

Over a Tom Collins supplied by Roger in the cocktail bar, Edward studied the girl in front of him. It was no hardship. She was very good to look at and he reckoned Warren Fairley was a lucky man. He said what was on his mind.

'Lucky man, your husband.'

'Oh, I'm the lucky one, I guess,' she said without affectation and Edward knew she was sincere. 'He's a great man. Do you know what I'd put on his tombstone if ever, God forbid, I had to think about such a thing? Patience on a monument ... that's what. His patience is just amazing. He puts up with unimaginable harassment, all sorts of slights and insults. It seems he can achieve nothing . . . I mean about what matters to him, the prejudice against black skins. He bears all this and never gives up hope.'

'Do you give up hope?'

'Nope, but I sometimes lose patience. It's no fun being taken for a pervert.'

'What do you mean?'

'You heard what that man Day said. A white girl has no business cohabiting with a black man. He called me white trash, mentally unsound . . . and a whole lot worse.' She spoke with such fervour that Edward was taken aback. 'I expect you think I'm a blonde bimbo with just enough sense to attach myself to a noble man.'

'I don't at all,' he said firmly. 'I think you are highly intelligent, determined and what I think I have heard an American friend of mine call a "cool operator". When I said Warren was a lucky man, I didn't mean just because you are a highly desirable woman – or rather, not only that – but because you are loyal and resourceful. If I may presume to judge, I would say you protected him rather than he protected you, great man though he is.'

Jane looked at her interlocutor with something like respect. 'I do my best,' she said, grudgingly.

'I think you do better than that. It's my belief that not only do you suffer with dignity the abuse of racial bigots and political enemies but you also tolerate your husband's occasional infidelities and soften, as far as you are able, the effects of his naive and sometimes reckless disregard for his own safety.'

She looked at him steadily and after a moment said, 'Meaning . . .?'

'Apologies! Verity – Miss Browne – would say I was being pompous; meaning, I don't think anyone tried to kill you in the steam room. I think the chloroform pad I found beside you belonged to you rather than a would-be killer. I think you wanted to make it seem as though you had been attacked. You had to make it look as though you had been very close to death without actually killing yourself. And you were very successful. Furthermore, I think you only thanked me for saving your life

167

to impress on me that you had been in danger of losing it – or to make sure that I had been taken in by your little charade.'

She blinked and said shakily, 'Why should I do that?'

'You had determined to kill Senator Day and to do it without attracting suspicion, either to your husband or to yourself.'

'So I pretended to stifle myself – is that it?'

'That's right, so no one would think you might kill the Senator. You played iller than you really were and it worked. I am right, aren't I?'

'You're very tough on me. Why should I want to kill Day?'

'He threatened your husband and he threatened you. You had plenty of motives – too many, some might say.'

She was silent and then said, 'Yes, you're right, I did kill that man. He was . . . a sex beast too. Did you know that?'

'What's a sex beast? He tried to rape you?'

'It amounted to that, I guess. He said he had always wanted me and if I let him . . . have me . . . he would stop persecuting us. He said if I didn't, he would have us before this new Senate Committee and stop us working in America ever again. I couldn't allow that. I said he could sleep with me if that was what he wanted, though it made my flesh crawl to think of it. He suggested we do it immediately but I said not in my cabin, and not in his either. I suggested the changing rooms of the swimming-pool. I knew most people would be up on deck for your race.'

'And what happened? I mean, obviously, you didn't sleep with him.'

'No. I suddenly thought: why would he leave me alone if I slept with him once? He had no morals, no principles. Why would he keep his side of the bargain?'

'So?'

'So as we walked beside the pool, I pointed out the emergency telephone and said I would use it if I didn't like what he was doing to me. He turned to look at it and then looked at me and grinned. I think that was what decided me – his grin. It was evil. He went over to the edge of the pool and looked down into the water.' She was speaking mechanically as if she were recounting a dream she only half understood. 'I picked up a hammer. I think it must have been left there by one of the men who had been checking the controls to the steam room. I hit him over the head with it and I heard his skull crack – you know? – like when you crack a walnut. He . . . he toppled into the water. He made an awful splash and I was afraid someone would hear, but nobody came.'

'What did you do then?'

'I didn't know what to do. I wanted to run away. I didn't want to look into the water but I had to. It was horrible – as though someone had tipped some dirty washing into the clean water. He was face down and his head . . . I could see the blood. And then I thought I did hear someone so I ran away.'

Edward said nothing while he considered this. Was she telling the truth or was it another lie? Did the story of the panicky girl hitting out to protect her honour square with the cool, competent woman who had told him to tell Verity to take her 'mitts' off her man? She had already proved she was a remarkably good actress. Was she acting now? She lowered her eyes, waiting for him to speak. 'Did you mean to kill him?' he said at last.

'I suppose so. I didn't think it would be so easy, that's all.'

'What did you do with the hammer?'

'I took it back to my cabin and threw it through the window . . . the porthole.'

'And then what did you do?'

'I had a shower and got back into bed.'

Edward was silent once more. Jane, her hand shaking, finished her drink and signalled Roger to bring her another. When the bartender had brought the drink and Edward had still said nothing, she continued, 'So what are you going to do about it? Turn me in?'

'Hell, I don't know,' he said wretchedly. 'That's what I ought to do.' He thought he saw a momentary flash of relief in her eyes but, if that was what it had been, why relief? Why did she want to be thought a murderer? Did she think she had checkmated him? Because that is exactly what she had done, he now realized.

She was still speaking, pleading, seducing him. It was difficult to resist. 'And ruin two lives for nothing?' The tears welled in her eyes but did not fall. 'You know, if anyone deserved to die, it was that man. He was an animal. No, that's not right. Animals aren't malicious and, if they *are* predatory, it's because they need to eat.'

Edward wiped his forehead and then got up and began to pace around. The bartender looked at him curiously. 'I admire your husband enormously – you must know that – and I agree Day deserved to come to a bad end but ...'

'Every good boy must turn in a killer? Is that it?' Her voice was hardening.

'I ... well, yes. I don't know!'

'And if you did tell the Captain or the police what I've told you, who would believe you? You don't think I would say this all over again, do you? I would deny it ... play the hard-done-by little girl. If it ever came to court, no jury would convict ... no jury north of the Mason-Dixon line, anyway. Is that what you want, to make a fool of yourself and make misery for us?'

'No, of course not, but murder isn't something you can just dismiss as trivial. Most of us have wanted to murder someone at one time or another but we don't ...'

'I agree, it's not a trivial thing to do but you can be driven to it. Do you think I might do it again?'

'Why not? If you get away with it this time, you'll be tempted to do it again. You said Warren's plagued by enemies ... enemies like flies to be swatted out of the way. Oh God, I wish you hadn't told me. Why *did* you tell me?'

'I read somewhere – and yes, I do read – that murderers require confession and then punishment but mainly they need to confess. I can do without punishment but it is a relief to tell someone. It's what drove Lady Macbeth mad, I guess, having to keep it to herself. I told you because you asked ... or, at least, I thought you suspected me and were determined enough to find out for sure ... and I thought you might understand.'

'And this checkmates me ... your confession? You may be wrong.'

'I may be wrong. Ask that girl of yours, Verity Browne. I'll abide by her decision.'

'You're prepared to gamble with ...?'

170

'Yes. Ask Verity Browne and then do what you think you have to do.'

Frank's head was still a confusion of love, anxiety and annoyance. He felt he had been treated like a child, bamboozled and teased. Philly knew what he felt about her and yet she hadn't seen fit to let him in on her terrible secret.

He was thinking so hard about what he would say to her when he met her that he actually bumped into her. This was the nature of their predicament. The *Queen Mary* might be one of the largest ships afloat but, as Dr Johnson said, if one was in the wrong mood it could resemble a prison. The exercise possibilities were many and varied but if, instead of deck tennis or squash, one simply wished to walk, every ten minutes or so one would meet another passenger engaged in the same pursuit.

'Ah, Philly!' he said inanely. He wanted to make some profound remark which would reveal him to be sensitive, tactful, supportive and wise. He had been juggling with several possible opening lines as he promenaded but, in the event, all he had come up with was, 'Ah Philly!'

'Frank,' she acknowledged him demurely.

'Come and have a drink or would you rather a game of deck quoits?' Remembering why Philly might not have the energy for deck games, he rushed on, 'Or no, what about backgammon? Or shall we just sit in these chairs and go to sleep?'

'Dear Frank,' she said amiably, 'what makes you so attentive all of a sudden? By all means, let's sit here and enjoy the sun. We may not have much more of it.'

Frank began to sweat. Why was it that even her most innocent remarks – about the weather, about there not being much more sun – made him feel she was referring to her own lifespan?

'Right, here we are. I'll put this rug over your knees. Are you warm enough?'

'Quite warm enough, thank you. Now tell me, what's all this about?'

'What do you mean?'

171

'You're treating me like a sick child.'

'But that's what you are!' he burst out.

'What has Perry been telling you?' she inquired gravely.

'He said . . . he said you were sick. He said you had leukaemia. Is that true?'

'It's true but . . .'

'Oh no!' Frank's shoulders slumped and his head fell in an extravagant gesture of despair. Philly smiled sweetly at the back of his neck.

'What did he say? That I only had a few weeks to live? He's so absurd. I shall probably outlive you all. This treatment I'm having is working. I feel hardly any tiredness now and . . .'

'Philly, is there anything I can do? You know I love you. I'll do anything . . . anything.'

'You're so sweet.' She put out a delicate hand and stroked his. 'Do you really love me? I think you do.'

'I do, I do. I swear it. Please, Philly, marry me, won't you? Say you'll marry me. Say it.'

He struggled out of his chair in an effort to go down on one knee but the chairs were so close together that this was impossible.

'Of course I'll marry you, if that's what you want.'

Frank stopped wriggling and looked at her. 'You will?' He had never thought it would be so easy and it rather floored him. Unconsciously, he had been looking forward to a period of delightful melancholy ending several months later – when it was almost too late – with a 'yes'. He had not even had to ask her twice. He would not admit it but he felt . . . cheated.

'That's wonderful! We'll get married in New York or Philadelphia. Where was it you said your family lived?'

'But what about your people? Your uncle . . . your father and mother? Hadn't you better tell them first?'

Frank was outraged. He was not a child. If he wanted to marry a girl, he damn well would, even if it meant running away to Gretna Green. 'Oh, they don't matter,' he said breezily before adding more doubtfully, as a vision of his mother's face floated into his mind, 'but of course I'll tell them.'

'They'll say "What do you know about this girl?" ' Philly went on sensibly. 'For all you know, I might be penniless.'

'What would that matter? I've got oodles of money.' He

172

waved his hands about. 'I wouldn't care if you were ...
Cinderella.'

'Darling boy,' she said dreamily. 'We'll be married and live
in a castle, just like Cinderella. I'd like that.' She closed her eyes
and seemed to sleep.

Sam was following Verity around like a whipped dog. The self-
confident young man, who had wooed and won the workers
gathered round his soap box outside factory gates a couple of
weeks previously, was now a rather ludicrous figure. At least,
that was what Verity thought. He would come up to her
metaphorically wagging his tail and maybe offering her – again
metaphorically – a dead bird in tribute only to have his peace
offering brushed aside. She had principles or, if not principles,
rules about whom she would sleep with. The problem was that
she had broken the first of these rules with the second of her
two affairs. Now she had almost broken it again and slapping
Sam was the only alternative to slapping herself.

In her defence, Ben Belasco, the American writer she had
slept with in Spain, had infiltrated her defences when she was
adrift and lonely in a country whose language she did not
speak and whose politics she did not understand. Moreover, he
had made it quite clear – in the way men do – that his wife,
back in the States, accepted his infidelities. She hadn't loved
Belasco, in fact he had repelled her, but inexplicably the sex
had been beyond her imagining. This relationship had ended
before she had left Spain after the disaster of the siege of
Toledo.

With Sam it was quite different. They were on a luxury liner
and, in a day or two, he would be back in the arms of his wife
and embracing his young son. That he should want to sleep
with her was flattering and, if she were honest, when he had
suggested she should go to the States with him, she had
anticipated that they might end up lovers. But the condom
lying on the photograph of his wife and baby had effectively
doused her lust and reduced him in her eyes. He was no longer
the political fighter and all-round nice guy she had thought
him and it saddened her. He was just another lying, cheating
man. Why had she not *sensed* that he was married? Had she

just not wanted to know? He had never said he was married but, of course, a man like him *would* be married. Was she a prig and a hypocrite? Possibly, but she would not forgive herself or Sam Forrest if they had a sordid, shipboard dalliance. Or was it, she thought wryly, that he had deceived an astute, worldly-wise foreign correspondent who ought not to have been fooled so easily? How did it go? Lead us not into temptation and deliver us from making idiots of ourselves.

Having made up her mind, she summoned him and, as usual, he came to her with his tail wagging. 'Have you forgiven me? Say you aren't mad at me. I can't help . . . you know . . . admiring you. We Americans don't have women like you who go and do things without husbands and so on. We like to put them on pedestals – not make partners of them.'

'You thought I was just some slut who would sleep with anyone,' Verity said unforgivingly. 'Anyway, we're not going to talk about that any more.'

'But you are going to talk to me?' he said, his eyes shining.

'We forgot ourselves. That's all there is to it but we stopped it in time. Our political purpose is what is important. We have to be worthy of that.' Damn it, she was sounding like the worst sort of prig. 'I just mean, I've got a job to do when we get to the States and I intend to do it.'

'If I can be of any help . . .'

'Thank you,' she said grudgingly. 'You may be able to help and, of course, I should like to meet your family.'

After a moment, Sam asked, 'Do you think I killed Senator Day?'

Verity was momentarily taken aback but answered honestly. 'You had motive and opportunity but . . .' she relented, 'since you ask me, I don't think you did. You may be a ratbag but I don't see you as a murderer. Who do *you* think killed him?'

Encouraged at being asked a question to which an answer was required, he replied, 'I'd vote for that fag art dealer, Bernard Hunt. A nasty piece of work and Frank says he has a motive. He says Day stopped him getting a top job in the art world or something. He was an expert at putting spokes in wheels, that man. No wonder he was killed. Good riddance, I say.'

'Yes, Frank told me about hearing Mr Hunt's confession but

I'm not sure. It's true he could have done it but did he have the will? He seems a weak, shallow man to me.'

'They're just the sort of men who commit murder,' Sam said eagerly. 'Strong men can live with slights and setbacks but weak men are spiteful. And Frank says he wasn't there when he and Corinth were racing.'

'Nor were several prime suspects – most noticably you,' Verity responded snarkily. 'Still, I agree he's in the frame. He calls himself a Communist sympathizer but I hope the Party can do without people like him sympathizing.'

Sam risked a tease. 'That's not very democratic of you. I'd say the Party would value a man like him – over you, I mean . . . but what would I know?' he added hurriedly.

She found Edward propped against a rail, gazing gloomily out to sea. He was smoking a cigarette which, given the stiff breeze, was not a very worthwhile pastime.

'There you are!' she greeted him. 'How's the knee? Shouldn't you be lying down quietly?' He looked at her strangely, wondering if Jane Barclay was right to entrust her fate to her. 'Stop looking at me like that. Have I got a smut on my nose or something?'

'Come with me,' he said, tossing his cigarette over the side and taking up his crutch.

'Where are we going?'

'To my cabin. I have something important to discuss with you.'

'About the murder?'

'Yes.'

'Good. I think it's time we thrashed out the whys and wherefores.'

'I know the whys and wherefores,' he said grimly. 'It's the "Does she go to the gallows?" I have to talk to you about.'

When they reached the cabin, Edward threw himself down on his bed and motioned to Verity to pour him a drink. 'Something strong. I think there's scotch in the cupboard.'

'Tell!' she commanded. 'I know, let me guess: Jane Barclay has told you she killed Senator Day.'

He raised himself on his elbows. 'Good Lord! How did you guess that?'

'You mean she really has confessed? I was joking.'

Edward gave her a concise account of their conversation and ended with the comment, 'It's hardly fair but she's left it to you to decide whether we tell the police or not.'

'I don't understand.'

'She said she would abide by your decision on what I should do with her confession.'

'Oh no! That's *not* fair. It's not my problem. You decide. I'm not having anything to do with it.'

'Well, it's not quite as cut and dried as that. If I were to tell the police, when we reach New York, that Jane Barclay has confessed to murder they would almost certainly think I was off my head. Particularly if, as seems most likely, she denied telling me anything of the sort.'

'Have you thought of something else? Just because she confessed to murdering Day doesn't mean she did it. She may know – or may think she knows – that Warren did it.'

'She could be protecting him? I hadn't got round to that. Still,' he said ruminatively, 'I'm almost certain her "accident" in the steam room was self-inflicted.'

'Could she have been trying to kill herself? It's possible.'

'She doesn't look the suicide type to me, and why do it in such a complicated and public way?'

Verity tried to shift the conversation away from Jane Barclay. 'Anyway, if you think a woman did it, why not Philly Roosevelt?'

'It's so unlikely. She's too weak, physically, for one thing.'

Edward thought privately that Verity was just a little bit jealous of Frank's attachment to the girl. It wasn't, of course, that Verity had any designs on his nephew's virtue but only a few months before he had almost worshipped her. Since the Spanish escapade, his admiration had visibly cooled.

'I don't know anything except that I'm going to do absolutely nothing which might send Jane Barclay to . . . the electric chair. It's quite barbaric and I don't approve of capital punishment.'

'Except for members of the aristocracy,' he reminded her.

'Except for them, of course.'

176

'And any Nazis caught, if you will excuse the pun, red-handed.'

'Them too,' she agreed.

'And ... be honest ... you don't want anything to happen which might affect Warren Fairley ... cast a shadow over his reputation.'

'He's a great man and a member of the Party – a leading member of the Party – but that doesn't put him above the law. It's quite absurd to think for a moment he would ever be involved in anything so ... so grubby.'

'Hmm. That sounds like me talking – a bit priggish. Of course, some people are above the law. Look at Hitler and Stalin. The law will never catch up with them.'

Verity said slowly, 'I have never seen any evidence that Stalin has committed crimes and to bracket him with Hitler is ridiculous. Perhaps I mean justice – not the law. Justice will catch up with Hitler.'

'I think you've been seeing too many Westerns. Wyatt Earp isn't going to ride into town and, if he did, he would probably be shot down before he could unbutton his holster. You must have learnt that in Spain.'

'It's not like you to be so cynical,' she said with dignity. 'I would have thought, if we shared one belief, it was in justice.'

'I believe in the possibility of justice but I also believe it needs a helping hand. Well, nothing's been resolved then? I'll have to tell Jane something.'

'Tell her we have decided to leave it to her conscience. Tell her to discuss the rights and wrongs of murder with her husband,' Verity said with sudden anger. 'You remember, of course, that a wife cannot be made to testify against her husband and vice versa. At least, that's the case in England. I assume it's the same in the States.'

At that moment there was a knock on the door and Frank put his head in. 'Oh, am I interrupting something?'

'No, come in. We were just discussing the nature of justice but I think we've finished ... for the moment. What can we do for you?'

'I'll go,' Verity said.

'No,' Frank insisted, 'I'd like you to stay. You'd know soon enough anyway.'

'Know what?' Edward said sharply. 'You haven't done something silly, have you?'

'I don't think so,' the boy said, with a trace of doubt in his voice. 'I've got engaged. That's all.'

12

Edward looked at his nephew incredulously. 'You've done what?'

'I think I'd better go,' Verity said once again, starting to get up from her chair.

'No, no, please stay,' Frank beseeched her. 'Uncle Ned, I don't know why you should be upset. She's a smashing girl and she's . . . you know . . . out of the top drawer. I mean, as far as there are top drawers in the States,' he added with embarrassment.

'I assume,' Edward said frigidly, 'that you have engaged yourself to Philly Roosevelt. Let's get that clear, anyway.'

'Yes, who else would it be? I don't go around proposing to every girl I meet, dash it.'

Verity was pleased to hear the spirit come back into his voice. He had obviously decided to fight and she always approved of standing up for oneself.

'Edward, don't be such a . . . you sound just like the Duke,' she ventured.

'I'll thank you to keep out of this.' The truth was Edward had a vision of his elder brother asking him what he meant by allowing his son to be shot at and then to become engaged to a girl he had known just three days. The term *'in loco parentis'* came into his mind and his blood chilled.

Frank, too, seemed a little disturbed by Verity's mention of his father. The Duke had not been pleased when he had run away to Spain but, in deference to the feelings of his wife, he had shown commendable restraint, grateful that the boy had returned unscathed. He had not even preached at him when he

179

had refused to return to school. He had been more bewildered than angry but, when he learnt that he had engaged himself to an American girl he had met on the boat . . . Frank cleared his throat nervously.

'I don't know why you are making such a fuss, Uncle. She's a wonderful girl and I love her. She's got leukaemia and I'll have to look after her, but I'll like that.'

'Leukaemia!' Verity said in alarm.

'Yes, Uncle Ned spotted it at once. I must say I didn't, but that's partly why her skin is so transparent . . . why she looks like an angel.'

'Let's get this straight,' Edward said, trying to be sensible. 'You've asked this girl to marry you and she has said yes?'

'That's right. Why do you keep on repeating it? She's as good as gold. In fact, it was she who raised it.'

'Raised what?'

'Whether you'd make a fuss. She asked me if my people would object and, of course, I said they wouldn't. Why should they?'

'Well, for one thing, the Roosevelts aren't quite what they seem.'

'What on earth do you mean, Uncle?'

'I used this miracle of modern technology,' he said, gesturing towards the telephone beside his bed, 'to check up on your new friends when I saw how stuck on the girl you were.'

'You checked up on Philly?' Frank was aghast.

'For your own good, my boy.'

'And . . .?'

'And the father is a disgraced politician serving five years for fraud. Their name is really Ravelstein and they make a practice of conning the rich and foolish.'

'I don't believe you!'

'Ask her.'

'Are you saying Philly isn't ill?' Verity demanded.

'She probably is ill. It's sympathy which gets them the cash they need. When you try to get out of your engagement, you will be asked to part with a decent sum of money – my guess is ten thousand dollars – if you don't want to be sued for breach of promise.'

'I don't believe you. You're just trying to frighten me. Anyway, if it's true, why didn't you tell me this before?'

'I saw no reason to interfere with a harmless flirtation. It never occurred to me that you would be silly enough to get engaged to the girl. Oh, and I have a theory. While Perry, you and I were running round the deck like headless chickens, your Philly was knocking George Earle Day on the head.'

Verity wouldn't let him get away with that. 'Hang on, just a moment ago you said you didn't believe it. You said – sorry, Frank – she wouldn't have the strength.'

'Well, I've changed my mind.'

'But why?' Frank said helplessly, and Verity's heart went out to him.

'Because the all-wise, all-knowing, all-blackmailing Senator knew exactly who the Roosevelt family were and was demanding his share of the profits. And how did he know, you ask? I'll tell you. Senator Day was an old friend and political associate of their father's.'

There was silence in the cabin, which was becoming hot and stuffy with so much emotion on display.

Frank looked as though he had been hit over the head with a blackjack. 'So what am I supposed to do?' He looked around him and Verity saw he was close to tears. She put out her hand to him but he ignored her, staring wild-eyed at his uncle who remained silent. 'Damn it! I don't believe you! Hell and damnation, why should I believe you?'

'Very well, wait and see. At the dance tonight, Philly will look entrancing and she will ask you . . . or Perry will ask you . . . for money. See if I'm not right.'

'Damn you . . . both of you. You've ruined my life. I'll never trust anyone ever again.' Frank flung open the door and left them.

'Weren't you a bit hard on the boy?' Verity said.

'He's got to learn to be careful. It's the same impetuosity that made him take off to Spain with that dreadful man, John Devon. He's got to learn not to wear his heart on his sleeve.'

'God, you can be so pompous. Weren't you ever young? Weren't you ever rash? You're just a . . . a rice pudding – soggy and indigestible.'

181

As the cabin door slammed for the second time, Edward decided he had every reason to feel sorry for himself. His knee hurt like fury. His best efforts at being a good uncle had earned him nothing but abuse. Jane Barclay had set him a moral problem to which there was no right answer and he still had to deliver his charge alive and kicking in New York. A shout half-way to a scream interrupted his self-pity and he struggled to his feet. The cry had come from the next cabin. Was he now to have Lord Benyon slaughtered by some Fascist madman virtually in front of his eyes? He cursed and cursed again.

'Sorry, Corinth, did I wake you?' Marcus Fern said. 'I managed to drop this briefcase on my foot. I don't know why it's so heavy.' He was alone in the cabin, sitting at the writing-desk working on some papers.

'I wasn't asleep,' Edward said shortly. 'I was just resting my knee. Here, let me give you a hand with that.' He leant over to help Fern lift the bag, which was lying on its side on the floor. As he did so he stumbled and nearly fell, pulling the bag violently as he tried to support himself against the wall. 'No damage done,' he began and then stopped. As he took a proper hold on the briefcase, a black object fell heavily to the floor. It was a .38 automatic.

Edward looked at Fern inquiringly. 'It's mine,' he acknowledged. 'I thought, if there was any trouble . . .'

'But I remember asking, after Barrett was killed, if anyone had a gun and only Sam Forrest said he had. Why didn't you declare it then?'

'I didn't think it was a good idea, that's all,' Fern said stiffly. 'How was I to know if one of the people in the cabin then might not be . . . you know . . . in the employ of the enemy?'

'You didn't think I was?'

'No, but I knew very little about you. As for Sam Forrest – who, as you say, was armed – what little I knew about him I didn't like at all. I thought you were far too ready to trust an American rabble-rousing union organizer with the safety of a government representative. There was no reason to trust you or your judgement. Forgive me for being frank but, in my business, I trust no one. Perhaps you think that odd but the

City is by no means the league of gentlemen some people think it is. Or, if it is, it excludes scholarship boys. I had a hard struggle to get where I am and I didn't get here by trusting people.'

'Doesn't that make for a lonely life? I'm sorry, I didn't mean to be rude.'

'I made a few enemies on the way but the friends I have made are not casual acquaintances. They've been tried and tested.'

'But surely you've never needed a gun? I can't believe that's the way business rivals fight their battles.'

'No, but when I knew I was to accompany Lord Benyon on this trip, I thought it wise to bring a weapon with me. Was that wrong?'

'No,' Edward said slowly, 'but I wish you had told me. Where did you get it, if I may ask?'

'I bought it last time I was in the States.'

'And you can use it?'

'I took a few lessons, yes. Now, if you'll forgive me, Corinth, I must get this finished before we reach New York. I gather that'll be about 3 p.m. tomorrow?'

'I think so.'

'The storm did not delay us as much as the Captain feared?'

'No. Will you be attending the fancy-dress ball tonight?'

'I hope to. Benyon says we ought to enjoy our last night on board before the rigours of our New York schedule.'

'Where is he, by the way?'

'I believe your man Fenton has taken him for a constitutional on the promenade deck. Good man, Fenton. You're lucky to have him. I can't be bothered with a valet myself but, I confess, sometimes it would be useful. I know Benyon means to ask you if he can take him – Fenton, I mean – as his valet while he's in the States. Without Barrett . . . I suppose he could hire someone in New York but we haven't really got time to interview servants and, anyway, could one trust a stranger?'

'Yes, well, of course,' Edward said, rather taken aback. 'It's up to Fenton. I know my duty,' he added with an attempt at jocularity.

As he passed through the smoking-room, he saw Bernard Hunt and Doris Zinkeisen huddled together in a corner deep in conversation. There was no one else in the room and they did not see him. Hunt was speaking in low tones but Doris Zinkeisen's shrill voice was audible across the room. Edward heard her say, 'I don't understand. It ought to have been done by now. He said there would be no difficulty but you know what . . .'

Not wishing to be an eavesdropper, he left the room but wondered idly if they had been discussing the repair of her mural. They were so earnest, however, he was inclined to think it was something more important, but what he could not guess.

He found Benyon walking on the promenade deck with Fenton a respectful two paces behind him. Benyon was in high spirits. 'I can hardly believe tomorrow we shall be on dry land. I have to say this voyage was more of an ordeal than I had anticipated. Poor Barrett and then that terrible storm. I wonder if I shall ever fully recover,' he added a little petulantly. 'Really, this trip – no offence to you, my dear boy – has been a nightmare.'

'I gather from Fern that you are planning to attend the fancy-dress ball tonight?'

'Do you know, I thought I might.' He sounded like a naughty child. 'I've always had a penchant for fancy dress. Let me tell you a story – in confidence, please! When I was an undergraduate, two or three friends of mine carried out the most joyful hoax. We dressed one of our number – I won't give you his name because he's now a distinguished government servant – in a toga, a turban and a false beard and we inspected the fleet.'

'You did what?' Edward exclaimed.

'I rang up the admiral at Spithead – who was a family friend as it happened – and pretended I was speaking from the Admiralty. I said the King of Bongo-Bongo Land was coming down to inspect the fleet and could he be shown over a battleship.'

'He didn't recognize your voice?'

'Not at all. It was a terrific lark. The whole thing went quite smoothly and we were greeted by the captain of the . . . of one of our great battleships and shown over with full honours. There was even a gun salute.'

'And you were never found out?'

'Never. Or rather, I think the truth did percolate through eventually but the Navy never said anything. They would have looked the most frightful asses if they had. It's a weakness of mine but I love hoaxes. There must be something irredeemably juvenile hidden inside this old body of mine.'

After lunch the sun came out and, though there was a cold wind, the First Class passengers seemed determined to make the best of what remained of their time on the *Queen Mary*. The promenade deck was a pleasant compromise between being inside and out. Protective screens, pierced by a number of vertically sliding windows, allowed passengers such as Lord Benyon, who were not particularly robust, to take their exercise without being exposed to the elements. The sun deck, immediately above the promenade deck, was also the lifeboat deck but the lifeboats were carried high up on davits so passengers could lean over the rails along the length of it. The after-end was used for a variety of deck games and it was there Edward encountered his nephew.

He was concerned that – as Verity had said – he had been too hard on the boy. From guilt above all, he had, he now thought, been too quick to dampen Frank's romantic attachment. He feared he might have humiliated his nephew which had not been his intention. He saw his role as that of a constitutional monarch – to warn and advise – but felt he should have found a gentler way of telling Frank that he had been taken for a ride. No one likes to think they have been made a fool of so he was relieved, if rather surprised, to find him playing an energetic game of tennis with Perry. Philly watched from the sidelines, looking fetchingly gracile in an outfit he had not seen before. The family might not be wealthy but they certainly dressed well. The mother, too, was there. Free, for once, from one of her headaches, she was sitting in a cane chair reading *Vogue* and watching her son.

Edward came up beside her and lifted his hat – a yachting cap he had bought on impulse in the Army and Navy while purchasing a new trunk for the voyage, the day before he left

London. Fenton had made it quite clear, without actually putting it into words, that he did not approve of the cap but Edward thought it made him look rather dashing.

'I say, good to see you are fully recovered, Mrs ... Mrs Roosevelt. Do you mind if I sit myself down here beside you?'

'Of course not, Lord Edward. I wanted to speak to you in any case. Isn't your nephew doing well? Perry thinks of himself as a good tennis player but Frank is beating him with ease.'

For a moment or two they sat in silence watching the two handsome young men display their prowess.

'I think my nephew is very taken with your daughter,' he ventured. 'She is delightful so I am not in the least surprised. I hope Frank isn't making a nuisance of himself. At his age, I know I was falling in and out of love like a yo-yo.'

Mrs Roosevelt turned to look at him and Edward found himself gazing into steady, grey eyes, by no means those of a neurasthenic and valetudinarian. He saw that she must have been a beauty when she was younger.

'I think you know, Lord Edward, that my name is not Roosevelt but Ravelstein. It's an odd conceit which you may find reprehensible but, wishing to distance myself from my husband, I chose to assume my maiden name.'

'I see,' Edward said awkwardly. 'Might I ask if you are divorced? Forgive me. That's impertinent.'

'Not yet. I decided to wait until my husband has completed his term of imprisonment and then decide what to do. I cannot forgive him for the shame he brought on the children and me but maybe I still love him. Time will tell. In any case, it is not in my nature to kick a man when he's down – isn't that the expression? Did you hear about my husband from that dreadful man Senator Day?'

'No, not from him,' Edward said, even more awkwardly. He did not want to admit that he had learnt her history from Major Ferguson. Fortunately she did not pursue the matter except to say, 'He was a horrible man and, I'm sorry to say, an associate of my husband's. Well, more than that, a friend of the family – or so we thought. When I found out he was on board, I'm afraid it brought on one of my migraines. I don't know why I should be so stupid but I could not bear the idea that I and my family should be the subject of gossip.'

'Of course not. And, if I might ask, did he try to . . .?'

'Blackmail me? Not overtly. He was, I think, otherwise engaged and I doubt he would have liked it to be common knowledge that his former business partner was serving a gaol sentence. He gave me the occasional "look", you understand?'

' "Meaning 'Well, well, we know', or, 'We could, an if we would'," that sort of thing?'

'I see you love *Hamlet* too,' she said with a smile. 'He certainly was a "smiling, damned villain".'

Edward was impressed, not just that she knew her Shakespeare but that she could talk so honestly about her predicament.

'Did you know his wife?' he asked.

'Not at all. He married after . . . after my husband and he had ceased to be friends.'

'But she must have known who you were.'

'I don't think so, unless he told her and I rather doubt that. I would guess he kept his business to himself.'

'What of my nephew and your daughter?' he risked. 'Do you think there is anything in it?'

'My daughter is not well. I have taken her to a good many doctors – that is, in fact, why we have been in London – but none of them can put forward a convincing diagnosis. The last one we saw – I mean the last one in New York, a Dr Barnes – said she was suffering from leukaemia and prescribed a course of arsenic trioxide but I don't know. The Harley Street consultant disagrees. To be honest, I don't think any of them know what they are talking about.'

'It must be very distressing for you.'

'What do I matter?' she said vehemently.

'She's very beautiful . . . Philly. She must have many admirers.'

'She has and she flirts abominably but I really believe she's not seriously interested in any of them. If she loves any man, it's Perry but she can't marry him.'

'Do you think she cares for my nephew?'

'As far as she can. He's been very kind to her and he's so good-looking. And of course,' she looked at him challengingly, 'he's the son of a duke. Even in our own disreputable age that goes for something.'

'I suppose it does, but you know Frank's a Communist?'

'That's part of his appeal, of course. To have a great position in society and not appear to value it . . . it's difficult for lesser mortals to resist.'

'Frank tells me he has engaged himself to Philly.'

'And you don't approve?'

'She is a very beautiful girl but . . .'

'But . . .?'

'They've known each other such a very short time. I wonder if it's wise. What do you think?'

'My dear Lord Edward, are you saying, as tactfully as you know how, that my daughter isn't good enough for your nephew?'

Remembering his own 'unsuitable' attachment to Verity Browne, Edward could hardly say that.

'No, of course not. She's a lovely girl . . . enchanting. I just want them to know their own minds. There is something about being closeted together on a great ship which can make us feel very intensely. The real world may make that intensity difficult to sustain.'

There was a pause and, once again, Edward was subjected to a long, cool gaze from those beautiful grey eyes. She seemed satisfied by what she saw. She said at last, 'I'll talk to my daughter, Lord Edward, and see how far this has gone. She's certainly not said anything to me about an engagement. Perhaps Frank misunderstood something she said.'

Edward touched his hat and left her, feeling that he had done all he could to put a brake on the affair without anyone losing face. He couldn't make his mind up as to how genuine the Roosevelt family were. They might be confidence tricksters, as Ferguson had hinted, or they might just be what they seemed – restless, rootless, *déraciné* Americans trying to find a place in the world under the shadow of the father's disgrace and the daughter's illness. Having talked to the mother, he was inclined to give them the benefit of the doubt.

For the rest of the afternoon, until it was time to prepare for the fancy-dress ball, he sat on a long chair beside Lord Benyon. He admired his industry and began to understand why he was so successful. Brilliance on its own is not enough. Persistence, hard graft and attention to detail are equally important.

188

Edward tried to read but, to his annoyance, kept dozing off. Whether it was the strain of the past few days or just being in this sea-borne hotel with nothing to do but watch and wait, he was lethargic and low-spirited. He thought he understood how the disciples must have felt when they fell asleep on the Mount of Olives having been told to watch and pray. He reprimanded himself for being flippant and, in an effort to wake himself up, limped over to one of the open windows and leant out to watch the sea and feel the wind on his face.

Despite everything that had happened, the passengers were determined to enjoy themselves on this, their last night at sea. There was an edge of hysteria to the excitement as they discussed their costumes and paraded in front of mirrors and their friends – like children preparing for a birthday party. In addition to the dance, there were to be prizes for the best costumes, games and entertainments and, of course, a banquet. The Purser was very aware that, as a result of the storm, many passengers felt cheated of the food and drink they had planned to consume at the Company's expense and were determined to make up for it.

All the public rooms – with the exception of the library, which was reserved for those few killjoys who wanted no part in the festivities – had been prepared for the feasting and dancing. The centrepiece was to be the great restaurant decorated with bunting, balloons and huge arrangements of flowers – though how these had survived three days at sea and rough weather Edward had no idea – and the lounge, now glittering with ice sculptures and 'starlit' under a canopy of tiny lights which blinked perpetually against the darkness. On the stage during and after dinner they would be entertained by celebrated artistes such as the magician, Jasper Maskelyne, and it was rumoured that Warren Fairley had agreed to sing Negro spirituals. This was where Henry Hall, who, on the wireless, had delighted the nation conducting the BBC Dance Orchestra, now conducted a band of some of the top instrumentalists from Britain and America, including the pianist Eddie Carrol. Several hundred couples could dance to the music without being forced to step on each other's toes. There was also dancing in the

Verandah Grill, to a piano, and plenty of places for couples to sit out the dancing. The cocktail lounge, the smoking-room and several smaller salons presented opportunities for secret amours and last-minute trysts.

It was this element which worried Edward. Benyon was determined to enjoy his last evening aboard the *Queen Mary*. He had, when not ill in bed, worked almost the whole time and had decided he had earned a few hours' relaxation before beginning his arduous round of lectures and meetings in New York and Washington. He would insist on having one dance with Verity but, in the main, his idea was to watch the young people enjoy themselves, smoke a few cigars and sample the excellent brandy.

'*Nuit d'épouvante et de plaisir, nuit de vertus et de crimes!*' he intoned, jocularly. 'I have always adored a *bal costumé*!'

'Well,' Edward said grimly, 'I wouldn't be surprised if it weren't a night of horror and crime, as you say.'

'And pleasure, Lord Edward,' Benyon chided him. 'Don't forget pleasure.'

How, Edward asked himself, was he to keep an eye on Benyon and distinguish friend from foe among the masked revellers? He had no wish to imprison his charge but he had to be protected.

He summoned a meeting of his little army in his cabin and divided the evening up into watches beginning at seven o'clock. Verity would take the first hour, he would take the next, then Fern, Sam Forrest and, finally, Fenton. If, by midnight, Benyon still had not gone to bed, Edward promised himself he would escort him to his cabin and, if he had to, lock the door after him.

The shops in the main hall were doing a roaring trade and Verity had splashed out on a bizarre head-dress which the shopkeeper had informed her was 'Brazilian'. It was a riot of yellow feathers and coloured beads. Edward said it looked as if a chicken had died on her head and been curried.

'And what do you wear with that?' he had asked.

'Not much,' she had answered cheerfully. 'Wait and see. It will be the most exciting thing you'll have to look at the whole evening.'

'I very much hope so. I would like a dance – or rather a hobble with you. Can I book a waltz or something slow?'

'No fear. You would be a liability. Oh well,' she said, seeing his face fall, 'I suppose I'll let you but . . .'

'I know, you will be keeping the foxtrots and the quicksteps for Frank and Sam.'

'I've made a few other friends on this trip, you know,' she replied tartly. 'Anyway, phooey to foxtrots and quicksteps. I'll be dancing charlestons and sambas . . . Have you seen me tango?'

'I've not had that pleasure but I would like to see you do . . . what's that other one? . . . the Chicken Walk, or do I mean the Bunny Hug?'

'If you mean the Turkey Trot, you won't see me do that – or not until I'm completely stonkered. And don't pretend you're an old man. Frank says he saw you skipping like the high hills the last dance they held at Mersham.'

'That was ten years ago,' Edward said gloomily, 'before I was a cripple.'

'Oh God, spare me the self-pity! Frank's promised to teach me the Lindy Hop – you know, because Lindbergh flew across the Atlantic? He says it's all the rage.'

'Huh!' was Edward's response. He wished he wasn't feeling so morose. He didn't want to be a wet blanket but he could not help dreading the evening ahead.

13

On the map on the dining-room wall, the model *Queen Mary* was shown within a few inches of New York. The Atlantic crossing was almost over and this fact appeared to induce a fever among the passengers so soon to disembark. The dancing before dinner was staid and respectable. Even the costumes, exotic as some of them were, had not yet released the carnival spirit in their wearers but there was a palpable tension in the air as if some signal was awaited.

Benyon, a sheet wrapped over his dress trousers and wearing a turban from the Purser's dressing-up box – he claimed to be Aladdin's uncle and financial adviser – presided over a large table at one end of the room. He had invited the Roosevelts to join them. 'We must have some feminine company,' he had insisted. Frank, seeming not to have heeded his uncle's warning, was sitting next to Philly. Or rather, they sat the way lovers sit – almost on top of one another, excluding everyone else and feeding each other titbits from a single fork. Perry, continually shooting covert glances at his sister and her lover, exhibited a desperate gaiety, and drank too much right from the start. He clearly welcomed the end of the voyage, whether because he hoped to have Philly to himself again or just because he was bored. Despite his laughter and frenetic chatter, Edward could not mistake the boy's deep-seated melancholy and found an echo of it in himself.

Perry was sitting next to Jane Barclay and they flirted amiably with Warren seeming quite unconcerned. He was next to Verity and on her other side was Sam who appeared to have recovered his spirits. Verity, on a whim, had abandoned her

'Brazilian' head-dress and had borrowed a dinner jacket from Benyon who was not very much bigger than she was. Edward thought her outfit adorable. He told her she looked like Vesta Tilley but Verity had never heard of her. When, rather laboriously, he explained she had been a music-hall artiste with a penchant for dressing up as a man, Verity borrowed Fern's monocle to complete the effect. When she kissed him unexpectedly, Edward was *bouleversé* and the blood came into his face. To be kissed by a boy, and to know it was Verity, was just too confusing in his current emotional state.

He noted, with a distinct feeling of satisfaction of which he was rather ashamed, that her attitude to Sam was subtly different. She no longer watched him with spaniel eyes but treated him as a friend and professional colleague, nothing more. When, forgetting himself, he attempted to flirt with her in the old way, he was treated to a glance of amused contempt which made him turn away in confusion. When he pontificated about 'working-class values' and 'international socialism', she seemed not to mind but did not respond with the enthusiasm she would have displayed twenty-four hours earlier. In the end, Sam transferred his attentions to Jane Barclay and joined Perry in chaffing her. She took obvious pleasure in being ragged by the two good-looking boys and the tension in her face eased. At first, she parried their teasing with sharp little asides but gradually lost the air of the hardened Hollywood actress she had spent so long cultivating and revealed the innocent, Nebraskan farm girl which, had she not been 'spotted' by some talent scout, she might so easily have remained.

Edward sat rather uncomfortably on a little gilt chair, his leg stretched out in front of him on another, and chatted with Mrs Roosevelt about foreign parts. She seemed to have been everywhere. She knew South America well – 'my husband's business interests', she explained laconically – but had never been to Africa and listened with commendable patience to Edward's stories of big-game hunting – of which, in truth, he had done very little – and of flying a little wood-and-canvas plane over the veldt.

'To be honest with you, Mrs Roosevelt, I don't call this travelling at all. Being cooped up in a luxury hotel for four nights can't compare with climbing in the Drakensberg with a gale blowing or flying across the desert in the knowledge that, if your engine conks out, you're a goner.'

She was really charming, he found himself thinking. She asked him to call her Madeleine and he found himself blushing. The charm of these people – it was as stupefying as incense! It was partly their costumes. Where had Philly found that Pierrette costume and – inevitably – Perry that Pierrot mask and pointed hat? He had made up his face with the sad, white contours of a clown and the little black mask completed the picture. As Edward looked about him, he noticed that there were several other Pierrots and Pierrettes and he came to the conclusion that seasoned travellers on the great liners brought outfits with them in anticipation of the ball on the last night. He himself had not dressed up, using his leg as an excuse, but now rather regretted it.

Despite the streamers, the champagne, the balloons and the fountain playing at one end of the room with Henry Hall playing at the other, the time seemed to drag. Edward was glad when dinner was announced and the band rested in favour of a pianist. The food was excellent: smoked salmon, then lobster or sole, followed by beef Wellington. How they had kept the lobster so fresh he had no idea. When the Purser came up, he told them, with a hand to his mouth, that if the lobsters were not eaten that night they would all have to be jettisoned – 'all eight hundred,' he added impressively.

Edward felt rather 'out of it' not dancing. He would have given anything to have taken to the floor with Verity who proved to be a surprisingly good dancer. Despite her talk of the Lindy Hop and the Turkey Trot, he had somehow imagined she would consider dancing to be a 'bourgeois' activity but, along with reading the Communist Manifesto, it must after all have been part of her extra-curricular activities. He had, in fact, danced with her once before, at a nightclub in London but, at the time, he had had other things on his mind than admiring her skill as a dancing partner. It was disconcerting to see her in Benyon's dinner jacket clasped to its turban-wearing owner. They were not dancing cheek to cheek, he was glad to note, but he itched to barge in between them and claim her for himself. He had never thought of Benyon as being physically attractive to the opposite sex but Verity seemed to be enjoying herself.

Perry and Philly were dancing together and, when Sam got up with Mrs Roosevelt, he was left alone with Fern. Dressed in breeches and a black cloak, his red hair flaming above his head, gave him a wild look but this was misleading. Fern would always have his wits about him.

'So, who do you think killed Senator Day?' Fern began without excuse or preamble.

'Oh, do we have to discuss that?' Edward replied, a touch irritably.

'I'm just curious, don't y'know. I had an idea you thought it might be me.'

'You're right, I did.' The pain in his knee made him speak bluntly. 'You had the opportunity and you were the last person to see him alive.'

'And what made you change your mind? That is, if you did change your mind.'

'You're too clever to be found with a corpse – if you had actually committed the murder.'

'That could have been a bluff.'

'Maybe. I certainly think you are ruthless enough.'

'Thank you!'

'You were at pains to tell me of the struggle you had to get where you are. However, when I met you down at the swimming-bath just after you had found Day, I was convinced by your description of finding the body: the green tie making the green line on the bottom of the bath look squiffy – that rang true.'

'Thank you again.'

'And you had no motive. The problem with Day is that too many people had a motive to kill him. To pick on someone who had no known motive seemed perverse.' Verity swung into view dancing a polka with Sam Forrest. 'Take Sam, for instance. Nice fresh young man but he had a motive. Day made an attempt to blackmail him ... pressure him into helping in some business venture.'

'I can't imagine that young man had much to be blackmailed about.'

'Oh, nothing serious – just girl trouble,' Edward said airily, wishing now that he had not mentioned it. 'You won't say anything about it, will you ... to him, I mean?'

'Of course not. So I gather you don't think he murdered Day either?'

'Like you, he had the opportunity. This blackmail attempt happened just before Day was killed – while we were racing round the deck, damn it!' Edward lifted his leg into a more comfortable position.

'When you fell over?' Fern asked innocently.

'When I slipped, yes. My knee's still dodgy after a car accident I had some time back.'

'But you don't suspect Sam of murder?'

'Of getting away with murder, I do,' Edward said grimly, watching him press Verity close to him as the polka became a waltz.

'Seriously?'

'Not seriously, no, otherwise I would hardly let him help guard our friend Benyon. Mind you, he doesn't seem to require much guarding at the moment.'

Benyon was proving to be an agile and graceful dancer and his new partner, Madeleine Roosevelt, obviously took pleasure in his company.

'But you think the man who murdered Barrett also murdered Senator Day and may try to harm Benyon?' Fern persisted.

'No, I'm pretty sure I know who killed Barrett. But, yes, he's still looking for a chance to stop Benyon fulfilling his mission.'

'Well then, why not arrest him?'

'I don't have the evidence, nor the authority. Benyon's well guarded now,' he said comfortably. 'I don't think he'll try anything tonight but, if he does, we are ready for him. When we get to New York ... if we ever do! – this trip seems to have been going on for weeks – then I'll hand him over to the police and see what they can do.'

'And the Senator's murder has nothing to do with the threat to Benyon?'

'I'm sure of it. In fact, I think I know who ... Verity, come and sit by me. Sam's had too much of you. I need attention. I'm an invalid, don't forget.'

Verity and Sam fell into their seats, breathing heavily after their exertions and calling for champagne.

'Look at Fairley and his wife. Don't they look ... exotic?' Fern said.

The flaxen-haired girl in a highly revealing dress – Salome, she had told Edward – looked as if she might be crushed in the embrace of her husband. He was wearing one of his Othello costumes. 'It's a part I play so often – type-casting, you may call it – that I tend to use my own costumes unless the director has very strong views. They certainly don't fit anyone else!' He was a magnificent figure in a soldier's short kirtle, a scarlet cloak slung over his shoulders. His powerful legs and arms glistened under greaves and he wore gold bracelets which lent a barbaric air to the whole.

After the waiters had cleared away the food, there was a mass invasion of the dance floor and Edward lost sight of all his table companions except for Warren Fairley who could never be lost in a crowd. He was now dancing with Verity. From his vantage point, Edward was in a perfect position to contemplate the festivities which now had something of a carnival air. As the Purser had been telling him earlier, fancy dress was both liberating and intoxicating. In a Pierrot costume or a toga, you were no longer yourself and if, for a moment or two at the beginning of the party, you felt faintly ridiculous there were always other people in even more absurd costumes. And the drink ... the champagne! How it lifted the spirits and, though the real world might take its revenge the following morning, who but a temperance man would think to remind you of it?

As a waiter refilled his glass for the third time, Edward thought he recognized Philly – but it might have been Perry. The twins were so alike and, in their Pierrot and Pierrette costumes, almost indistinguishable. They appeared to relish the confusion over their identities. Such charm! Was it a curse or a blessing? He sighed. Why was it he felt quite sure the Senator's murderer was someone he knew – rather than one of the other swirling figures whom he had not met? There were seven hundred First Class passengers and any one of these – in theory at least – might have done the deed. And then there was the crew. Was the Purser a murderer? He had every opportunity. There was nowhere on the ship he couldn't go, but no ... it was too absurd. And the Captain? He smiled to himself. No doubt the poor man felt like murdering someone but who could be more respectable . . . more like an archbishop than the captain of this great ship.

'What are you smiling about?'

Fern had dropped back on to the gilt chair beside him, his red hair now partially hidden under a sombrero.

'Fern, is that you behind that mask?'

'It is indeed,' he said a trifle breathlessly. 'I am Zapata, who I am led to believe by your nephew was a Mexican bandit.'

'He led the Indian *pueblos* in their fight to regain their ancestral lands.'

'That's what I said, a bandit. I suppose he died with a sword in his hand? I had to leave my sword in my cabin. I kept on tripping over it.'

'As far as I remember, Zapata was murdered by a man he considered a friend but I may be wrong. I'm sure he had a sword in his hand though. But that cape, Fern, it must have had an effect on you. Didn't I see you dance the fandango with a rather beautiful gypsy girl?'

'Ah, yes, a fandango? It might have been a fandango. It certainly left me a bit puffed.'

'What was her name?'

'Whose?'

'The gypsy's.'

'Oh, I couldn't tell you. It's not the sort of thing you ask a gypsy in mid-fandango. You know, Corinth, I thought I saw Barrett across the dance floor.'

'But Barrett's dead.'

'I know he's dead, old man, but all the same . . .'

'Where did you think you saw him?'

'Over there, by that huge vase of flowers.'

'It must have been your imagination, but what say we go over and look?'

'Oh, I very much doubt he would still be there.'

'Why didn't you go after him?' Edward said, getting to his feet with some difficulty.

'I told you, I was dancing. I don't dance often. In fact, I can't think when I last did dance but dash it – I think I'm rather good at it.'

198

They walked across the room, buffeted by dancers. Edward almost howled after one bruising encounter and he wasn't mollified when he discovered it was Verity who had kicked him.

'Edward! Gosh, sorry! Oughtn't you to be in a chair? This is too rough for you.'

He gritted his teeth and said nothing. They got right across the room without seeing anyone who might be Barrett. Edward was just beginning to wonder how he would ever get back to his table when Fern took him by the arm. 'Look! There, in the corner.'

A man was slouched in a chair, very drunk or deaf because, when Fern called to him, he took no notice. His back was towards them but there was something about the jacket . . . Edward hopped over and almost overbalanced as he laid his hand on the man's shoulder. For a second he thought he must be dead. They were definitely Barrett's clothes – the jacket, the Leander tie, the shirt even – but it wasn't Barrett.

'I say, I say . . . look here, whaty'doing?'

'I'm so sorry,' Fern said. 'We thought you were a friend of ours, a man called Tom Barrett. Do you know him, by any chance?'

The man had a walrus moustache, was aged about seventy and was puce in the face. He was very drunk and it looked as though that was his normal condition.

'Barrett? Barrett? Never heard of him. Is this some sort of practical joke?'

'I say,' Edward put on his silly-ass voice, 'dashed sorry and all that but you couldn't tell me where you got those clothes, could you? It's a regimental tie, isn't it? I can't for the life of me think which regiment though? The Guards, d'y'think? No, not the Guards.'

'I've no idea what the fellow's talking about,' the old buffer said querulously. 'I got these togs from the Purser's dressing-up box, if you must know. Now clear off, will you. I need a drink.'

'Of course, of course, sir. May I know your name, so I can stand you a drink tomorrow?'

'No, you bloody well can't. Now go away or I'll call . . . I'll call the Captain.'

Fern and Edward threaded their way back across the room. When they were seated again, Fern said, 'What do you think of that? Looked as though he was telling the truth . . . about where he'd got the clothes. Do you think the Purser murdered Barrett?'

'Don't be an ass, Fern. It was just a place to hide the clothes – and a damn good place.'

'Why not toss them overboard?'

'Might have been seen. This was much more innocent. If he'd been spotted, he could easily have made up some excuse. The dressing-up chest is kept in the Purser's office. People in and out all the time and no reason to lock it up.'

Fern was disappointed. 'So we're no further on then?'

'Oh yes, we're further on,' Edward said but refused to elaborate.

The stage darkened and then into a spotlight walked the Purser who announced that, while Henry Hall and his band took a break, they were to be entertained by, as he put it, 'stars from London's glittering West End'.

This meant, to begin with, an energetic top-hatted and white-tied duo of tap dancers who modelled themselves on Ginger Rogers and Fred Astaire. What they lacked in elegance they made up for in energy and the girl had a figure which drew wolf-whistles from certain of the diners who were, as Sam said, 'tanked up'. When they withdrew to a good hand they were replaced by the magician, Jasper Maskelyne. Looking every inch the matinée idol in top hat and tails, he embarked on a series of tricks and illusions which soon had the attention of even the rowdiest of the diners. Edward had heard Maskelyne's name but never seen his act and was curious to find out how much of a charlatan the man really was.

He certainly had an air about him and he began with a fast-flowing series of traditional tricks which he performed with visible irony as if to say, 'Isn't this what you expect me to do?', ending with the inevitable white rabbit drawn from his top hat. But after the rabbit, he seemed to surprise himself by finding in the hat a whole host of objects from a flat iron to a ladder and ending, once again, with a white rabbit and a seemingly endless rope of flags. He never spoke a word but his face was mobile and expressive. As the final white rabbit hopped off the stage, he gave an exaggerated yawn and looked first to one side of the stage and then the other, as if for help. He beckoned to a couple dressed, Edward guessed, as Antony and Cleopatra, sitting at a table by the stage and invited them to come up to him. At first reluctant, at the urging of their friends they climbed on to the stage and stood beside Maskelyne. Edward had no idea if these were genuine passengers or the magician's assistants but, if the latter, they played their parts convincingly.

Edward watched as Maskelyne brought out a massive saw and heard a groan beside him. It was Verity.

'Typical male hatred of the female. Watch, if you can bear it. He's going to cut her in half.' As if he had heard her, Maskelyne looked at his saw with displeasure and crushed it between his hands, as if it were a concertina, reducing it to a paper chain. The girl looked relieved but then anxious as he placed her on a bed and offered her male friend a hoop which he seemed to be urging him to encircle the bed. Since the bed was on a plinth, this was clearly impossible. Maskelyne looked annoyed and, taking the hoop from the young man, passed it without any difficulty over the girl as if she had gone through a tunnel.

The audience gasped and the young man once again took the hoop and once again failed to pass it round the girl and the plinth. Maskelyne took the hoop back and, instead of using it himself, rolled it into the wings. Then, passing his cape in front of the girl on the bed, he gradually raised it as if he were taking off a mask or lifting a curtain. As he did so, the bed with the girl on it rose slowly from the plinth and hovered above the stage. Verity grasped Edward's hand and everyone in the room watched in silent amazement as the magician twisted the bed in the air and guided it around the stage before lowering it gently back on the plinth. He helped the young woman up and seeming, naturally enough, rather dazed she and the young man took a bow. The applause was considerable but there was an unease in it. They had been tricked – of course they had been tricked – but what was the nature of the trick? Where were the wires? Where were the pulleys which must have raised the bed?

'Golly,' Verity said, 'that *was* magic! How did he do it? You always have an explanation for everything, Edward. You explain.'

'I'm afraid I can't. I remember one man I knew – a member of the American Magic Circle – talking about "misdirection".'

'Misdirection? What's that?'

'Well, basically, you make the audience look one way while what's really happening goes on somewhere else.'

'What?'

'I don't know, V. I just mean it's an illusion. You have to be made to think something's happening even when you know, rationally, it can't be.'

'Thanks for nothing,' Verity said. 'Come on, Sam, give me some more champagne. Oh look, it's Warren!'

Warren Fairley was climbing on to the stage to be greeted by a wave of applause. He held up his hand and there was silence almost immediately.

'I hadn't intended to sing tonight. My songs can be a little sad for a night like this when we are all enjoying ourselves and looking forward to docking in New York tomorrow.'

There were cries of 'No' and 'We're staying put.'

'However, we mustn't forget that two men have died on the *Queen Mary* during this voyage. One was a man I did not know but I believe to have been honourable and a friend to justice. The other was no friend of mine and an enemy to the cause of racial equality.' There was an uneasy murmur and Edward had a horrible feeling in the pit of his stomach that there might be some unpleasant barracking from some of the younger and drunker partygoers who might think they were being lectured. But the moment passed and Warren, pulling himself up to his full height, went on, 'But, friend or enemy, I do not condone violence. I have seen too much of it and I know that hate and violence only breed hate and violence so, for these two men, I offer up this.'

He had no use for the microphone which stood at one corner of the stage. Quite alone in a single spotlight, with no accompaniment of any kind, he began to sing. For Verity it was the most moving thirty minutes of her life and, when she looked at Edward, he saw tears were streaming down her face. She was weeping for herself as much as for anyone else. He touched her hand and she held on to his. They could not take

202

their eyes off this man who had suffered so much for justice and whose vision of a righteous world never failed, even when there was no possible reason for hope. Here was a man who had outfaced disaster and the murmur of his audience, low and respectful, seemed to acknowledge this.

He sang, almost without a break, the Negro spirituals with which he had first come to fame. These songs of pain and regret, faith in the Lord, and stoic endurance of suffering were powerful enough. Verity was not alone in finding her face wet with tears and Edward felt his heart swell with anger at these poignant reminders of man's inhumanity to man. He knew that Fairley was singing for all the dispossessed, not just black Americans. He was remembering the itinerant white fruit pickers starving in California amongst so much wealth; the women and children of Spain living in the rubble of what had once been their homes, and the Jews and Communists rotting in German prison camps.

Finally, he told his audience, he was going to sing for them a song written for the Federal Theater Project. He explained that this was a government-sponsored organization with which he had been involved since it was founded two years before. It operated throughout the States employing actors and actresses, writers and stage staff, who had been without work for some time. They performed in disused theatres, barns and tents or in the open air. They reached audiences who had never had a chance of seeing theatre before and were therefore viewed as subversive by many men of substance, particularly politicians. Some of the plays they performed raised issues of economic and social injustice and, unsurprisingly, Senator Day had been one of those demanding the Project be suppressed.

'I am going to sing you one of their songs, called "Ballad for Americans". It says what I believe about America.'

He stretched himself, as though summoning up all his forces, and began – his voice at first sweet and low but gradually gathering power until the whole room, huge as it was, seemed to reverberate. The words were simple enough: a list of all the races and religions which made up America – Irish, Negro, Jew, Italian, French, English, Spanish and Chinese. Then came a list of the wide range of religions and beliefs held by these far-flung people – Baptist, Methodist, Catholic, Mormon,

Quaker, Jew and so many more. When the ballad came to its rousing finish, the whole audience rose to its feet to applaud both the singer and the sentiments.

It hadn't needed anyone to point out that the *Queen Mary* was a microcosm of the world – a hundred races and creeds – all hoping for something from the New World which the Old World could not give them. At last Edward was able to disagree with Dr Johnson: the ship was not a prison, nor yet a slaughterhouse. It was a frail vessel of hope, a message in a bottle tossed into the sea, one day to find its answer. They had all weathered storms and dangerous seas to reach their goal and Fairley had made them feel their lives were not worthless – mere bric-à-brac tossed hither and thither at the mercy of a cruel wind – but had meaning and value.

The Purser hurried on stage to thank the performers and urge the dancers to take to the floor again, nervous that the mood had become too sombre. Henry Hall's band scraped away energetically and dancers drifted back to the floor. Edward watched a little enviously as Sam swept Verity back into the dancing and soon he was left alone again. Even Benyon was back in the arms of Mrs Roosevelt and Marcus Fern had found his gypsy again. However, just as he was thinking he might go back to his cabin and rest on his bed, he was joined by Warren Fairley.

'May I . . . ?' Fairley said, gesturing to the chair next to his.

'Of course! It would be an honour. Your performance – it moved Verity to tears and made me feel what a spoiled, privileged life I have led.'

'Lord Edward – please don't think I was not also feeling guilty about the life I am leading. After all, what was I doing singing to First Class passengers? Was I not upholding a different kind of segregation – economic segregation? Come – why are you not dancing? How silly of me – your knee! What bad luck . . . though I am glad to have a moment alone with you.'

'Please, is there anything I can do?'

'It's about my wife . . . I gather she made some sort of mad confession to you. You didn't believe a word of it, I hope?'

'I thought she was protecting you. I guessed that she had

got it into her head that you had killed Senator Day but after what you said on stage . . .'

'You didn't really think . . .?'

'Can you blame me? Your wife thought . . . feared you might have taken it upon yourself to . . .' Edward hesitated, 'right a wrong, and she's no fool.'

'That's it. You are most astute. Jane may look like an empty-headed starlet but she's no fool. In fact, I rely on her entirely. This may sound melodramatic but I literally couldn't live without her.'

Edward paused, waiting for Fairley to say something more, but he didn't. He adopted an air of abstraction and looked out into the dancers. Finally he said, 'So you don't suspect either of us?'

'I didn't say that. Your wife is a formidable person and you are, as you say, fortunate to have her. I think she would do a lot to protect you.'

'But not murder?'

'In certain circumstances I think she might take extreme measures to keep you safe.'

'I know it.' His face was grave. 'She is the light of my life . . .'

' "O my fair warrior!" '

'What? Oh yes – that is how Othello greets his Desdemona after the storm. But tell me, Lord Edward, do you know who murdered the Senator?'

'I believe I do.'

'He was an evil man.'

'The murderer?'

'No, the murdered man. As you quoted *Othello* at me, what say you to persuading "justice to break her sword"?'

'You mean, not pursue the murderer?'

'That's what I mean,' Fairley agreed.

To mark midnight and the beginning of their last day at sea, or for some other reason Edward could not guess at, the ship's siren sounded. Low-pitched and haunting, the sound seemed to carry with it the whole history of departure, longing and loss. God knew what would face them at journey's end. The omens were not good and there was the promise of foul weather. He decided he would be better able to face whatever the new day might bring after a few hours' sleep. He would ask Frank to take charge of Benyon.

As he got to his feet, a piercing pain in his knee made him sink back into his seat.

'Are you all right?' Verity had appeared out of the crowd like the rabbit from the hat. 'You look white as a whatsit.'

'My knee, blast it! I'm not sure I can use it at all. As soon as we get on shore I'm going to have to see a real doctor. Can you give me a hand, V? I thought I might retire to the cabin and try and get some sleep.'

Like two sailors rather the worse for wear, Edward and Verity staggered down the stairs. It was all so absurd. Warren's achingly sad songs had left Verity drained of emotion. Weakened by all that had happened in the four days they had been at sea, she was now as prone to laughter as to tears and propping up Edward was a very funny thing to be doing. He was the tall, strong man and she was the small, bird-like female who just happened to be dressed in a dinner jacket.

When they got to the cabin, Verity tumbled him down on his berth and somehow – who could say how? – she tumbled with him. For a minute, they lay there exhausted, breathing heavily, very much aware of each other. Edward had her in his arms and it seemed criminal not to take the chance of kissing her. She tasted odd, he thought – salty with tears, her scent spiced with sweat, her flesh warm and sweet on his lips. It was a heady brew and he was intoxicated.

'V,' he said at last, removing his lips from hers, 'I've been a fool. What you said about not wanting to marry . . . you're right, of course. It wouldn't work.'

Verity stirred. 'What do you mean, "it wouldn't work"?'

'Well, you said you weren't the marrying sort. That it would make us both unhappy.'

'Oh damn it, Edward,' she said, raising her head. 'Don't take what a girl says about marriage so seriously. You caught me at a bad moment. I thought I was in love with somebody else. Ask me again.'

He was amazed – nonplussed – and his heart started beating a rat-tat-tat in his chest. 'Verity – darling, infuriating Verity, will you marry me? Say you'll marry me – that is, if you don't happen to be in love with anyone else at the moment. We'll argue, we'll fight, we'll be unhappy, but at least we won't kick ourselves for not having tried.'

Verity was silent. Then she said, 'I'm a pain in the backside most of the time. I'll go off and leave you for months on end and I may not always manage to be completely faithful. The Duke won't like it. I won't have children – not yet anyway – and I don't have respectable friends.'

'I know all that but I'm not perfect either. At least, I don't think I am.'

She tried to cuff him but he held her thin wrists in his hands and she was powerless. 'You don't think it would be a good idea to sleep together first – to see if we fit?' she whispered in his ear. 'You might not like me. I might not be very good.'

'I'd teach you,' Edward said, and this time she did kick him.

'Ow! Blast you, that was my knee! I'll never walk again. I know it.'

'Don't swear at me. That doesn't bode well for our marriage.'

'So you are going to marry me?'

'I don't know. You haven't asked me yet, not properly.'

'Damn it, V, I can't get down on one knee for obvious reasons but I'm asking you now. Will you please marry me?'

The sound of what could only be a gunshot in the next cabin made them jump apart. Verity scrambled off the bed, leaving Edward to follow her as best he could. She tried Benyon's door and, to her surprise, the handle turned and she almost fell into the room.

'No need to worry,' Frank said, clutching his arm. 'Just scraped my flesh.' He was standing beside the armchair in which Benyon was sitting, very white but undamaged. They both looked rather ridiculous in their fancy dress. Benyon still had on his sheet but the turban had gone – and Verity had to resist a nervous laugh. Thank God – she found herself thinking – Frank not dead, Benyon not dead. What if, while she and Edward had been in each other's arms just a few feet away . . .? It didn't bear thinking about. In the same instant, she registered the existence of the other person in the room, Major Cranton. He had an automatic in his hand and it was still pointed at Lord Benyon.

'Give that to me, please,' she said like a bossy headmistress and walked over to the Major. 'You can't start shooting people on the *Queen Mary*. It just won't do.'

It was a ridiculous thing to say but somehow it had the desired effect. Rather sheepishly, the Major gave her his gun and then sank to a crouch, his back supported by the wall of the cabin, and put his face in his hands. 'They said I wouldn't do it,' he said miserably. 'They said it and they were right. I'm useless.'

'I don't know who you are but –' Verity began.

'But I do,' Edward interrupted. Leaning on his stick, his face creased with pain, he said again, 'I do. This is Captain Blane ... Lionel Blane. I thought I recognized him when I first saw him three days ago.' He limped over to Frank. 'Hey, are you hurt, my boy?'

Benyon chipped in. 'He saved my life. He stood in front of me and threw a pillow at that man.' He pointed at Cranton and Edward saw his outstretched arm was quite steady.

'You're all right, Benyon? Not hurt?'

'No, but Frank . . .'

'I thought I had better try and put him offside.' Frank tried to sound nonchalant but he was now very pale as his wound began to pain him.

'Verity, use that telephone to summon the doctor and the Captain, would you? I think I would be happier if this pathetic specimen was safely lodged in the brig.'

He examined Frank's arm. The shirt was torn and there was a three-inch runnel where the bullet had grazed his arm. It was bleeding but the crease made by the bullet was not very deep.

'And V, get me a clean towel from the bathroom, will you? Thanks. How did he get in, Frank? I thought I told you to keep the cabin door locked.'

'It was locked but I heard a knock on the door and I thought it was you so . . .'

'So?'

'So I opened it and there was this fellow holding a gun. Sorry, Uncle, I suppose I was rather silly.' His voice wobbled a little. 'Do you know this man, Uncle?'

'I haven't *met* him before but I have seen him. During the

Cable Street riot, you remember, V? He was standing a few paces behind Mosley.'

'You weren't being nasty to Frank, were you, Edward? You're not such hot stuff when it comes to guarding people, you know. I think he's a hero.' She beamed at Frank and he smiled back but there was still no blood in his face. The shock of what had happened was only just beginning to hit him.

'I wasn't blaming Frank. I was angry with myself. I ought not to have let this happen. So, V, you don't remember seeing Blane at the riot?'

'I remember the Cable Street *protest*,' she said deliberately, 'but I don't remember seeing this worm before. You say he's one of Mosley's lot?'

'He was but I gather that, about six months ago, he and one or two other nut cases split off from that organization and founded their own little group. They call themselves the Imperial Fascist League – isn't that right, Blane? – to combat "Red Revolution".'

There was no answer from the man crouched on the floor – just grunts which could have meant anything or nothing.

The phone in her hand, Verity snorted, 'Well, I don't think the Red Revolution has much to fear if this . . . object is an example of its enemy. Anyway . . . Oh, Captain, sorry to bother you but we've arrested a man trying to murder Lord Benyon . . . yes, here, in his cabin. We wondered if you could send down a couple of heavies to cart him away . . . yes, put him in irons until we reach New York. Thanks . . . and can you send the doctor down? I'm afraid Lord Corinth has caught a slug in his arm. Nothing to worry about . . . Oh good, thanks.' Verity put down the receiver. 'They're on the way. The Captain sounded rather annoyed, I thought.'

'I say,' Frank objected, 'I mean, dash it, don't be so casual. I might be bleeding to death.'

'Well, you aren't, are you?' she said rather sharply. 'Here, let me have a look. No, as I thought, just a graze. It's almost stopped bleeding. Edward, give me the towel. You're going to fall over if you're not careful.'

'Ouch, Verity, that hurt! Oughtn't I to be offered brandy? They always offer the wounded brandy in the flicks,' he said reproachfully.

'Don't be a baby, Frank. In Spain I saw lots worse than this.'

'Yes,' Benyon broke in, 'but we're not in Spain. We're on the *Queen Mary* where people aren't supposed to shoot at one another.'

Verity was immediately contrite. 'I know, I'm sorry. I didn't mean to sound unsympathetic. I'll get the brandy. I expect we could all do with some.' She was actually trying to stifle her panic at the realization of how close the boy had been to death but her concern had manifested itself as a reprimand.

'Benyon, sure you're all right?' Edward asked again, needing reassurance that the worst had been avoided, though more by luck than anything else.

'Yes – a bit shocked. It's not often someone pulls a gun on you – at least, it's never happened to me before and I sincerely hope it won't happen again. But, thanks to Frank, I'm fine. Miss Browne's right: he's a hero. He saved my life.' He looked as though he could hardly believe what had happened. He wanted to do something to make it real – to shake the boy's hand, for instance – but, as Frank was holding a towel round his wounded arm, that wasn't practicable.

'How do you know all this . . . about Blane or whatever you called him?' Verity demanded of Edward. 'And I don't understand why he wanted to murder Lord Benyon.'

'I checked with . . . a friend of mine in London . . . on the telephone, don't you know.' He tried to sound casual. He had remembered that Verity did not know about Major Ferguson and would certainly not approve of his relationship with him. 'He . . . my friend did a bit of research and then cabled me back with the info. Blane's bunch of Fascists want above all to be taken seriously. Mosley doesn't rate them and Ribbentrop certainly doesn't. Ribbentrop gave them this little test. They had to stop Lord Benyon from meeting the President and perhaps persuading him to support us – financially at least – in standing up to Hitler. The only thing which can stop him now is American intervention and the Nazis will do everything they can to prevent it. That's right, isn't it, Blane?'

There was no answer from the man crouched on the floor, who was rocking backwards and forwards as if in some sort of trance.

'And it was Blane's lot who took a pot shot at the car on our way to Southampton?' Frank asked.

'I don't doubt it. They failed with that but they had Blane on board so they must have thought they still had a chance. But they hadn't counted on you being on guard. Well done, my boy! I'm proud of you.'

Verity wasn't listening. She was standing in front of Frank. 'Look, I'm sorry. I must have sounded like a pig. I meant what I said. You're a real hero and if I wasn't worried about your poor arm, I would kiss you.'

'Oh, that's all right. Thanks a lot though.' Frank sounded pleased but embarrassed. There was some colour in his cheeks again. 'By the way, did you know your lipstick's gone all wonky?'

'Has it?' she said, wiping her mouth with the back of her hand. 'I fell when I tipped your uncle on to his bed.'

'Oh, I see. So that's why he's got lipstick all over his face.'

'This isn't the time to be talking about make-up,' Edward said brusquely. 'What were you doing here anyway? I thought you would have gone to bed, Frank. I mean, thank God you hadn't but . . .'

'Of course not! You told me *you* were going to bed and I was on duty. It was my watch. We've been having a most awfully interesting chat, haven't we, sir?'

Benyon nodded. 'The boy's got a sound head on his shoulders, Corinth.'

'If I can keep it there,' Frank quipped.

'What were you talking about?' Edward was curious.

'Oh, you know, economics, world peace – that sort of thing.'

'Hmf,' was all Edward found to say. He was impressed with his nephew's sang-froid and felt very much to blame for not having been there when he was needed. Blane was still crouched on the floor, his face in his hands, whimpering. Unable to take out his irritation on anyone else, Edward snapped, 'Do shut up, Blane. We can hardly hear ourselves think with all that weeping and wailing.'

'And if you're looking for sympathy,' Verity added, 'you won't get it. You killed Tom Barrett, didn't you?'

Blane began to wail – a soft, keening noise which chilled the blood. 'Stop that awful noise, man,' Edward commanded but he took no notice.

'I think he's off his head,' Verity opined. 'Not that that's any excuse in my book.'

Fenton and Marcus Fern arrived but there was nothing for them to do, other than fuss round Lord Benyon and administer first aid to Frank, until the doctor came a minute or two later. When the Captain appeared, looking harassed but relieved, with a couple of his officers, the cabin started to look over-crowded and feel stuffy. Blane was taken away, still sobbing. The doctor insisted that the rest of them leave him to minister to his patient in peace so they all filed next door to Edward's cabin. The Captain was angry with himself and with Edward. He had read Major Ferguson's cable about Blane but Edward had talked him into agreeing not to put him in irons immediately but to wait until they reached New York where they could hand him over to the authorities. Edward had come to the conclusion that he was too pathetic a character to be a threat but he had underestimated the man – not by much but enough. He blenched. His judgement had been faulty and he had put two lives at risk.

When the doctor had seen to Frank and prescribed bed, Verity and Edward were summoned back to escort him to his cabin.

'Gosh!' Frank exclaimed, yawning hugely. 'I think I'd sleep even if we hit an iceberg.'

'Please,' Edward shuddered, 'that's just about the only disaster still waiting to happen.'

They then returned to help Fenton put Benyon to bed. The doctor had given him a sleeping draught but he hardly needed it. He was quite exhausted by the night's events and, if he was to greet the American press the next day – which was already this day – he had to get some sleep.

Verity and Edward were too strung-up to sleep and, at Edward's suggestion, they returned to his cabin. Fenton doled out brandy and then left them alone. Fenton, too, was feeling bad that he had not been where he could have been of use. He was off duty and had been partying with friends in the Tourist lounge. Edward told him not to be silly. 'It wasn't your watch. It was Frank's and he acquitted himself well. And so did you,

212

V. You got the gun off him as though you did that sort of thing every day.'

'Thanks. I was just so cross I didn't stop to think. So Cranton – I mean Blane – was one of Mosley's men?'

Edward was stretched out on his bed and Verity perched on the end of it.

'Yes, but in the end he was too extreme . . . too batty even for the BUF.'

'It was he who attacked Doris Zinkeisen's mural?'

'Yes. It was a mistake but he just couldn't resist it. She was everything he hated and her black lady taunted him. He just had to show the world what he thought of it.'

'But Bernard Hunt saw him with the bucket of paint.'

'Yes, he was fortunate Blane did not try to kill him.'

'Was Blane really a Major?'

'No, a Captain. He served in the Worcestershire Regiment during the war. Did quite well as a matter of fact. He became a chum of a fellow officer – one William Joyce.'

'Mosley's propaganda chief?'

'Yes. They had it in for what they called "Jewish Communists" – ironically mostly Conservatives who, in their jaundiced eyes, had betrayed "the cause". Rabid anti-Semites, of course. Special Branch infiltrated their organization right from the start and has several agents in place so we knew they'd try to do something to prove they were more than a talking-shop.'

'You mean Special Branch has agents in the . . . whatever you called it . . . the Imperial Fascist League?'

'Oh yes – fully paid-up members.'

'Golly, isn't that a bit underhand?'

'You sound like me,' he smiled. '"Not cricket" and all that bosh.'

'No, I mean . . .'

'You mean you're wondering how many of your Comrades are actually Special Branch?'

Verity sounded put out. 'No! Yes. Anyway, how do you know so much about it? I'm suspicious.' Edward made no comment and fortunately she chose not pursue her suspicions. 'We know our enemies will stoop to anything. It's a compliment really.' She thought for a moment. 'But he did kill Barrett. He may look pathetic but he is a killer.'

213

'That's right. I don't doubt Barrett recognized him immediately and I suppose Blane knew he had been rumbled. Lured him down to the cold store for a "private chat" or something and bashed him over the head.'

'Killed him in cold blood, as it were. But Barrett was armed. Surely he shouldn't have allowed . . . ?'

'Yes, I fear he must have underestimated Blane, as I did. We'll know more when we've questioned him.'

'What will they do with him when we reach New York?'

'I don't know. They may arrest him but my guess is that they'll tell Captain Peel to take him back to England to be dealt with.'

'Won't he need extraditing or whatever you call it?'

'Maybe but they'll want to avoid any publicity. They may say the murder happened on a British ship, possibly in British waters, so it's nothing to do with them. We'll have to see.'

They were silent. Then Verity said, 'Well, I suppose it's bed for us . . . I mean we're both pretty whacked . . . and I can see your leg's hurting.'

She was still wearing her black tie, though she had shed the jacket. With her short hair and brilliant black eyes, she looked like some adorable boy and Edward wanted nothing more than to kiss her. He propped himself up and said, 'V, before you go . . . unfinished business? Please . . .'

'Oh God! Do you really want to? Won't you regret it in the morning?'

'I'll only regret it if we don't. Please, Verity . . .'

She put her hand over his mouth. 'Don't plead. I like my men to be masterful. Hey! What are you doing?'

'*Viens dans mon lit, viens sur mon coeur.*'

It was awkward undressing with a gammy leg, lying on a bed. In the end, he gave up and so, half-undressed, still wearing his socks, he took Verity in his arms. The bunk wasn't as big as he remembered and they had to be quiet so as not to wake Benyon in the next-door cabin. Whenever he moved, Edward felt a pain in his knee which made Verity laugh and him swear. But even if it wasn't quite the display of fireworks it might have been under different circumstances, it was still good enough for him to feel that, in some indefinable way, it was right.

14

Verity had slipped back to her cabin before the sun was more than an orange glow on the horizon but she was acutely aware she was not unobserved. Sam 'happened' to open his door a crack as she passed and, though she pretended not to see him, she felt his eyes on her back as she closed her door. It was too late, or rather too early, to go to sleep so she showered and then went on deck. As she stared out at the sea, pearl-grey in the dawn, she felt she had crossed the border of a foreign country, even if there was no stamp in her passport to prove it. She was calm now and her head was clear. She must not let her resolve weaken, whatever she had said with the pressure of his arms about her. Marriage would be a disaster for both of them, she was certain of it, but she had initiated an intimacy which, as the marriage service put it so succinctly, for better or for worse would last a lifetime.

It wasn't the sex – or rather the sex was just a sign of a deeper intimacy, the product of his having watched over her as she grew from innocent child to become a woman of some experience, all in the space of eighteen months. She felt that their commitment to one another would be the deeper for not being formalized by a conventional wedding ceremony. She tried to imagine herself in a virgin-white dress, veiled to preserve her modesty and attended by a flock of bridesmaids, and she laughed aloud. Without benefit of clergy, they had made a voluntary and equal promise – one to the other. It was not the promise of the wedding vows. Nobody owned anyone – she was not going to be Edward's property. They were not to make babies together; she would certainly not 'obey' him and she was enough of a realist to know that it was possible she might love other men. However, their first loyalty would always be to one another and in loss, disappointment, even despair, they would find in each other a support and strength – gifts which, she knew, many married couples could not or would not grant one another.

It was symbolic that their coming together had been on board a ship in the middle of the Atlantic. On dry land they would be *somewhere* but here they were *nowhere* – without the ties and restraints that so often rubbed at a marriage like a horse's harness. Marriage would have made her feel trapped by all the expectations Edward's family would have of her: the expectation that she would give up her career and 'settle down', breed and turn to bridge afternoons and church charities and, above all, their – quite understandable – expectation that she would fail. She would not be dependent on him in any material way and would keep the respect she had already earned of him by simply being true to herself. The disapproval of society she could bear without much anguish.

'Mind if I join you?'

The voice was dark and the American accent like ground coffee. 'Oh, it's you, Sam.'

'Yes, it's me. Shouldn't it be?'

'It's your ship as much as mine.'

'I know, and the ocean's kinda large too. Still, I thought you might say there wasn't room enough for the both of us.'

She looked into his clear eyes – almost the colour of the sea – the broad shoulders which spoke of hard manual work and the strong chin. She remembered why she had liked him so much and was inclined to think she had been hard on him – not that she regretted her refusal to sleep with him. It was funny how being in love – she supposed she was, in her own peculiar way, in love with Edward – made her want to be kind to all her friends.

'Looking forward to seeing your wife and son? What did you say her name was?'

'I didn't but her name's Marty and he's called Richard, or rather Dick – after my father.'

'Who was your father?'

'That's such an English question!'

216

'How do you mean?'

'In the States it's who you are, not who your father is.'

'Unless it's Roosevelt,' she said drily.

'*Touché*,' he said. 'But let me answer your question. Who are "my people"? Who was my father? Some might say nobody. I'd say he was a great man. He came over from your country maybe fifty years ago. He had nothing – no parents living, no money, no schooling. He could hardly read – taught himself by working his way through *The Pilgrim's Progress*. I guess it was his Bible. He always went to it when he needed wisdom. Anyways, he had a tough time – did all sorts of labouring jobs, then got himself a job as a longshoreman – what you would call a docker. That was difficult. Jobs were almost hereditary – passed down from father to son.'

'But you didn't inherit his job?'

'No, I didn't. My pa met a real nice girl and they had me and he vowed I'd have the schooling he didn't get. I was bright enough, I guess, and he was proud enough of me but then he got up and died. He was just sixty.'

'So then there was just you and your mother?'

'You might say so but my father lived on in our house long after he had shuffled off that "mortal coil" – oh, yes, my pa liked old Shakespeare too and made me read him. What I mean is – he taught me my principles – about when to fight and when to turn the other cheek, about ... I don't know ... withstanding corruption. There's a lot of it about.'

'Even in your union?'

'Specially there, or at least that's where I notice it most. A guy'll sell out to the bosses or take back-handers. Some of it you can put down to the compromises you're expected to make to get some of what you want – negotiation. But some of them – good men in their youth – forget why they're where they are. They get the taste of money! Maybe it doesn't smell, as that Roman emperor said, but it does taste good, that's for sure – dirty but good. Don't think I'm pretending to be what I'm not. It's just because I'm human that I made that pass at you.'

'I'm sorry, I shouldn't have slapped you.'

'No, I deserved a slap. What hurt much more was that look in your eye which said I had lost your respect, failed some test.'

'Please, Sam . . .'

'No, let me have my say. I felt like a heel. I love my wife and son. They're the best things in my life and I ought to have had respect for them and for myself.'

Verity wondered if this didn't amount to calling her a whore but decided he did not mean it to sound that way so she let it pass.

'I guess all this rigmarole is just to say I'm sorry. Forgive me?'

'Sam! Of course I forgive you.' She took his face in her hands and kissed him on the lips. 'There, I forgive you.'

'Not butting in, I hope?'

Edward was standing behind her, leaning on his crutch with a quizzical smile on his face.

'We were saying goodbye,' Sam said. 'You're a lucky man, Corinth.'

'I know that, Sam, but thank you for reminding me.'

When Edward and Verity were alone together, neither wanted to talk about love and lust. Words seemed beside the point when everything worth saying couldn't be said – or at least not yet. Instead, Verity said, 'Have you thought any more about Jane Barclay's confession?'

'What? Do we tell the New York police? Or do we believe it?'

'Both, either.'

'Jane definitely faked that attack on her in the steam room. She's a strong-willed lady and perfectly capable of an act of violence to defend her husband and herself. Don't forget they have both been harried and harassed by people like Senator Day for a long time. Perhaps the insult at the Captain's table was the straw that broke the camel's back.'

'But you don't think so?'

'Well, you see, V, at the ball last night Warren made a point of telling me that her confession was nonsense.'

'He did, did he? So what? A wonderul man like Warren would never suspect his own wife and, even if she had convinced him she had done the deed, he would naturally do what he could to protect her.'

'You don't think Warren could have killed Day? If he saw

Day at the swimming-pool with his wife, might not jealous rage . . .?'

'*Othello?*'

'Too neat perhaps?'

'Let's look at our other suspects and see who we can eliminate.' Verity thought for a moment. 'I suppose Sam Forrest is the strongest suspect. He came up from the bowels of the ship just before your idiotic race with Frank and Perry. He admitted he had resisted Day's attempt at blackmail. In a moment of rage, he could have hit him over the head. We know he's used to living in the violent world of American union politics and, to prove it, he carries a gun.'

'And you think he could use it?'

'In certain circumstances but, of course, he didn't use it on Day.'

'No, he was hit on the head by some unidentified blunt object, probably the hammer missing from the toolbox of the man repairing the controls to the steam room.'

'Does that suggest the knock on the head was unpremeditated? You would hardly go to kill someone without a weapon.'

'I don't know, V. I think the idea of killing Day was premeditated even if the actual killing was not.' They were silent, thinking things over. Then Edward said, 'Stop being objective about Sam. Tell me what your instinct is. What's your gut feeling?'

'Feminine intuition?'

'No, I just respect your judgement of character.'

Verity was pleased. 'I think he is basically honest and not a violent man. The fact that he refused to do some deal with Day which might have made him very rich supports my view. I don't think he did it.'

'Nor do I,' Edward said and they smiled at each other with relief.

'Who else?' Verity persisted. 'What about Marcus Fern? You said that, rather surprisingly, he carries a gun.'

'Yes. He's a tough cookie and he keeps on asking me about Day – or at least he did last night. He has come up the hard way, he says so himself. A boy from the wrong class without

219

family, with no one with an established City position to help and protect him. You have to be very good to beat the system and you would probably fight hard to keep what you had won.'

'I should think so! He's the exception which proves the rule. It's exactly what we in the Party object to – the "old boy" thing, the shake of the hand, the nod and the wink. He's probably a Mason. That's the sort of club he might be allowed to join.'

'Yes, well, that doesn't make him a murderer but it does mean he's capable of being tough when his back's against the wall.'

'But what's his motive? Why would Day have had anything against him or been able to blackmail him? I agree that, having fought his way up to become a confidant of men like Benyon, he has a lot to lose but there's absolutely no evidence he had heard of Day before that moment at the Captain's table. Is it likely their paths would ever have crossed? I doubt it.'

'You're right but the jury's still out on him. He's an enigmatic man.'

'You've got that look on your face, Edward. I think you know who killed Day.'

'I don't know what you mean, V. What look?'

'Don't play the innocent with me. That look of having trapped a mouse . . . you can't fool me. Out with it.'

'You sound like a dentist. I tell you what, you get on with investigating Bernard Hunt. Try and find out where he was when Day was hit on the head. He gives me the creeps so much I really can't talk to him . . . He put his filthy paws on Frank . . .'

'Don't be silly, Edward. Frank's a big boy. If he can throw a pillow at a man with a gun, he can cope with Hunt. Talking of Major Cranton, I mean Blane, why did he do that awful thing?'

'Murder Barrett?'

'No, I can see he panicked when he recognized Barrett and knew that Barrett had recognized him but why did they end up in the cold store and why did he . . . you know . . . take all his clothes?'

'Blane was desperate to get rid of Barrett before his cover was blown so he persuaded Barrett to meet him "to do a deal".

After all, Barrett couldn't have Blane arrested just for being on board.'

'He was travelling under a false name on a false passport. If the Captain had locked him up he wouldn't have had a chance of taking a shot at Benyon.'

'The passport would be a matter for the immigration authorities in New York. The Captain couldn't have locked him up for that.'

'But how did it happen – the killing, I mean? Barrett was an experienced Special Branch man. How did he allow himself to be outwitted by Blane?'

'I don't know yet. No doubt we'll find out when Blane talks but I expect Barrett did what I did.'

'What was that?'

'Underestimated him. Blane seemed a pathetic character and, of course, he was but I forgot that weak men, inadequates, can still do damage. The meeting took place near the kitchens. There was so much going on down there – so many cooks and scullions and what-not rushing around – that, paradoxically, it was just the place they could meet without anyone noticing. Blane managed to knock him unconscious and then dragged him into the cold storage room.'

'But why take his clothes? To humiliate him?'

'I would guess for a more practical reason. Barrett was only unconscious and not dead. Maybe Blane didn't feel like hitting him again. He didn't find it easy to work himself up to carrying out an act of violence, like shooting Benyon. Anyway, it might have been messy. He wouldn't have wanted blood on his clothes. An easier option must have occurred to him. Naked, Barrett would die very quickly from hypothermia.'

'Ugh, how horrible! But why hook him up among the carcasses – that was disgusting.'

'For the same reason. Hiding him among the carcasses would delay discovery until he was dead.'

'Poor Barrett! Secret policemen aren't my favourite people but what a horrible way to die.'

Edward was uneasy. Was *he* a secret policeman? After all, he took his orders from one.

Verity was talking again. 'So you think Hunt killed Day? Is that what I'm to try and establish?'

221

'No. I want you to eliminate him if you can. I believe I do know who killed that bad man but I need to think about it. Perhaps it's not my job to bring Day's killer to justice.'

'You mean it's not your job but maybe it's your duty?'

'In a naughty world, oughtn't we to do our bit to clean it up?'

'Don't parlourmaids sweep the dirt under the carpet?'

'We don't approve of that, do we?' Edward said primly. 'In fact, we have had occasion before now to criticize the police for doing exactly that.'

Verity sighed. 'You must do what is right. Surely that is the one principle we both believe in and you've only got a few hours in which to do it. We dock about five this afternoon. The Purser told me we're a bit behind schedule. It's now . . .' She looked at her watch. '. . . seven. Can you wrap it all up in ten hours?'

'I suppose so.'

'When did you know who had killed Day?'

'When the conjurer took the rabbit out of the hat.'

Verity found Bernard Hunt eating breakfast, a copy of the ship's newspaper propped up against the toast rack in front of him.

'Might I join you or would you rather be alone?' Verity inquired, with one of her most persuasive smiles. 'It's probably rather awful eating breakfast with someone who's almost a complete stranger but, I don't know why, I feel that – when we all troop off the *Queen Mary* – some sort of chapter will close and we've not really had a chance of getting to know each other.'

'By all means join me, Miss Browne. Waiter! Bring a chair for the lady, will you, and . . . coffee?'

'Yes please.' She offered another smile to the waiter. 'I wanted to ask you if . . . if there had been any more news . . . about the Poussin.'

'Oh that,' Hunt sighed. 'It's a great disappointment but there we are. *La commedia è finita*. There's no point in brooding. Actually, Miss Zinkeisen's been most helpful.'

'Miss Zinkeisen?'

'Yes, I told you we know each other quite well and she was grateful I got her the commission to design the mural in the Verandah Grill. Anyway, she is going to introduce me to some of her Hollywood friends. The thing is, apparently, many of these film stars like investing their earnings – and you've no idea how much some of them earn – in property and art rather than stocks and shares. After the crash, the stock market doesn't seem a sensible place to put one's little all and if there's a war – God forbid – the whole system will probably collapse.'

'I do hope so,' Verity could not help interjecting.

'As a Communist, you mean?'

'Yes, of course. It's what we are working for.'

Hunt looked dubious. 'The funny thing is, all that rubbish Marx talks about the capitalist system – I don't really hold with it. I'm an art dealer – a parasite, I suppose you might say. If there are no Lorenzo de Medicis to buy and Michelangelos to sell . . .'

'Hey!' Verity said, trying to talk with her mouth full of toast and honey, 'I remember you saying the artist ought to be an artisan with a secure place in society – like a postman or a carpenter – and that he should have a salary and not be subject to market demands.'

'Did I say that?' Hunt was vague but his small eyes were beady. 'How very clever of you to remember, my dear.'

Verity did not like be called 'my dear' particularly by someone who, if not a card-carrying Communist, was certainly a sympathizer and therefore ought to have known better.

'Yes, you did.'

'I must have been in one of my theoretical moods. I'm afraid I'm such a weathercock – not consistent . . . not consistent at all.'

She had a feeling he was mocking her. 'So you are going to be art adviser to the stars?' She, too, could mock and Hunt looked a little embarrassed.

'If you put it like that, yes, that's the idea.'

Verity suddenly remembered why she was having this conversation. She was trying to find out if Hunt could have killed Senator Day. She must turn on the hot tap again and warm up the conversation.

'I think it's a brilliant scheme,' she said confidingly. 'If you

223

get to know the powerful people in Hollywood, it will help get them on our side.'

'Which side is that?' Hunt was still not mollified.

'I mean if Day's friend, Senator Dies, gets his un-American whatever-it-is . . . un-American activities committee . . . off the ground, the government will use it to clamp down on Communists.'

'Oh, do you think so?' Hunt sounded vague again. 'I don't know anything about politics.'

Verity felt she wasn't getting anywhere. She ought to have him eating out of her hand by now but, instead, she could sense she was losing him. She'd better get to the point.

'Talking of Senator Day, I wonder who did kill him? Have you any ideas?'

'None at all. Does it matter? Someone did us all a good turn. Let's leave it at that.'

'But I can't help being interested,' she persisted. 'I was watching the race when it happened. You were too, weren't you?'

'The race? You mean that silly rush round the deck when Corinth got hurt? Why should I watch that?'

'So where were you then?'

'Do you really want to know?' A gleam of malice ripped the vagueness from his face.

'I do,' Verity said stoutly.

'You'll be shocked.'

'I doubt it.'

'No? Well then, I'll tell you but you musn't breathe a word – especially not to your friend Corinth. I'm sure *he* would be shocked. You know that boy who's always running about in a brass-buttoned uniform?'

'One of the pageboys?'

There were a dozen or so pageboys available to fetch and carry, take messages and otherwise make themselves useful to First Class passengers.

'There is only one,' he said reproachfully, 'worth looking at, that is. Rudi. You must have seen him. Red-haired, such a cheeky boy. Anyway, Rudi and I were in my cabin when the good Senator was getting himself killed.'

224

'What were you doing with Rudi in your cabin?' she asked faintly.

'What do you think we were doing? He was cleaning my shoes for me.'

When Edward was regaled by Verity with this story, he laughed outright.

'What are you laughing about?' she said crossly. 'That horrible man was perverting some boy in his cabin and you laugh.'

'I'll get the Purser to have a quiet word with Rudi but I think you'll find he *was* just polishing Hunt's shoes – even if Hunt hoped he might be available for something else. Haven't you noticed how he worships Jane Barclay? Rudi is a red-blooded heterosexual boy, whatever Bernard Hunt might wish to the contrary. Still, he may well be able to give Hunt an alibi. I think he knew just what you were up to, V, and wanted to tease you.'

'Well, I'm glad you think it's funny. All I can say is you'd better be right about Bernard Hunt. I would be quite pleased to be able to say he was a murderer.'

'But he's a Comrade!' Edward said in mock horror. 'What can it matter if a Comrade is a killer provided he kills on the Party's instructions?'

'He's not a member of the Party,' she replied coldly.

He knew he had gone too far. 'I'm sorry, V. Forgive me? Please!'

She stalked off in high dudgeon. Golly, Edward thought. A few minutes ago they had been proclaiming eternal love to one another and now they were back to their normal squabbling. He shuddered. What would marriage be like? He shuddered again.

He was just turning to hobble down to the lounge – he couldn't go back to his cabin because Fenton had begun packing – wondering if it were too early to get a drink when he bumped into Frank.

'I say, Uncle Ned, can we have a word? There's something I've been meaning to say to you.' His manner was formal as

225

though he had asked to see the headmaster, and Edward repressed a smile. He thought he knew what was coming.

'I was just going down to the lounge. We can find a quiet corner there. It's too early for people to be having drinks,' he added with regret.

The leather armchairs were so deep and wide that it made confidential conversation difficult but there was no one else in the place except a waiter whom they dismissed as they seated themselves.

There was a pause. Edward looked at his nephew expectantly but the boy seemed unwilling to begin so he said, 'How's the arm?'

'Oh, it's all right. The doctor insisted on making me wear this sling but I think it's just to make me feel important.'

There was another pause and Edward tried again. 'I don't know why but I can't seem to hate that man Blane even though he killed an innocent man. He just seems so pathetic.'

'You might feel differently if he'd killed me or Benyon,' Frank said tartly.

'You're right, of course. I was being stupid. The inadequates make us suffer for their inadequacies. Hitler is using us to make up for his. Have you read Freud?'

'No. Look, Uncle Ned, I didn't want to talk to you about Freud.'

'Of course not. What do you want to talk to me about?'

'The Roosevelts – Perry and Philly.'

'Are you still engaged to Philly? She's a charming girl.'

'No, I'm not. I don't know what happened. I wanted to ask her if she really loved me or if she loved my being a lord and all that tosh and being . . . you know . . . rich. We were dancing and she felt like . . . like gossamer in my arms and I swear, if she had said she did love me, I would have married her whatever Father said . . . or you . . .'

'But . . .?'

'But, before I could say anything, she put her hand over my mouth and led me off into a corner and told me she was sorry but she couldn't marry me.'

'Did she give any reason?' Edward inquired mildly.

'She said she was ill and that it wouldn't be fair on me. I said that didn't matter. I would help her get better.'

226

Edward winced inwardly. If the girl had wanted to take that as a renewal of Frank's offer, she would have had every right to do so.

'And what did she say?' He spoke gently but there was an undercurrent of anxiety in his voice which his nephew must have sensed.

'I ... meant it ... I would have stood by her,' he said with dignity, 'but she wouldn't hear of it. She said she wanted to get well first and then if we met ... well, it would be different.'

'That was very fair of her.'

'Yes, it was, and I let her persuade me. I don't why I still feel a bit of a cad. She is the most lovely thing ...'

'I know she is, Frank. She's enchanting but you are still very young.'

Frank looked at his uncle with dislike. 'That's not a very original thing to say. If I'm old enough to be shot at, I'm surely old enough to know when I'm in love.'

'Sorry, Frank. I didn't mean to be patronizing. Was that what you wanted to tell me?'

'Yes – I mean no. There is something else.' He was clearly wrestling with himself. Edward lit a cigarette and waited. 'You remember our race?'

'I do,' Edward said, tapping his leg.

'Yes, of course you do. I mean, that was when Day was murdered, wasn't it?'

'Yes.' Edward was curious, wondering what was coming next.

'Well, I don't want to ... I'm probably mistaken but ...'

'But what, Frank? You may as well spit it out.'

'The thing is, Perry wasn't there.'

'Not there? But I saw him race.'

'Not there all the time. You raced first and you fell and we all clustered around you. Then – I don't know – five minutes later, I ran and then ...'

'And then Perry ran.'

'Yes, but there was a period of perhaps ten or fifteen minutes when Perry just wasn't around.'

'I thought I saw him but, it's true, I was in pain and concerned that I had made a fool of myself.'

227

'You may have seen Philly and thought she was Perry. I noticed they were wearing very similar colours.'

'She wasn't wearing white tie and tails.'

'No, but she was dressed in that rather wonderful black trouser-suit with the white collar. I thought she looked absolutely . . .' His voice had taken on a note of excitement which was soon replaced by anxiety as he remembered what he was saying.

'You think we might have mistaken Philly for Perry while he was rushing downstairs to knock Day on the head? Is that it?' He spoke brutally, wanting Frank to face the implications of what he was saying.

'I'm sure he didn't but . . . but I thought it was possible. He had a motive . . . what Day had done to their father . . .'

'And he had opportunity and a sort of alibi.'

Frank looked miserable. 'Tell me I'm wrong, Uncle Ned.'

'I had thought the same thing,' he confessed. 'It occurred to me when I was watching the magician – Jasper Maskelyne. He was working by "misdirection" – making the audience look in the wrong direction so they did not see the wires that made the "levitation" possible. He made us think we were seeing something when actually we were seeing something else. But even if Perry did mislead us about being on deck when actually he wasn't, how could he possibly know that Jane Barclay had positioned Day in exactly the right place, on the edge of the pool?'

'They might be in cahoots. I got the feeling from something Perry said to me that they had met her and Warren in England.'

Edward considered this. 'But even then . . . even if they – Jane and Perry – had planned this between them, how could she have timed it so perfectly?'

'What if Philly had been with Jane – watched her lure Day to the pool and then rushed up on deck and more or less taken Perry's place as he went down and did the deed?'

Edward sucked on his cigarette. 'It's possible,' he agreed. 'Look, you've done well, Frank. You've overcome a perfectly justifiable feeling that you might be betraying a friendship to tell me your suspicions. That was right of you but I don't think you are correct. I think Perry *was* on deck while I was making a fool of myself and you were racing. I'm sure I can find

228

witnesses and I'm sure I didn't mistake him for his twin. So forget all about it. You concentrate on Benyon and leave the rest to me.'

'Gladly, Uncle. Phoo! What a relief to have got that off my chest. I'm glad you think it's nonsense though.'

'I didn't say that but . . . Anyway, you cut along and leave me to meditate.'

With a wave of his hand, Frank got up quickly and made off. Edward sat for a further five minutes, chewing over what Frank had told him and then, with a sigh, reached for his crutch and limped off to find the Roosevelts.

15

There was an almost tangible air of excitement among the passengers. As though heaving off a blanket preparatory to getting out of bed, they were beginning to throw off the intimacies they had encouraged in the days at sea. Maids and valets were opening suitcases while stewards fussed around them trying to justify the tips they were anticipating. Edward knew he could safely leave Fenton to do his packing as well as Benyon's.

A little reluctantly, he strolled along to the Roosevelts' cabin. He knocked on the door and Mrs Roosevelt called, 'Come in.' The twins, he saw to his relief, were not present. Mrs Roosevelt was half seated, half lying on a sort of ottoman. She had a handkerchief in her hand and the scent of cologne was almost overpowering. Around her, suitcases lay open but no attempt had yet been made to fill them.

'Are you all right, Mrs Roosevelt?' Edward asked with concern.

'Oh, Lord Edward, is that you? Take no notice. I have one of my headaches, that's all. I always get one when we arrive in a new place. I suppose it's knowing I have to make the effort to pack and get off the boat.'

She gestured vaguely to the suitcases.

'Would you like me to summon the steward to help you pack?'

'That's so kind of you but please don't worry. Philly will be back shortly and she'll take charge. You know, Lord Edward, behind that air of being beyond the ordinary – not quite of this

230

world, I think was how you once put it – she is, actually, very well organized and quite determined.'

There was a very slight edge to her remark and Edward wondered if the twins did not occasionally bully their mother, but perhaps she was a woman who needed a little bullying.

'I've noticed that, Mrs Roosevelt. Philly knows what she wants and how to get it but she does it so charmingly we are all persuaded it was our idea in the first place.'

They looked at each other and smiled like two conspirators who had dared to criticize their gaolers and felt the better for it.

'I understand from my nephew that he is no longer engaged to your daughter? I hope I haven't been guilty of . . .'

'That was all such nonsense. Frank is a dear boy but it was a shipboard romance – that's all.'

'I do hope we can see something of you all in New York. Where will you be staying?'

'The St Regis to begin with and then we may take an apartment. It depends what the doctor says.'

'Yes of course. Philly . . . what do you really think? Is she . . .?'

'She's not well. She hardly eats but that's not it. I really don't know, Lord Edward. I sometimes think it is better not to know. To know might be to have no hope.'

'I understand,' he said gently. 'Tell me, Mrs Roosevelt, did you know Mr Fairley before you came on board?'

'In London, do you mean?'

'Yes, or I wondered if you had known each other in the States?'

Mrs Roosevelt considered. 'I never met either of them before but I do believe Philly and Miss Barclay saw something of each other in London.'

'I thought they must have. Do you happen to remember where they met?'

'I believe it was at dinner with the ambassador, dear Mr Bingham, who is now so ill. Yes, I wasn't able to go, I remember. I had a migraine but I think Philly mentioned that terrible man Senator Day had been there as well. Oh dear! I suppose one shouldn't speak ill of the dead.'

The door opened with a crash and Perry appeared, breath-

231

less. 'Corinth! Have you come to visit Mother? How kind of you. You must excuse me. I've been playing shuttlecock with Frank and I'm quite pooped. I thought I might have a shower before I put on my "landing-in-New York" clothes.'

'Then I shall leave you. I too must pack – or rather watch Fenton pack as he won't let me interfere. He is transferring his services to Lord Benyon for the duration of his stay in America – at least I hope that's all it will be – so I must learn to look after myself.'

'I'm quite sure you can do that,' Perry replied. 'Verity – Miss Browne – was telling me about your life in South Africa. I gather you – what's the expression? – "knocked about a bit" there.'

'You musn't believe all Verity's stories,' Edward said smoothly. 'She is a journalist, don't y'know. Have you ever read anything accurate in a newspaper when the subject happens to be something you know about?'

'I'll tell her you said so,' Perry said, laughing. 'We won't say "goodbyes" because I am sure we will see you before we disembark.'

'And I was just saying to your mother – in New York, too, I hope.'

As Edward closed the cabin door behind him, he heard stifled laughter and he wondered what they really thought of him. Did Perry imagine he was a complete fool? He thought he needed a drink – it was now eleven o'clock. He made his way to the cocktail bar and found Roger, the barman, deep in conversation with Jane Barclay who was sipping something violet-coloured through a straw.

'I hope I'm not interrupting, Miss Barclay . . . Roger, gin and tonic please.'

'Not having one of these?' she asked, thrusting the list of cocktails under his nose.

'No, thank you. As often as not they make me feel dizzy. I think it's the colour as much as the taste.'

'You're right, I guess. Roger, this is quite repellent. I can't think why you recommended it.'

'I say, Miss Barclay . . .' Edward began.

'Jane. I feel after all we have been through, you know me well enough to call me Jane.'

He was aware he was expected to invite her to call him Edward but he did not. Instead, he said, 'I am pleased to have bumped into you, Jane. I wonder if you would mind if we go over to that table in the corner? There's something I want to say to you before we part and this seems like a good opportunity.'

He thought he noticed her go a shade paler but she only replied, 'How fascinating. Yes, of course. Roger will bring over your drink.'

When they were seated out of earshot of the barman with their drinks and a plate of olives on the table between them, she said, 'I suppose you want to tell me that Verity – Miss Browne – has decided you should turn me over to the New York Police Department.'

'That's not my job. I merely wondered if you would satisfy my curiosity on a certain matter?'

'If I can.'

'When you confessed to having done away with Senator Day, you gave me the impression that your motive was to protect your husband.'

'That was my motive. Day had made Warren's life a misery and threatened to do worse – said he would haul him in front of some Senate Committee he was involved in and have him banned from ever working in the States again. You may not think it but Warren is very highly strung, very emotional. His politics and his work are the only two things he cares about and, if he was prevented from working, I think it's possible he might kill himself.'

Edward raised his eyebrows. 'But he could always work in Europe.'

'He's an American through and through. It's in the States he needs to find his audience. Apart from anything else, there's no movie industry outside Hollywood to speak of. He'd starve. He'd shrivel up and die.'

'You said there were only two things he cared for – his work and his politics. I think you forgot the third thing.'

'Meaning?'

'Yourself. He's no fool. He loves you. I've watched him look at you. He may flirt with other women but it's almost out of politeness. It's only you he loves.'

233

Jane flushed. 'I hope so,' she mumbled.

'That's why he could never survive losing you to the electric chair.'

She winced. 'You're very blunt.'

He went on remorselessly. 'He would know you had killed to protect him and he would feel so guilty. In fact, he knows – or thinks he knows – already. At the ball last night, he came over specially to tell me to take no notice of your confession.'

She looked up abruptly. 'He did? But how could he know? Did you tell him?'

'No, but there is one other person who might have told him, isn't there?'

'I don't know what you mean.'

'Don't be silly, Jane. You know who I mean – Philly Roosevelt. It was she who lured Day to the edge of the swimming-pool so you could knock him on the head and you made the confession the way you did to leave her out of it . . . to protect her.'

'Why . . . why do you think that?'

'Mrs Roosevelt – who, by the way, I am convinced knows nothing about this – told me you had all met at the American Embassy in London. I guess you found out somehow that the Roosevelts, too, had suffered as a result of Day. He was Philly's father's business partner. While he ended up in gaol, Day went on to make a political career and a fortune.'

'What you don't know,' Jane said wearily, 'is that Day had debauched Philly when she was just a child. He was the most horrible lecher. I told you he offered to protect Warren if I agreed to be his mistress. Anyway, he was a family friend of the Roosevelts. He used to read the twins children's stories.' She spoke with utter disgust. 'She was only ten when he first . . . fumbled her. Then, when she was fifteen, he raped her. Oh no,' she went on, seeing Edward's face. 'Nothing was ever said or admitted, though I am sure Perry must know or at least suspect. Philly said it happened in his office in the Senate. He said he wanted her – had always wanted her and, if she gave herself to him, nothing bad would happen to her father. She refused and he forced himself on her . . . on the leather couch in his room. She told me she still can't smell leather without wanting to vomit. And he never stopped wanting her. It was easy for her to persuade him, when they met up again on the *Queen Mary*, that she might become his mistress. When it came to sex, he was as vain and gullible as most men.'

'Why did she tell you what Day had . . . had done to her if she hadn't even told her mother?'

'We had a heart-to-heart in the little-girls' room when we met at the ambassador's dinner. Anyway, she was ready to talk.'

'How do you mean?'

'Philly had been going to a psychoanalyst in London. He had made her face up to the trauma of being raped and it made her angry for the first time.'

'Why angry so long after . . .?'

'Before that, she thought *she* had sinned . . . that *she* was the guilty one. It sounds mad, I know, but she believed it was in some way *her* fault she had been raped.'

'And was that what made her ill . . . mentally?'

'The rape? Yes, so the analyst said. Philly had this feeling of being dirty and she hated eating because that made her feel dirty too – all that flesh. So she ate as little as she could and washed.'

'Washed?'

'Like Lady Macbeth, you remember. She washed her hands ten or twenty times a day and had at least three showers a day.'

Edward recalled how Mrs Garton, Benyon's sister, had explained *The Magic Flute*: a story of cruelty – of harsh and unjustified punishment. Was that the meaning of this killing? Philly had punished herself for a sin she had not committed. The Senator had been punished but was it justice or unjustified retribution? He felt unqualified to pontificate.

'And she never told her mother?'

'She knew her mother was already suffering from seeing her father go to gaol for fraud but I believe she did know. Her migraines – I think they come from a subconscious knowledge of what Philly has been through. Anyway, Mr Roosevelt – or Ravelstein, I should say – was not saved from gaol despite Philly's ordeal. Even Mrs Roosevelt swore they would never speak to Day again.'

'Wasn't she surprised when she discovered he was a passenger on the *Queen Mary*?'

'She just thought it was a dreadful coincidence but it brought on her headaches. She hardly dared leave her cabin.'

'But it wasn't a coincidence, was it?'

'No, we found out through the embassy that he was going back to the States on this ship and we made sure we were on it too.'

'You meant to kill him?'

'We did.' A smile of satisfaction, even of triumph, creased her face.

'And now she's better?'

'Oh no, I wouldn't say that. Not better. I can't see her ever being better in the way you mean but at least she feels the job has been done. Her father has been avenged.'

Edward looked worried. 'I had noticed her washing but I put it down to her being so delicate.' He grimaced. 'I've had a terrible thought. When you said the job had been finished, could that not mean she might . . .?'

'Have nothing more to live for?' Jane gasped. 'Oh God, I didn't think of that.'

'I think we should go and find her,' he said urgently. He had remembered one other thing Mrs Garton had said about *The Magic Flute*: 'No wonder Pamina tried to kill herself.'

'I have this awful foreboding. Do you know where she is? She wasn't in her cabin a moment ago. Perry was there with his mother. He said he had been playing shuttlecock with Frank. Perhaps Philly was watching. I never thought to ask him.'

'I saw her not long ago. I think she was heading towards the promenade deck.'

'I was there earlier. There was hardly anyone around. Everyone's packing, I suppose. I'd just feel easier in my mind if I had spoken to her.'

They walked quickly out of the cocktail bar and made their way on deck. It was strange how small the ship seemed when one was trying to avoid someone and how big it was when one was looking for someone. There was no one playing deck games so they decided to walk round the ship.

236

'You go one way round and I'll go the other so we can be sure we don't miss her,' Edward said.

He set off towards the bow and, though he came across two or three acquaintances, none of them admitted to having seen Philly. Then, at the furthest point where the deck turned back on itself, he saw a flash of white. It was Philly. He ran, or rather limped, the few yards that separated them. She was standing on the second rung of the rail which ran round the deck. He called out her name and she seemed to hear him because she turned her face towards him, was hit by a sudden gust of wind, tried to steady herself and lost her balance.

Edward made a grab for her but missed and, with a cry of horror, saw her topple over. As he launched himself towards the rail, his knee gave way under him and he fell on the deck almost weeping with the pain. Jane Barclay appeared at that moment and knelt beside him.

'Lord Edward, are you all right? Shall I call the doctor? Oh, your poor leg.'

'Over the side,' he gasped. 'She went over the side. I couldn't stop her.'

'Philly?'

'Yes, Philly. She fell . . . I couldn't stop her. Oh God!'

Fearfully, Jane got up from her knees and went to look over the rail. She could see nothing. The sea was just the rolling, featureless, sheet metal it always was. Then she looked directly below her. On the lower deck lay the broken body of the girl in white. There could be no doubt that she was dead. She lay on her back, her head twisted awkwardly to one side, and blood poured from it making an angry halo of red on the wooden deck. Then people began to gather about the body, obscuring Jane's view.

'Jane, what is it? What are you staring at? Philly . . . is she . . .?'

There came a scream of anguish that chilled his blood. With a great effort he pulled himself to his feet and heaved himself over to the rail. He could not suppress a groan. The little crowd below him parted. Perry had his twin in his arms. He was kissing her ruined face but, in his agony, he raised his head and saw Edward and Jane staring down at him in horror.

'This was your doing,' he cried. 'I hope you are satisfied!'

Did he mean he blamed Jane for making his sister a murderer or did he mean Edward for not having stopped her falling to her death? With the pain in his leg and the pain in his heart Edward did what he had never done before and fainted.

When he came to, the first thing he saw was an anxious-looking Verity. He was lying on his bed but how he had got there he had no idea.

'Thank God! The doctor said you would come round but I was beginning to think you –'

'Tell me it was just a nightmare!' he interrupted, grasping her hand.

'It wasn't, I'm afraid. What happened? Jane said you were looking for Philly and you fell and . . .'

'I saw Philly climbing over the rail but I . . . I couldn't reach her. My bloody knee . . .'

'Did she mean to kill herself, do you think?'

'I don't know . . . perhaps. Oh God! How has Frank taken this? Do you think he'll ever forgive me?'

'It wasn't your fault you couldn't get to her.'

'He won't see it that way. He'll blame me for having driven her to her death. If I hadn't gone on with my wretched sleuthing I wouldn't have . . .'

'. . . found out the truth?' Verity finished his sentence. She was suddenly angry, though not with Edward. 'You mustn't blame yourself for that. The truth is the only thing worth going after. You did not drive her to her death.'

'She wanted to kill herself and I didn't stop her!'

'Maybe she did. Maybe she couldn't live with herself any longer. That was her decision. But for her sake and her mother's we must call it an accident.'

'Verity! Can you still love me?' he asked wretchedly.

'I love you more when you doubt yourself than when you are certain,' she said. 'And I love you for loving the truth. I have said so much about what makes us different but I haven't said what it is which brings us together.' She leant over and kissed him on the lips. 'I love you because you care about the things I care about. We care about facing up to the truth. It's not easy. It's not comfortable. We'd all much rather live cosseted by lies and half-truths. It would be easier if we could live in some pretend world, like this boat, but even here, behind the fancy dress, we see reality ugly enough but *real*. You and I are different, aren't we, Edward? We have the courage to meet the truth face to face whatever mask it wears. Without that we are nothing.'

Verity was speaking with an earnestness he had never heard before. He opened his mouth to say something but she pressed the palm of her hand over his lips. 'I know you want to get up and face the music but you are just going to have to wait. Doctor's orders. You stay here and rest. I'll go and see what is happening. I'll be back in five minutes . . . promise.'

It seemed all the passengers were on deck to watch the great ship navigate the Verrazano Bridge – to gasp with pleasurable horror when it appeared certain she would not fit beneath it, only to sigh with relief as she slipped safely through, neat as an ivory ball sliding into the pocket on a billiard table. Then that first unforgettable glimpse of the Statue of Liberty and Ellis Island beyond it, peopled by the ghosts of so many thousands of immigrants in search of a brave new world in which to begin their lives again.

There was some cheering and a general feeling of exhilaration coupled with some apprehension on the part of the un-American contingent, as Senator Day might have put it. The police and immigration authorities came on board and even the most blameless of the foreigners felt they were under scrutiny. Everyone had something to hide and it was a relief that the police seemed uninterested in discovering what. No doubt they had enough problems without needing to add to them gratuitously. Edward gave a full account of seeing Philly fall over the rail and it was agreed that it was a tragic accident.

Mrs Roosevelt was remarkably stoical about her daughter's death. She knew Philly had been living on borrowed time. She had been spared the lingering, painful death the cancer would have brought her. And then there was the murder. Edward had expected to be abused by a hysterical woman but Mrs Roosevelt either knew or guessed more than he had supposed of her daughter's reason for being on board.

He saw nothing of Perry, whom the doctor had sedated and who was being nursed by Frank. Feeling cowardly, he did not seek out the two boys and, when Frank did appear, Lord Benyon seemed to keep him very busy.

As they waited for their passports to be checked, Edward caught Jane Barclay looking at him. She raised her eyebrows in mute inquiry. He pretended not to see her. She could sweat a little longer, he thought spitefully. It was some small punishment for her part in the whole debacle.

He had thought long and hard about where his duty lay in identifying the Senator's murderer to the police. The New York police had been happy to accept the Captain's verdict that the Senator's death was an accident. He had been gazing at the swimming-pool and had fallen in, hitting his head as he did so. He could not swim and so drowned. It was as simple as that. They interviewed none of the passengers, with the exception of Marcus Fern who described finding the body in the pool, and appeared satisfied. Perhaps they did not wish to annoy some important people, Edward thought uncharitably.

And yet, murder was not some trivial misdemeanour to be brushed aside as though it were of no importance. The Senator had been a bad man and the world was well rid of him, but who were Jane Barclay and Philly Roosevelt to take on that task? The killing was murder; it was premeditated and carried out with determination. They had counted on there being no police on board the *Queen Mary* to investigate, and it was bad luck for them that he had been on board and the Senator's death had got mixed up with keeping Benyon safe. Philly had paid the price asked of her for revenging the harm Day had done her. Jane had not. He wondered whether, if Philly had not been to the psychoanalyst, she would have done what she did. It was one area where he was presumptuous enough to disagree with Freud, whose theories he generally respected. He did not believe that it was always necessary to face up to childhood trauma, or at least not in public. He accepted that to *know* the truth about oneself was necessary if one wished to call oneself a mature human being but to proclaim it to the wider world could cause unforeseeable damage to innocent parties. At best, the truth was a 'blunt instrument' and should be

240

wielded with care. So often 'blunt instruments' became murder weapons. But how specious was his argument? He *knew* who had killed the Senator – it was no longer a suspicion, he *knew*. If he remained silent, did that not make him an accessory to murder? Did not keeping silent put him on a par with those who made no protest when a fellow citizen was taken from the streets and sent to a camp or shot out of hand with no semblance of a trial? He put this to Verity who told him he was in danger of sounding self-important.

'There can be no comparison. You are not killing anyone or informing on someone. A class-enemy . . . an enemy of the people is dead. It is not incumbent on you to shop the killer. You are not Father Brown. You're not justice personified.'

So Edward kept silent. He liked Jane Barclay and he admired Warren Fairley whose life would be ruined if his wife was accused of murder. He felt guilty about Philly's death and the pain he had caused his nephew and Philly's twin and mother. These were his reasons for keeping silent, not Verity's casuistry, but still . . .

Verity and Sam had had some trouble with the immigration officer who checked their passports. She had seen Benyon take Professor Dolmen and his wife up to one of the officials and say something to him. The man had laughed, patted Dolmen on the back and then stamped his papers. How come the officer had seemed much less willing to let *her* enter the States? Were Nazis more welcome than Communists? It seemed so. The immigration officer questioned her closely about her reasons for visiting the United States and appeared to know all about her political affiliations. Humiliatingly, she had to call Edward over for support and he had to use all his charm to get the man to relent. It was her first lesson in the reality of American politics. The United States might be a democracy and it might welcome the huddled masses but the true democrats as she defined them – Communists – were greeted with suspicion. Evidently, *she* might pollute the atmosphere even if Dolmen did not.

The FBI agent, Henry Fawcett, also came on board before the

Queen Mary docked, and Edward reported on the events that had led to Tom Barrett's death and Blane's attempt to murder Lord Benyon.

'Well, I guess you've had a busy time,' Fawcett said with a grin, 'but you can relax. We're taking Blane off now and we'll interrogate him. I'll need a statement from you, of course, and your nephew.'

'What'll happen to him?'

'Don't know yet but I expect we'll ship him back to England for your people to deal with.'

'I'm heartily glad to be turning over my badge to you, Sheriff,' Edward said, recalling a Western Verity had made him sit through. 'Keep Lord Benyon safe. It's been a hell of a job getting him here in one piece. I'd hate to see you mess it up now.'

'We'll do our best,' Fawcett said, laconically.

When Bernard Hunt, arm in arm with Doris Zinkeisen, said his goodbyes to Edward and Verity, he confessed that he was gambling everything on becoming a Bernard Berenson figure to the rich and famous, advising on art and buying for his clients.

'If it comes to nothing, I might have to settle for the Courtauld after all,' he joked.

Edward kissed Doris and was almost drowned in *Acqua Di Parma*. Perched on her head like pastry on a pattypan she wore a *Queen Mary* beret crowned with a representation of the ship. It looked quite absurd but Edward found he had become fond of this madcap. She was spunky, eccentric and not without talent. Her mural in the Verandah Grill might be vulgar but it had the energy and zest for life of its creator.

'Darling, if you ever visit Hollywood, come and see me. You could give dear Errol Flynn a run for his money.'

Verity looked doubtful. 'Don't you mean Franklin Pangborn?' Pangborn normally played down-trodden clerks or put-upon waiters.

'Miss Browne,' Hunt said carefully, 'we must keep in touch. As you said to me earlier, we have something in common.'

He and Doris had gone before she thought to ask what it

242

was they shared. If the answer was Communism, he might go a long way to making her change her political opinions.

Lord Benyon was greeted by a small but determined group of press and by the British Minister in New York, who whisked him through customs and into an official car, with Fern and Frank at his heels.

Jane Barclay and Warren Fairley were the main attraction for the press. The cameras flashed, capturing Fairley at his most noble and Jane at her most glamorous. The contrast between them was dramatic – the huge black man and the blonde with the hour-glass figure – but Edward was inclined to think they were both 'tough cookies'. As they said their final goodbyes, Jane kissed Edward and whispered in his ear, 'Shall we see you in court?'

Edward whispered back, gesturing at Fairley talking to the reporters, 'Warren holds court. I don't. As the Boers used to say, "*Alle zoll recht kommen*" – all will come right in the end.'

Jane looked at him. 'Is that so? I guess I must take that as a decision not to prosecute. You're not quite the stuffed shirt people take you for, are you?'

'I accept that as a compliment,' he responded.

She kissed him again. A reporter, cigarette stuck in the side of his mouth and wearing the uniform of his trade – shiny suit and porkpie hat – took their photograph. Scenting a story, or at least juicy gossip, he indicated Edward with a nod of his head. 'Who's d'guy, Jane baby? Some limey by the look of him. Is he your latest "daddy"?'

She winked and said out of the corner of her mouth, 'I should be so lucky.'

Edward looked round for Verity and saw her all alone reading a newspaper. She seemed on the point of tears.

'V, what's the matter? What's that you're reading?'

'Nothing,' she said bitterly, 'just a review of my book in the *Times Literary Supplement*, no less.'

'And it's not favourable?'

'No,' she said shortly. 'You read it.'

Edward took the paper from her and read the review. It was unsigned, as was the policy of that distinguished publication.

243

'Miss Browne has the easily raised emotions of the ill-informed. It appears she does not speak Spanish. She saw mainly socialists. She accepted her facts from them. Visiting Spain for the first time and having the usual blindness to character endemic in the politically minded, she seems to have been carried away by the facial fervour of her friends, their flashing eyes and fervent gestures. She might have seen the same exalted manner in Fascists, priests and peanut vendors.'

'How beastly,' Edward said when he had finished the review. 'I suppose you don't know who wrote it? Not one of your friends, anyway.'

'I don't know who wrote it but I wish he were here so I could wring his neck.'

Edward knew better than to offer easy sympathy. An angry Verity was better than a sobbing Verity. She was tough and he knew she could take whatever was thrown at her.

'Who was the kind friend who gave you the paper?'

'One of the people with the man who came to meet Benyon. Do you think it's some sort of warning to me?'

'How do you mean?'

'"We know you are a member of the Communist Party so behave or else . . .".'

Edward thought it was entirely likely.

'It's a good book, V, and it tells the truth,' was all he said, however. He was distracted by a shout of greeting.

'Edward darling. I've come to fetch you away. How wonderful to see you again. But what's this? You're on sticks. Have you been wounded chasing murderers?'

The woman who had just elegantly slid her long legs out of a Rolls-Royce was Amy Pageant, an old flame and the daughter of Lord Weaver, the owner of the *New Gazette* which employed Verity. Edward had first met her singing in a London nightclub when she was quite unknown and he had watched her become one of Broadway's most feted stars.

'Amy! What are you doing here?'

'Aren't you pleased to see me?'

'Of course I am but how the devil did you know I was on the *Queen Mary*?'

'I heard just by chance. Ronald read it in the *New York Times*.

They list all the important passengers. But you haven't met Ronald, have you? He's too divine and we are going to be married, aren't we, sugar? Just as soon as we have time.' She kissed Edward on both cheeks. 'He's money. I don't know why but I never seem to have quite enough,' she murmured.

Edward glanced at Ronald. Plump, smiling, silent, clearly proud to be seen with Amy Pageant, he seemed like the perfect escort.

'Verity's here . . .' Edward said, looking round for her. 'Oh, she seems to have vanished. No, there she is with Sam Forrest. Sam,' he called.

''Bye Corinth, glad to have met you,' Sam shouted. 'I hope you don't mind but I'm taking Verity off to meet some friends.'

'Won't you introduce me?' Amy broke in.

'I apologize. Sam, come over here a moment, would you? May I introduce you to Amy Pageant? Amy, this is Sam Forrest. You might think he was too young but he is, in fact, a senior figure in the labour movement on this side of the Atlantic.'

'Mr Forrest, how nice to meet you.'

'Miss Pageant, it's an honour to meet you.' He took her hand and, for a moment, Edward thought he was going to kiss it. 'I have seen several of your shows. You're wonderful.'

'Oh, you dear boy! How sweet of you. You must come to one of my parties. I think we're going to be *great* friends. And Verity . . . is that really you? I hear you are quite famous now. Daddy's always talking about you.'

Verity was cross. She did not like being patronized by Amy Pageant and she did not like the way she talked to Sam or the way Sam looked at her. Then she reminded herself that Sam was a married man and she wasn't having an affair with him. She glanced at Edward but he too was looking at Amy.

'Where are you staying?' Amy demanded.

'At the Algonquin.'

'No, no. You must come and stay with me. The apartment is quite big enough. Don't you remember?'

'I do and I also remember that there's only one spare bedroom. It's very kind of you but Verity and I might as well stick to our plans.'

Verity smiled at him gratefully. For a moment it had looked

as though she was going to be left quite alone and, hardened foreign correspondent though she was, she had felt a moment of panic.

'If you won't come and stay, then you must come and have dinner with me tonight. I'm not in a show at the moment so I'm quite free.'

Edward was fairly sure the invitation did not include Verity but he said firmly, 'That would be lovely, Amy. We'd like that, wouldn't we, V?'

Amy looked a little put out but she accepted defeat gracefully. 'Good, that's settled then. Sam – I may call you Sam, mayn't I? – you'll come too, won't you?'

'I'd be honoured,' he said, bowing over her hand again. Verity snorted.

'Edward, shall I drop you off at the hotel?' Amy said. 'Sam, Verity – where are you off to?'

'I'm taking Verity to meet some of my union people on the way to the hotel. We'll take a cab but thank you, Miss Pageant.'

'And you, Edward?'

'That would be very kind of you, Amy. Fenton, my man, has gone with Lord Benyon and, as you can see, I managed to twist my knee so I'm a cripple. By the way, my nephew, Frank, is here too. He's acting as Lord Benyon's secretary, or bag-carrier.'

'Frank! I'd love to meet him. Is he as good-looking as his uncle, Verity?' Verity opened her mouth to reply but Amy had not stopped for a response. 'Bring him this evening as well and Lord Benyon, too, if he can make it. Bring everyone! Let's have a party. I haven't had an English party for absolutely ages.'

'Amy, it's so good to see you.' Edward was suddenly overwhelmed by memories of the six months he had spent in New York watching her blossom into a star. 'You're looking wonderful – more beautiful than ever.'

In truth, she was looking beautiful but there was an air of artificiality, of strain almost, which had not been there when he had last seen her eighteen months before. He wondered if her life was quite the bed of roses she pretended. She had said she was not in a show and implied that it was by choice, but was it?

He looked at Verity. She was not cocooned in a silver fox fur, and she wore no jewellery – not even a ring. Her make-up

246

was restricted to a slash of red on her lips. She was small and Amy was tall. She could never be called glamorous but, in making the comparison, he realized how much he loved her. There must have been something in his face which Verity recognized because she smiled back and took his hand.

'We won't be long,' she said. 'Sam'll drop me at the hotel in an hour or two. You're sure you don't mind me coming tonight, Amy? I don't want to play gooseberry.'

'Don't be silly,' Amy said, sounding at once more natural and more sincere. 'I'd love you to come. You don't have to worry about me and Edward. The past is the past – *nostalgie de la boue* – that's all.'

'That doesn't sound very complimentary,' Edward laughed, feeling relieved. 'I'll just go and see about our trunks and then I assume we have to go through customs?'

'Yes, but that won't take long. Ronald, go with Edward and make everything happen, there's a dear.'

A yellow cab stopped and a window was wound down. It was Mrs Roosevelt. 'Lord Edward, I was looking for you to say goodbye.'

Edward raised his hat and looked troubled. 'I hope you don't think I was avoiding you. How is Perry?'

'Didn't you know? He's gone with Frank. Lord Benyon has very kindly taken him with him . . . to distract him I suppose.'

'I am so sorry . . .' It seemed absurd having this conversation on a busy dock with Amy at his elbow, listening avidly.

'I do understand.' She put out a gloved hand and touched his. 'It might have been the best thing . . . I can't tell. Goodbye for now, Lord Edward. I am sure we will see you while you are in New York. And don't blame yourself. Perry doesn't, I promise you.'

When the cab had gone, Amy said, 'I think you have a lot to tell me. I thought a few days on the *Queen Mary* would be a rest cure but I'm beginning to suspect it was anything but.'

'It had its moments. For one thing, there was this terrible storm . . .' Verity stopped in mid-sentence. There was the man Edward had introduced her to as Bill Stephenson, shepherding the murderous 'Major' into an unmarked car. Two exhausted-looking women trailed behind them, the wives of two bullying bigots – a southern senator and a half-deranged would-be Nazi.

247

Both, in different ways, were their husbands' victims. The Major caught her eye and smiled . . . was it impudently? She could not be sure.

Edward returned, having arranged for his and Verity's baggage to be sent on to their hotel. 'Right, let's get going. Customs seem uninterested in what we might be smuggling.'

'As long as it isn't Communism,' Verity could not resist saying.

'Verity's been telling me you had a storm at sea. Was that when you hurt your leg?' Amy inquired, almost jealous at having missed the excitement.

'Not just then but it's true – isn't it, V? – we were almost lost on a dangerous sea.'